Aftershock

KG MacGregor

Bella
BOOKS

2008

Printed in the United States of America on acid-free paper

First Edition

Editor: Cindy Cresap
Cover designer: Stephanie Solomon-Lopez

ISBN-10: 1-59493-135-6
ISBN-13: 978-1-59493-135-2

In memory of my father
1931–2007

Acknowledgments

As I stated in the acknowledgments for *Without Warning*, the first book in the Shaken Series, it's been a thrill to have the chance to go back to an earlier book and retell the story. Thanks to all of you who wrote after reading *Shaken* to let me know how the story moved you, and especially to those who shared the trials and triumphs of these characters. Many thanks once again to Cindy Cresap, whose contribution always makes a better book. On the technical side, my appreciation goes out to Karen and Jenny for their help in cleaning up the copy. They find the extra words, the missing words, the wrong words and places where I simply assumed you would read my mind and know what I meant.

About the Author

Growing up in the mountains of North Carolina, KG MacGregor dreaded the summer influx of snowbirds escaping the Florida heat. "If it's tourist season, why can't we shoot them?" she said. Now older, wiser and intolerant of extreme temperatures, she divides her time between Miami and Blowing Rock, NC. A former teacher, KG earned her PhD in journalism and mass communication, and her writing stripes preparing research reports for commercial clients in the publishing, television and travel industries. In 2002, she tried her hand at lesbian fiction and discovered her bliss. When she isn't writing, you'll find her either on a golf course or a hiking trail. Please visit her at www. kgmacgregor.com.

Chapter 1

"I bet this is pretty in the daytime," Anna said, peering through the windshield into the darkness.

From the quirk in Anna's voice, Lily knew her chain was being yanked. "Funny, Amazon. We should have been here two hours ago." A sign for Yosemite National Park flashed by on the passenger side.

"But at least we made it."

"No thanks to you," she groused, thinking about the awkward request she had made in court two days ago. "I practically lied to a judge to get my client's hearing postponed so we could leave early. And then I find you covered in grease from head to toe."

"It took longer than I thought. I wasn't going to drop a hundred grand for a car without being sure it was perfect."

Lily tried not to smile, but it was useless. In truth, she had been thrilled upon arriving at Anna's BMW dealership to find her in a jumpsuit with her long dark hair pulled through a ball cap.

Still, it had delayed their start by two hours while she finished her work and got cleaned up. "I can't believe you'd spend that kind of money for a car."

"The Z-eight's a classic. There were only a couple of thousand sold here in the US. I would have bought one a few years ago when they first came along, but I had my eight-fifty back before it was crushed in the earthquake."

"I thought you liked your six-fifty now."

"I do, but it doesn't have the character of one of the limited editions, especially something as hot as the Z-eight."

"And just what do you need a hot car for? Are you single?"

They both burst out laughing.

"No, honey."

"Good answer."

Lily breathed a sigh of relief when they finally reached the ranger station. Ten minutes later the park would have been closed for the night.

"The campground is here," the ranger told her, pointing to a corner of the map. "Just stay on this road and you'll see a sign in about two miles."

"Thank you," she answered, dropping the parking permit on her dashboard.

After several minutes of creeping along the two-lane road, Anna gestured ahead. "Isn't that the sign she was talking about?"

"Yeah." Lily slowed and turned on her blinker. "Thanks for doing this."

"I should be thanking you. They're my friends."

"I know, but you know how much I love camping. I'd rather be meeting them here than at some resort."

Anna picked up Lily's free hand and brought it to her lips. "You know how much I like camping too."

"Oh, please. You like camping about as much as you like cooking."

"But I'll do either with you." Anna pointed to a red 4Runner with Washington plates situated between two giant redwoods. "There they are."

Lily's headlights shone upon a bright blue two-person tent nestled against the underbrush nearby. Two women, both in jeans and jackets, sat huddled atop a weathered picnic table, obviously on the lookout. She pulled the X3 into the space behind the other vehicle and turned off the engine.

"The one on the left is Carolyn," Anna said. "The other one is Vicki."

"And the one in the bandana bouncing up and down?"

"I'm guessing that's their new Labrador."

Lily sucked in a breath and readied herself to meet Anna's friends. She wanted to make a good impression, especially after hearing that Anna had gone to Seattle for advice about their relationship. Carolyn and Vicki had heard all about her, and now it was time to live up to their expectations.

"I would never have believed it in a million years," Carolyn boomed as they got out of the vehicle. "Anna Kaklis is wearing hiking boots and blue jeans. Where's my camera?"

Lily liked Carolyn instantly. Not only did she obviously know Anna very well, she knew just how to goad her and bring out a smile. She was just as Lily had pictured from Anna's description—tall, with short curly hair, its deep red tint most likely from a bottle. Her partner Vicki was petite, with wavy brown hair pulled tightly into a ponytail. She stood off to the side, gripping the puppy's leash. They looked fit and "outdoorsy," both characteristics to which Lily could relate.

Anna crossed the campsite quickly to embrace her longtime friend. "If you're going to take a picture, let me give you something pretty to look at."

Lily slid her smaller frame under Anna's outstretched arm. "I'm Lily, in case anyone was wondering."

"Did you dress her up like this?" Carolyn asked.

"I did. But she drew the line at the flannel shirt."

"She's prissy, isn't she?"

3

"Yeah, but I kind of like that about her," Lily said, tightening her arm around Anna's waist.

Anna gestured toward Carolyn. "Please allow me to introduce you to Carolyn Bunting, who was Cal Poly's official class clown. And this woman who puts up with her nonsense is Vicki Hurst."

"And this is Zack," Vicki said, loosening the leash enough for the pup to charge ahead and pounce on Anna.

"Dogs love me," Anna said. "Every time we go visit Lily's mom, her basset hound follows me everywhere I go."

"I'm glad to meet you all," Lily said, shaking hands with the women and stooping to give Zack a friendly scratch. "Anna's been afraid to have me meet her friends. Makes me think there are some awful stories out there."

"Oh, there are," Carolyn said. "And we're going to have such fun telling them."

Anna ran her hands through her hair. "Why did I ever agree to this?"

"Because you love me," Lily said. "Now why don't you guys catch up while I set up the tent?"

"I'll help," Vicki offered, handing the leash to Carolyn before following along behind. "Anna said you guys bought a new Trango—except Carolyn laughed at her because she called it a tango. That's the one we've been looking at."

Lily chuckled as they walked toward the X3, impressed that Anna had even come close to remembering the name of their tent.

Anna and Carolyn warmed their hands beside the fire as Lily and Vicki worked to set up the rest of their camp. Overnight temperatures were heading into the low thirties, typical for April in the Sierras, so Anna was glad she had taken Lily's advice about bringing warm things.

"I'll have you know I'm getting to be an old hand at this

4

camping thing," she said, stretching out to pet Zack, who was tied to the picnic table, where he chewed contentedly on a rawhide bone.

Carolyn had lined up four mugs and was warming milk to make hot cocoa. "Define old hand."

"The first time I went was when Lily took me to Silverwood Lake with a bunch of kids from foster care."

"And have you been since?"

"Twice. But this trip's special because Lily says we get to share a sleeping bag."

Carolyn laughed heartily. "Admit it, Anna. You like this lesbian thing."

"I like that lesbian thing over there very much." Anna appreciated how easily she and Carolyn had reconnected after their ten-year hiatus. "Everything you and Vicki told me about this was right on the money. All she needed was for me to show her how I felt."

"I'm looking forward to getting to know her."

"She feels the same way. She has a couple of lesbian friends that we do things with in LA, but she always says we need to socialize more. Both of us are bad about working too much."

"She's a little thing. Does she push you around like Vicki does me?"

Anna laughed. "Oh, yeah. Anything she wants."

Carolyn shook her head in apparent dismay. "I never thought I'd see Anna Kaklis whipped."

"It's not so bad." Anna nodded in the direction of the tent, where Lily was bent over forcing a stake into the ground. The sight of her rear prompted a lascivious smile. "See what I mean?"

"Boy, this is going to take some getting used to."

"Everything's different now, Carolyn. I feel like Lily walked into my life and turned the lights on."

"Something tells me you and I are going to spend the whole weekend talking about how lucky we are."

"You're probably right." Anna lowered her voice. "There is something I want your opinion on. But we can talk about it tomorrow."

"You know I can't stand it when you do that. I have to know right this second or I'll go crazy. I'll be up all night. I'll bite my fingernails down to the nubs. I'll—"

"Shhh! I just want to talk about what comes next," Anna whispered.

"Ahhhh . . . that's a talk I don't want to miss. You're serious about Lily."

"Very."

"Can I be your best man?"

"No, thanks," Anna said, shuddering to recall her failed marriage to Scott Rutherford. "One humiliating extravaganza was enough for a lifetime."

"And what about Lily? Has she already had an extravaganza?"

"No." Anna frowned. Technically, Carolyn was right. If they decided to make a commitment to each other, Lily deserved a ceremony if she wanted it. "Maybe I can get her to elope."

"There's a thought."

"You don't think I'm jumping into this too early?"

"When was it you came up to Seattle?"

"A year ago last January."

Carolyn shrugged. "That seems like plenty of time to know what you want. But if you're worried about it being too soon, maybe it is."

The last thing Anna wanted was to make another mistake in her life when it came to romance. Almost two years after her divorce, she still shuddered to think what an embarrassing blunder her marriage had been. If only she had paid attention to her doubts instead of expecting them to resolve on their own. At least she didn't have reservations like that when it came to Lily. What she did have, though, was a huge case of nerves about making another commitment.

6

Lily and Vicki approached the fire, which was dying out for the night. Anna held out an arm and pulled Lily close while Carolyn fixed the mugs.

"Their camping stuff's better than ours," Vicki said.

"That's all right. We can steal it while they're making out." Carolyn handed Lily the first cup. "Look at them. They can't keep their hands off each other. Remember when we were like that?"

"No, not really," Vicki deadpanned.

Anna burst out laughing at Carolyn's quizzical look.

"She loves me . . . honest," Carolyn said. "Just last week she said something nice to me for no reason at all."

Anna kissed Lily just above her ear. "Didn't I warn you these two were nuts?" It was a rare treat to feel comfortable with openly showing her affection. Lily didn't seem to have the same reticence about public displays, but Anna held back unless they were with lesbian friends. Eloping was looking better all the time.

"I hate to break up the party, but we should probably hit the restroom and turn in. We have to save some firewood for tomorrow night," Vicki said. "Did you guys bring food? We're supposed to lock it up in the bear bin."

"I'll get it," Anna said. She wanted to give Lily a few minutes to chat with Carolyn—or rather, give Carolyn the chance to get to know Lily a bit. She had no doubts they would like each other, but she wanted her Washington friends to see what a prize she had. She stowed their food and locked the bin, returning to the fireside just in time to follow the group to the restroom.

"I hope you like the way I set things up," Lily said as they returned to their tent.

"Oh, this is nice," Anna said softly as the beam from the flashlight revealed the layout of their small quarters. Lily had spread out their sleeping bags on top of a double air mattress, covering both bags with pillows and two thick blankets. "So we're not going to sleep in our sleeping bags?"

"We might have to if it gets a lot colder, but this should be enough if we wear sweat suits and cuddle. And if you share the covers."

Anna chuckled. It wasn't that she was a blanket hog. But somehow, her long legs pulled their covers loose nearly every night, leaving them piled on the floor—and Lily shivering—by morning.

"You know how much I like to cuddle," Anna crooned. She enveloped Lily in a hug and brought her down to the blankets.

"Oh no, you don't, Amazon. Lose the boots. You'll get dirt in our bed."

Anna kicked off her hiking boots and set them under the rain guard outside the tent.

"Now put these on." Lily handed her a set of navy blue sweats and zipped the tent entry.

By the light of the flashlight, Anna pulled off her fleece jacket, long-sleeved T-shirt and bra, shivering against the chill as she hurried to tug the sweatshirt over her head. Then she squirmed out of her jeans, but before she had time to pull on the sweatpants the light went out and an arm went around her waist and pulled her backward onto the blankets.

"Not so fast," Lily whispered, pushing her hand under the elastic of Anna's panties. "It isn't often I get to make love with you in the wild."

Anna felt her body tense. "But they're like . . . ten feet away."

"Then you'll have to be quiet for a change . . . not that I don't enjoy those lovely sounds you make when you come."

Despite her fears of being overheard, Anna couldn't fight her growing arousal as Lily stroked her intimately. "I get so wet when you do that," she whispered.

"I know." Lily covered her mouth with a kiss and continued her caress. Slowly, she eased into a position where she could press her center into Anna's thigh, matching her movements to the rhythm her fingers tapped against Anna's clitoris.

Anna drew a deep gasp as the fire built beneath Lily's touch.

And when Lily pressed harder, she thrust her hips up in demand. "Oh, Lily."

"Shhh . . ." Lily gently laid a finger across her lips to keep her quiet, all the while increasing the speed of her strokes. "Are you going to come for me?"

Anna nodded frantically, gritting her teeth to keep quiet as the sensations erupted between her legs. Lily smothered her moan with a deep kiss, before tracing her slicked fingers along their lips as the climax ebbed.

She pulled the blankets over them as Anna worked to catch her breath. "Think you'll be warm enough, Amazon?"

Chapter 2

Lily was awakened by the same sensation that had sent her off to sleep—Anna's lips against her brow. Soft voices outside told her Carolyn and Vicki were already up and about. "Good morning," she murmured, snuggling deeper into Anna's embrace.

Anna answered with a tighter squeeze and another kiss.

"You were good last night. You only pulled my covers off once." After that, Lily had tucked them underneath the air mattress on her side.

"I tried to make up for it by sleeping on top of you."

"That was nice . . . my human blanket."

"Can we pitch one of these in the backyard? I don't think I've ever slept so well."

"You always sleep well right after you come," she whispered.

"Do I really?"

"Yep."

"And what about you?"

"I sleep better when you sleep better."

"That sounds like a pretty good deal if you're me."

"Don't you know"—Lily rolled on top of Anna—"that making you happy is all I care about?"

"But that works both ways, you know." Anna ran her hands down Lily's sides. "You shouldn't just let me fall asleep on you like that."

"We're not keeping score, honey. I love it when I can help you relax." Not that she didn't also love Anna's touch. For someone who had never been with a woman before, Anna had shown very few inhibitions in their sexual explorations. It was hard to believe she once had reservations about expressing herself sexually.

"We probably should get up," Anna said, nudging her from her thoughts. "I hear them outside."

"Vicki told me she was making breakfast burritos."

"Now I know we should get up."

Lily resisted the urge to cop a feel when Anna pulled the sweat suit off and changed back into her clothes. They emerged from the tent to find Carolyn sitting at the picnic table with a cup of coffee, intently studying a map of the park. Vicki had four plates lined up beside her camp stove awaiting a scoop of scrambled eggs.

Zack began to bounce in place as soon as he saw Anna. She obliged him with a friendly scratch before peering over Carolyn's shoulder. "Have you figured out where we're going?"

"It's about two and a half hours from here to the valley. We'll have a great view of the falls from there."

"Sounds like a good place for a picnic."

Lily poured their coffee before stooping to pet Zack, who never took his eyes off Anna. "I'll camp with you anytime, Vicki. I like a woman who cooks."

"We're a two-fer," she answered. "Carolyn loves to clean up."

Carolyn frowned. "I think it's possible I left Washington with the wrong woman. This one just doesn't seem to know me at

11

all."

"I'll help you with the dishes, you whiner," Anna said, offering a hand to Vicki as she set the plates on the table.

"Oh, Lily," Carolyn moaned. "Will you pass me the hot sauce?"

Lily recognized immediately the teasing reference to last night's intimate exchange, and in mere seconds, Anna's face turned a deep red. Lily patted her thigh beneath the table and shot her most lascivious grin at Carolyn. "We're happy campers this morning. How about you?"

"If Carolyn doesn't behave herself, it's going to be quite a while before she's happy again," Vicki said.

Once again, Carolyn's face morphed to a frown.

Anna snorted, her blush dissipating. "And you said I was whipped."

Lily was sorry she had missed that conversation. It would have been interesting to hear what Anna had told Carolyn to warrant such an impression. At any rate, she was glad to see Anna get past her initial embarrassment about being overheard last night.

As Anna helped Carolyn clean up, Lily readied their daypacks, packing only water and trail mix in Anna's. In her own, she loaded her basic provisions, plus their camera, binoculars and a few things to share at lunch. She saved room for their jackets, which they would surely shed as the temperature climbed.

After breakfast, they set out on the four-mile hike to the meadow beneath Yosemite Falls, the majestic centerpiece of the national park. Lily fell in step with Carolyn on the point, while Anna and Vicki brought up the rear, where Zack was faithfully at Anna's heels. "Do you and Vicki hike a lot?"

"We used to, but we haven't been in a couple of years. As you can probably tell, Vicki works out about four times a week. She's in great shape. I've been so busy at work, this is the first time I've gotten off my butt since January."

Lily slowed her pace, curbing her energy to accommodate Carolyn and Anna. Eight miles was a long hike for anyone, but especially for those who weren't used to it. She had coaxed Anna out for a four-mile hike a couple of weeks ago at Escondido Canyon near Malibu, their longest ever. If she was lucky, Anna would get the hiking bug from this trip and make it a part of their regular routine.

"Anna told me all about going up to Seattle last year. I'm glad I finally get a chance to thank you guys for steering her my way."

Carolyn laughed. "You should have seen her. She was a mess. She was so crazy about you and she didn't have a clue what to do about it."

"Whatever you said was perfect. She came home and swept me right off my feet."

"Anna can do that without even trying." Carolyn looked over her shoulder to see Anna and Vicki deep in conversation. "Did she happen to tell you I used to be in love with her too?"

"She mentioned it. And she also said you were always one of her favorite people." In fact, her relationship with Carolyn had been the catalyst for Anna to open up and talk about her earlier sexual experiences. She said she might have discovered her sexuality much sooner if Carolyn had offered her that option back in college. Instead, she had explored her sexual side with a casual boyfriend, a disappointing episode that had left her wary of intimacy.

"I'll probably always think of her as the one that got away, but I'm a big believer in destiny." Carolyn looked again over her shoulder. "And that other woman back there was my destiny. There isn't one thing I'd change about my life if it meant not finding her."

"I know what you mean. Some nights I lie awake thinking about how we both just happened to be in that mall during the earthquake."

"That really was an amazing story. And then Anna said you ran into each other out of the blue after that. So you two probably know a little about destiny too. You were meant to be together."

13

Lily toyed often with such thoughts, but she was careful not to read as far into her future with Anna as Carolyn hinted. The invitation a year ago to move into Anna's home was proof they were serious, but there was no lifetime promise implied. She sometimes wondered if Anna could make another vow like the one she had made with Scott.

Lily had a thing about commitment, something she figured was a remnant of bouncing around in foster homes before finally being adopted. It wasn't just two people staying together day after day, even if that implied permanence. For Lily, it was a spoken vow to always be there, a mutual understanding that this was the life you wanted forever. That's what she had asked of Beverly, her last lover, who had been so spooked by the prospect that she bolted. Lily wouldn't repeat that mistake with Anna. No matter how much she wanted to hear the words, she accepted that their relationship would have to be on Anna's timeline.

"Those were weird times back in college," Carolyn said, snapping Lily's train of thought. "I had to face the fact I was a lesbian because I couldn't deny the feelings that I had for her anymore. I wish I had just told her."

"I don't think coming out is easy for anyone."

"What about you? When did you figure things out about yourself?"

"I was a freshman in high school. My friends were drooling over Tom Cruise, but I was hung up on Jodie Foster. And not just her movies—I wondered about how she took her coffee, how she kissed . . . that kind of stuff. That's where my teenage fantasies started to go."

"So what was it like being gay in high school?"

"Not a picnic, I have to say." Though the sting was long gone, Lily still remembered the painful betrayal of people she thought were her friends. "In high school you have to be like everyone else. When you're gay, you don't really fit in anywhere."

"What about your family? How did they deal with it?"

"It's just my mom and me, and she's always been supportive.

One of our family friends was a lesbian."

"You're lucky. My parents didn't speak to me for about four years after I told them. We talk now, but only because Vicki made me reach out to them again."

"Anna still gets a hard time from her dad, but I think he's coming around." Over the past year, Lily had made a good bit of progress with George, joking with him openly about his misgivings in hopes he would begin to take it all in stride. Though Anna had never said as much, Lily knew his approval was important to her, and she never wanted to give George any reason to feel his daughter had made a poor choice.

"George? He's a piece of work," Carolyn said. "But I think there's a nice guy under there if you can get through."

"I think so too. I need to win him over for Anna's sake."

"Let me tell you something about Anna." She lowered her voice. "She studies on things a lot before she makes up her mind, and she took her time with you. She knew her dad wouldn't be crazy about this, but she didn't give him a vote. Whatever grief she expected from him, her relationship with you was worth it."

Lily barely heard the last part. She was stuck on the part about Anna taking her time. If they were to move from what they currently had to a committed relationship—assuming Anna could even do that again—it might be years before it ever happened. The only thing that was certain was that it would have to come from Anna, because Lily wouldn't risk ruining things again.

"I officially like her," Carolyn announced as she fell back to walk with Anna. Vicki and Lily had forged ahead with Zack, who had energy to burn.

"I knew you would. She's really something. Did she tell you about how she grew up?"

"She said she came out in high school. That was about it."

Anna related Lily's tale of abuse and neglect at the hand of her biological mother, her grueling time spent in foster homes,

15

and her eventual adoption by her teacher. "A lot of people would have been screwed up for life after that, but Lily turned it into a source of strength. Now she works with people like that in a legal aid clinic. She's an incredible person."

"I can sure see that. And I can see why you'd be thinking about what comes next."

Anna sighed. "Except my track record on commitment sucks. Why would anyone believe Lily was any different from Scott?" She asked her question quietly, not only because she didn't want Lily to overhear, but also because the subject unnerved her.

"It doesn't matter what anyone else believes. You and Lily will make your promises to each other."

"Maybe that's my real question. How do I convince myself it's different this time?"

Carolyn clapped her hand on Anna's shoulder. "If you're looking for some magic sign, forget it. Cupid isn't real."

"I was afraid of that."

"It's all on faith, Anna. You're just going to have to throw yourself back out there and make up your mind it's worth working for—because that's what relationships are. It takes a lot of work to overlook someone's flaws when you know you're going to be dealing with them forever. And if you're too chicken to promise you'll do that, then maybe you shouldn't."

"Lily's biggest flaw is she forgets to change her oil when she's supposed to. She has way more to overlook about me than I do about her."

"That's the whole idea. You put yourself out there for each other. Then you both promise to accept all of it and to hold together no matter what."

"I did that already, remember?" Anna said, her frustration evident. They were talking in circles.

"But did you do it with someone you truly loved? I don't think so, because you would never have given up on Scott if you had really loved him."

Anna considered Carolyn's words. Yes, she had given up on

Scott, admitting to herself she didn't want their marriage badly enough to work as hard as she would have had to in order to get past their problems.

"But if what you feel for Lily is something you never want to lose, maybe you're ready to try again. The thing I don't understand"—Carolyn stopped to catch her breath—"is how we both ended up with women who can't sit still. Whatever happened to good old-fashioned sloth?"

When they reached the meadow shortly after noon, Anna collapsed in the grass, eagerly accepting Lily's offer of bread and cheese. Beneath the towering magnificence and thunderous roar of Yosemite Falls, Anna had to admit Lily's love of nature was a worthwhile pastime. If she could hand off some of her duties at the dealership to her sales manager, she could take off on Saturdays and join Lily on her hikes.

"Hey, you two. How about a smile?" Carolyn clicked her camera. "That's going to be a great picture."

Lily fixed chicken stir-fry on the camp stove for dinner, one of Anna's favorites. As she cooked, the others took advantage of the time to rest, lounging in low-slung chairs with their feet next to the fire. Anna and Carolyn were exhausted when they got back to their campsite, and would probably be sore tomorrow. It was hard not to feel sorry for them.

"Should I set the table, or do you want to just fix a plate and sit by the fire?"

"I'll give you a thousand dollars if you'll fix my plate and bring it to me," Anna said. She sounded serious.

"Keep your money, Amazon. I'll fix your plate. In fact, why don't you all stay put and I'll serve you?" No one argued, but Vicki did jump up to help her clean the dishes afterward.

"Can someone tell me why this dog thinks I'm his mother?" Anna asked. Zack was stretched out beside her, his head nestled on her feet.

Carolyn nudged the dog with her foot, but he didn't move. "It's very cute, Anna. If you want to take him home, I guess we could get another one."

"Don't listen to her," Vicki said. "She'd cry all the way home." She leaned over and whispered something into Carolyn's ear.

"Vicki and I are going to let you guys in on a little secret, something we haven't told anyone." Carolyn took Vicki's hand and smiled. "Zack isn't the only one joining our family. My lovely wife here has been paying regular visits to her fertility clinic—"

"So many that we'd started calling it the futility clinic," Vicki interjected.

"But we finally got some good news last week. We're going to be mommies."

"That's fabulous!" Lily exclaimed.

"You sneaky things. I can't believe you didn't tell us the second we got here." Anna hauled herself up gingerly to give both women a congratulatory hug.

"And I can't believe you hiked eight miles today," Lily said.

Carolyn chuckled. "It's nothing compared to what she usually does."

"Would it be too personal to ask . . . ?" Anna looked from Carolyn to Vicki and back.

"We did in vitro," Carolyn said. "You fertilize the eggs in a Petri dish and plant them in the uterus. And get this . . . they're my eggs." She buffed her nails on her vest.

"That is so cool," Lily said. "She's having your baby."

"I know. I'll get to pass out cigars."

"Another little Carolyn running around . . . who would ever have guessed it?" Anna said, still beaming at the news.

Lily loved sharing in their excitement, especially since she and Anna were the first friends to know. For the next hour, they heard all about plans for the nursery, day care after Vicki went back to work, and an exhaustive list of baby names.

The night air grew chilly as the fire died down. Carolyn stood and stretched, pulling Vicki to her feet. "I guess we should turn in. I don't know about you guys, but that hike today kicked my butt."

"I think this one would agree." Lily helped Anna from her chair. "Oh, by the way . . ."

Carolyn and Vicki stopped and turned back.

"I promised Anna a massage tonight. She sometimes moans when I do that." She shot Carolyn a wink and guided Anna toward their tent.

Wriggling into the cramped space, they changed into their sweats for the night.

"I think it's your turn to moan tonight," Anna whispered.

"I told you this morning. We're not keeping score." She eased Anna down on the mattress. "I was serious about that massage. You need to let me rub the soreness out of your legs or you won't be able to walk tomorrow."

"I can hardly walk now." Anna rolled onto her stomach as Lily knelt between her feet.

"This is probably going to hurt a little." She gripped the calf muscles through the sweatpants and started to squeeze, gently at first, then with more pressure. Her hands traveled to the soft tissue at the back of the knee, where she tenderly caressed the spot on the side that was injured in the earthquake over two years ago. Next, she kneaded the tightened hamstrings until she felt them relax, finishing with the firm buttocks . . . which was very possibly Lily's favorite feature of Anna's beautiful body. "Is that better?" The silence told her that Anna had fallen asleep. "Sweet dreams, Amazon."

Anna stared out the window on the drive home, lost in thought about her future with Lily. So much had changed inside her in the past two years, but looking back, it was undeniable the seeds of love had been planted when they were trapped together in the Endicott Mall after the earthquake. How else could she explain the longing she felt to find Lily again and be with her?

She had discovered so much about herself in their brief time together, especially since they moved into their Brentwood home last summer. She had learned the give and take of everyday life with a partner, no longer needing as much of the private time she used to crave when she lived with Scott. And now she understood the value of talking about things openly and the senselessness of keeping feelings inside. But mostly, she knew real love—how to express it in words, in actions and with her body, how to receive it without doubt or obligation, and how to nurture it to make it grow.

Carolyn and Vicki's big news had pushed the question of commitment even closer to her heart. The only time she and Lily had ever spoken about children, Lily had seemed adamant she didn't want any of her own. Granted, that was before they had become lovers. But the question was different now—would Lily want children with her? And if not, was that something Anna was willing to give up?

Yes, she realized with clarity. The life she wanted forever was the one she had with Lily, no matter what else it brought, or didn't bring.

"You're staring at me, Amazon."

Anna laughed, her face warming from having been caught. "Give me a break. This is Bakersfield. What else is there to look at?"

"Now there's a compliment. I'm cuter than Bakersfield. Be still my heart."

"You're cuter than everything. How's that?"

"What good is a compliment when I have to beg for it?" Lily reached over and took her hand. "Did you have a good time this weekend?"

"Yes, I did. I have a confession to make."

"What?"

"I sort of like camping."

"Do you really?"

"I don't want to go every weekend . . . or even every month, but it's a fun way to spend time with friends. We should go sometime with Sandy and Suzanne."

Lily looked at her dubiously. "Are you serious?"

"Sure. We need to do more things you like instead of spending all of our free time with my family."

Lily picked up her hand and kissed it. She loved Anna's family, and was especially close to her stepsister Kim. "You're sweet. But I enjoy being with your family, so you don't have to feel like it's a burden on me."

"I know. And I love the way you torture my father, but we should try to get out more with other lesbians. It's fun when we get to be ourselves."

"Excuse me, but did you just refer to yourself as a lesbian?"

"I did not." Anna looked away to hide her smile. This was one of their running jokes.

"Are you sure? Because I'm almost certain you did."

"You must have misheard."

"So that bit about getting out with other lesbians . . . I misheard that?"

"Oh, I said that. But I was talking about getting out with lesbians other than Vicki and Carolyn, or Sandy and Suzanne."

"So you didn't mean other lesbians besides us?"

"Oh, no. That would mean we were both lesbians," Anna said, still smirking.

"And you're not."

"I didn't say that."

"Which is not the same as not saying it."

"Yes, whatever you just said."

"You drive me crazy, woman."

It was Anna's turn to pull Lily's hand for a kiss. "At least that settles which one of us is crazy."

Lily shook her head and smiled. "So what did you think of Carolyn and Vicki's news? Wasn't that cool?"

"It was. With both a baby and Carolyn, Vicki's going to have her hands full."

21

"I thought the same thing. Vicki waits on her hand and foot."

"She doesn't seem to mind it. I think she just likes that," Anna said.

"Maybe, but if you were pregnant, I'd be doing everything for you—fixing dinner, cleaning up, taking out the trash. Oh, wait. I already do those things. Is there something you want to tell me?"

Anna burst out laughing. "I'm not pregnant, but that doesn't prove I'm a lesbian."

"You're hilarious, Amazon."

"You know, I woke up thinking about babies. I like having a nephew I can spoil totally rotten, especially since I can give him back to my sister. I always thought I would have children, but I haven't felt that urge in a long time."

"Did you and Scott ever talk about having kids?"

"More than that. We actually tried for a couple of months just before we ran into his ex-girlfriend and their baby. And what was really freaky was right after that happened, my period was late. I was climbing the walls. God, what a mess that would have been."

"What do you think you would have done?"

Anna shuddered to think about it. "I would have stayed married. And I probably would have been thrilled with my baby and miserable with everything else."

"You'd be a great mom, Anna."

Ironically, her decision to try to have a child with Scott was something she had hoped would bridge their differences and help them connect. She didn't need those things in her relationship with Lily, but it was almost sounding as if Lily was open to the idea. "Kids are a big commitment."

"Yes, they are," Lily said.

Anna had another commitment in mind first. All she needed was the right romantic moment to test the waters. Then maybe they could elope.

Chapter 3

Moments like these were Lily's favorites.

It was rare for her to wake before Anna, but when she did, she relished the chance to watch her in repose. Anna had migrated in the night to the center of the bed, twisting the blankets along the way to leave a bare hip exposed. If this was like every other Monday, she would awaken soon already in work mode, the instantaneous creases of her brow a sign she was thinking about marketing or payroll . . . and she would smile because she loved everything about the car business.

That was one of Lily's favorite things about Anna, that she enjoyed her work so thoroughly. But they had struck a deal when they moved in together not to take for granted the time they shared at home. Both tried hard not to bring home work unless it was absolutely necessary, even if it meant staying late at the office on occasion.

Lily felt good about how their relationship had progressed.

In many ways, they were behaving like partners, each taking responsibility for certain things. Knowing Anna's aversion to the kitchen, she had agreed to handle the cooking and grocery shopping. Anna managed the household finances, which included paying for someone else to clean the house, maintain the pool and care for the lawn. Lily had bucked this arrangement earlier, feeling that such luxuries were beyond her means. Anna had thought her silly for resisting the help, insisting Lily had no obligation to work off a debt just because Anna made more money. They settled the question of disparate finances once and for all when Anna sarcastically suggested she sell the house and they buy something smaller they both could afford.

Another good sign for them was how easily they seemed to talk about things. Anna had finally opened up about her sexuality, and was learning to give voice to her wants and needs without getting embarrassed. And through her trust and total lack of inhibition, she had become the best lover Lily had ever had.

By all accounts, Lily felt they were moving toward a commitment, meshing their lives as though they expected to stay together. Eventually, Anna would surely recognize that her prior mistake had been the choice of Scott as a partner, not marriage itself.

Lily had no such hurdles. She would marry Anna tomorrow.

"That's right, a Cinco de Mayo sale, weekend after next. A full-color double truck." Anna spoke crisply into the speakerphone, using the newspaper lingo for an ad stripped across two pages.

Her father loomed in the doorway, waiting while she finished the phone order.

"No, just the usual for this weekend. I'll have Brad send you the VINs this afternoon." Anna waved her father in. "Thanks, Steve. So long."

"I can't believe you're still nice to that jerk. He had a lot of nerve pulling that stunt down in San Diego."

"Pfft." She waved her hand in the air. She had told her family the whole story of Steve French's presumptuous gambit at the Hotel del Coronado, reserving a room and champagne on the off chance she might stay with him for the night. "I got over it. Lucky for Steve I didn't turn Lily loose on him. She would have tied his teeth in knots."

"You should have asked for a new rep."

"That was personal. This is business. He does a great job with our account, especially since that fiasco. I think he works harder for us than he used to."

"Still, you shouldn't have to put up with that."

"It was my own fault for mixing business with pleasure. You warned me about that." She gestured toward a chair in her cluttered office. "You want to talk about something?"

"I'm having another birthday, you know."

"Believe me, Dad. We all know. You remind us every day."

"We reserved the big round table at Empyre's on Saturday night. I might have some big news."

Anna leaned back and studied her father with amusement. "This is interesting. What kind of big news?"

"You'll have to show up on Saturday if you want to find out. But I'll give you a hint." He leaned forward and lowered his voice. "I'm more likely to tell you if you bring me a nice present."

She rolled her eyes dramatically. "Is Jonah coming? If you want me to come, you have to guarantee he'll be there." After all, her nine-month-old nephew was the center of the entire Kaklis universe.

"Are you kidding? He's the only reason I invited Kim and Hal."

Anna loved her father as a father, but she adored him as a doting grandfather. "And Lily is invited, of course?"

He gave an exaggerated groan. "I suppose so."

Anna wasn't quite sure when she realized this was merely his shtick. Over just a few months, Lily had met his resistance with offhanded humor, wearing him down. If this level of acceptance

25

was the best he could manage, she could live with it.

"Sounds good, but let me check with her first." This was going to put a dent in her romantic weekend plans, but it would give her a little more time to plan everything so it would be perfect. The idea of getting away for another weekend soon was growing on her.

Lily pulled her X3 into the valet line at Empyre's. The steady rain, though much needed in Southern California, had ruined her plans for a hike today. But Anna had surprised her by coming home at lunchtime, and they had spent the whole afternoon napping on the couch while basketball games played in the background.

"Did Kim have any ideas about what your father was up to?"

"She thinks he might be planning some big trip for their twentieth anniversary, which is next month. She was over there a couple of days ago and saw a bunch of brochures."

"Your dad only acts like a beast. In reality, he's a teddy bear."

"What did you get him for his birthday?"

"A digital picture frame with nineteen pictures of Jonah, and that one of us at Yosemite."

"He'll love it . . . until he gets to that one."

"That's the whole idea. He learns to associate smiling and being happy with seeing us together."

"It may take more than that."

"I know, but I couldn't figure out how to gift-wrap a lobotomy."

They reached the entrance and got out. Lily pocketed the valet check and walked around to loop her arm through Anna's as they walked in the door. The maitre d' nodded his hello and they proceeded to a large round table near the back.

"Look. Jonah saved me a seat," Anna said excitedly, hurrying to sit next to her sister. "Come to Auntie Anna, little man."

Kim looked relieved to give him up, and relaxed against her

husband's shoulder. Lily was thrilled for Kim and Hal. Their son was a handsome, healthy child with a sweet disposition. Though at nine months, he still wasn't sleeping through the night, and the weariness showed on his mother's face.

"Where's George?" Lily sat next to Anna, leaving empty the two seats beside her.

"They're running late," Kim said. "Mom was at our house all day with Jonah while Hal and I papered the guest room."

Anna held Jonah up and made a wide-eyed face. "Tell your daddy there are people who hang wallpaper for a living so he can sit and daydream about when he used to go out on his boat."

Kim snorted. "You seem to forget I'm married to an accountant."

"Look at it this way, Anna," Lily said. "Martine's been with Jonah all day, so you don't have to share him tonight."

She bounced the baby gently on her lap. "That's true, isn't it?"

George and Martine cut through the crowd to join them, and Hal jumped to his feet to hold his mother-in-law's chair. George seated himself next to Lily, glancing briefly at the wine list before ordering two bottles of his favorite for the table.

"Good evening, Lilian," he said formally, turning to face her.

"My, aren't we polite? I'm not moving out, George."

"You keep saying that. But it's going to get crowded when Anna's new husband moves in."

"I hate to tell you this, but Anna's new husband is a wife." Under less playful circumstances, she would never have said something so presumptuous, but she loved the contortions such a prospect produced on George's face.

He tasted the wine and motioned for the waiter to fill the glasses. "Give her a little extra . . . and be sure to bring her the bill."

Martine talked about spending the day with baby Jonah as everyone nibbled on olives, peppericcini and feta chunks. The waiter filled their wineglasses again before taking their order, and at George's signal, brought two more bottles.

Chattering between Anna and George, Lily became aware she was getting a nice buzz from the merlot. It felt good to relax, even though she and Anna had lounged around all afternoon. Thanks to their time with Carolyn and Vicki last weekend, she had been mired all week in thoughts about what was next for their relationship. She reaffirmed her decision that bringing it up with Anna was out of the question. Though they talked about everything else, Lily wasn't about to risk setting off a panic about making another commitment so soon after Scott. The ball was in Anna's court. It was up to her to decide what she wanted, and Lily would force herself to wait.

She smiled as she watched Anna fuss over Jonah. "He looks good on you, sweetheart," she whispered. "You're a natural."

"You want to hold him?" Anna asked.

Lily almost laughed at the expression on Anna's face. It was obvious she was only being polite. No way did she want to give up the baby. "No, that's okay. I mean I do, but he looks happy where he is."

As if on cue, Jonah sputtered and laughed, waving his arms up and down as Lily made exaggerated happy faces. His delighted squeal commanded the attention of the entire table.

Once dinner was ordered, all eyes finally turned to George. The excited smiles around the table made Lily giddy with joy at being part of this celebration, whatever it was.

"So what's up, Dad? Spill it," Anna said eagerly.

George leaned back and smiled at the expectant faces one by one. "Where should I start?"

"You mean when," Kim said. "And the answer is now."

"Very well." He chuckled and took a sip from his wineglass. "My sixtieth birthday has given me a reason to reflect on my blessings. I have a wonderful family and a loving wife. And thanks to Anna's hard work, I sit at the top of a very successful business. I've been thinking that I'd like to start spending less time with that business and more time with my family, especially this beautiful woman beside me and that little fellow over there." He took Martine's hand and nodded toward the infant, who was nodding off in Anna's arms. "And who knows, I might even enjoy playing a little more golf."

Everyone turned and exchanged astonished looks.

Anna was the first one to find her voice. "What are you saying?"

"I'm saying I've decided to retire."

Martine was obviously flabbergasted. "George, do you mean it?" She was already out of her chair reaching for her husband.

"Absolutely, darling." They shared a hug and then a kiss so deep everyone looked away embarrassed.

George then turned to Anna, who seemed stunned by the news. "Anna, I think you're ready to move up into the big chair now. I know this is going to mean a lot more work for you, and I wouldn't mind helping out on a part-time basis. But I wouldn't be doing this if I didn't think you were ready to take the helm."

Lily grinned at Anna's stupefied look. She had listened for hours on end to Anna's ideas for the dealership when the day finally came for her to take charge. But neither had expected it to come so soon.

Martine could hardly contain her excitement. "Does this mean I can start planning a real vacation?"

George smiled at her and looked at Anna. "I'll have to ask the boss if I can have a little time off, but I'm in pretty good with her, so I think she'll say yes. Besides, I already have a little trip in mind."

Anna finally broke into a sly grin. "I think a vacation is a great idea, Dad. In fact, you should make it a long one. I have to order new furniture and get your junk moved out of the corner office." She handed Jonah back to his mom, stood and walked behind Lily to give her father a hug.

"Congratulations, sweetheart," he said. "You're going to make a great boss."

Lily beamed at the news, excited at what this meant for all of the Kaklis family, but especially for Anna, who she knew relished the opportunity. Premier Motors was in for some very dramatic changes, many of which would take everyone by surprise. But having the chance to implement her vision for the dealership was a dream come true for Anna. She took Anna's hand as she slipped back into her chair and raised her wineglass in salute. "I'm so proud of you, honey. This is exciting."

Anna clinked her glass and took a sip, while Lily drained the last of hers. George quickly reached over and refilled the glass.

"When does this all happen?" Hal asked.

George pulled a packet from inside his jacket. "Pretty soon, I think. I've booked us on a cruise of the Greek Isles to celebrate our twentieth anniversary. We leave a week from tomorrow."

"The Greek Isles!" Martine clapped her hands together. "You sneaky devil."

"I figured you deserved something special for putting up with me for so long."

"What about us?" Kim asked. "Don't we deserve something too?"

"What did you have in mind?"

"You could keep Jonah and send Hal and me. That would be nice."

Martine shook her head. "Not this time."

Anna dug through her purse on the floor and pulled out her planner. "We should call our agency first thing Monday and ask them to prepare a press release. You can let the staff know at the end of the day and it will come out in the business section of Tuesday's *Times*."

George's look was priceless as Anna immediately fell into her new role as the dealership's CEO. Lily couldn't resist leaning over to whisper her taunt. "Not that she's in a hurry or anything."

"I wonder if she'll stay through dinner," George whispered back.

Anna missed the playful exchange, her mind obviously elsewhere. Suddenly she turned to her brother-in-law. "Hal, are

30

you ready to come to work in the car business?"

Hal was too surprised to speak, but Kim was grinning from ear to ear.

"Seriously, I've got some things in mind that could be fun for a bean counter like you. At least think about it."

"You certainly aren't wasting any time," George said.

"You only gave me a three-day notice. I have to hustle." She nodded toward Hal. "If Hal comes on board, I can let go of the financials and pay more attention to operations and marketing."

"Who's going to manage your inventory?" George asked.

Lily knew that had been his primary responsibility. She almost volunteered that Anna would have to buy and train a monkey, but stopped herself, aware that the wine was making her silly.

"I'm going to let Brad handle that. It makes sense to give the sales manager total control over the lot."

"That's enough business," Kim said. "I want to hear more about this cruise. Hal can take me to Greece as soon as you get back."

Throughout dinner, Lily listened with envy as George filled them in on the details of their trip. She and Anna were overdue for a real vacation. The two-day camping trip to Yosemite had been their longest getaway since becoming lovers a year ago. Something on a faraway beach would be perfect.

As the plates were cleared, Jonah began to fuss.

"Someone else is hungry now," Kim said.

Anna patted the baby's head. "You can feed him here. We don't mind."

"I mind. I fed him just before we got here. I'm trying to get him on a schedule of eating again at nine and going right to sleep. That's our only hope of him making it through the night."

Hal stood up and collected their belongings. "I guess we should go."

"How long am I going to have to wait for your decision, Hal?" Anna asked.

"You'll probably have a message on your answering machine when you get home tonight," Kim said. "You caught him after a

31

bad week at work."

"Good. I can get him cheap."

"Don't count on that."

Anna chuckled and started to rise.

Lily did the same, and was pleasantly surprised when George offered a hand to help her to her feet. She couldn't resist ducking under his arm and twirling, a move that told her the wine had definitely gone to her head. "You dance divinely, George."

"You think that's something, just wait till you see me dance at Anna's wedding."

"You're throwing us a wedding?"

George shook his head drearily as everyone else laughed.

"No more weddings for me," Anna said. "One was enough."

Stung by Anna's retort, Lily lurched away from the group toward the cloakroom. Suddenly conscious that her actions would be seen as pouty, she shook off her soured mood and tried to smile. Anna had always said her ill-fated marriage would have been far less humiliating had it not been for the lavish wedding. No wonder even the word carried such baggage. She stopped and waited until Anna caught up.

"This is such wonderful news, Anna."

"It's going to be a madhouse for a while . . . and Dad probably doesn't know it, but his timing is perfect."

"What does that mean?"

"I'll tell you later. If he hears what I'm up to, he might change his mind."

The group's departure was typically chaotic. Hal was sent with the valet tickets to order the cars, Martine retrieved the raincoats and umbrellas from the coat check, and Lily ducked into the ladies' room.

Anna took one last opportunity to cuddle with Jonah while Kim put on her raincoat. She was hopelessly in love with the little guy, enough that she entertained the fleeting thought of talking again with Lily about someday having a baby of their own. The notion deserved serious consideration before dismissing it altogether.

But her father's announcement tonight had given her a new set of immediate priorities. Rumors about Sweeney Volkswagen going under had her salivating at the possibility of expanding Premier's auto empire.

She smiled when Lily returned from the restroom and her father helped her into her coat. It was impossible not to appreciate the way their relationship had grown. Both of them deserved credit for smoothing out the rough spots—Lily for meeting her father's objections with humor, and her father for simply letting those objections wilt. No matter what either of them said, they cared about each other in their own special way.

Lily joined her at the door the moment her X3 appeared. Anna stepped in just as she reached for the keys. "Oh no, you don't."

"Probably not a bad idea," Lily said in agreement. She climbed into the passenger seat and immediately rolled down the window.

As Anna walked around the back of the vehicle, she heard Lily shout.

"Hey, George! You have to be nice to me now. I know your boss."

Anna laughed and strapped herself into the driver's seat. "Buckle your seatbelt, baby."

Lily complied, fumbling a little with the catch.

"Did you have a good time?"

"I must have. You're not letting me drive."

"Every time I looked over there, Dad was filling your glass. I bet you had a whole bottle."

"It's hard to keep count when someone else is pouring."

"If I were you, I'd plan on sleeping late." That was Lily's usual defense against a hangover. Not that she often drank to excess . . . but she enjoyed kicking back on the weekends. They both worked hard during the week, so Anna didn't begrudge her the chance to relax. She too enjoyed a glass of wine here and there, but never so much that she wasn't able to drive them home. "I might go in to my office for a little while tomorrow. Is that okay?"

"Measuring for new drapes?"

Anna chuckled. "Something like that."

Lily's hand crept over the console and into her crotch. "What if I have other plans for you?"

"Then I . . . might have to do some . . . multitasking." She grasped Lily's hand and pulled it to her lips. "I love you."

When they reached their home, Anna triggered the automatic opener for the garage door and pulled the SUV alongside the black Z8 she had acquired last week. The sleek two-seater convertible was longer and more powerful than BMW's mass model, the Z4. She felt bad for the seller—a Hollywood producer facing bankruptcy—but his misfortune was her gain. She'd had her eye out for one of the rare roadsters since losing her 850 in the earthquake.

As she stepped out, she realized the rain on the concrete floor had made it slick, a danger given Lily's unsteady state. "Stay there. I'll come around."

Together they huddled under an umbrella and hurried across the driveway to the side porch. "Our next house is going to have an attached garage." Anna slipped in her key and pushed open the door to the family room.

Before she could even kick off her wet shoes, Lily was covering her face and neck with passionate kisses. Anna happily accepted the greeting. "Somebody's feeling sexy tonight."

"We're celebrating."

"And just what are you celebrating?"

"I'm sleeping with the boss." She bit Anna's earlobe and whispered roughly, "I have a surprise for you upstairs."

Anna felt a surge of excitement as she followed Lily up to the master suite.

Lily set the tone immediately for what she had in mind, pushing Anna backward onto the bed. "Off with that dress, Amazon."

Anna complied, scooting out of the cocktail dress and tossing it onto the bedside chair. Under Lily's watchful eye, she then slipped off her stockings.

"Keep going or you won't get your surprise." Lily rested one knee on the end of the bed.

"I definitely want my surprise." She unhooked her bra and tossed it aside. Then she slid out of her panties and leaned back against the shams, waiting for Lily to take her.

Apparently, that wasn't what Lily had in mind. Piece by piece, she undressed as well, caressing her own body as it became bare. When she was fully nude, she scooted closer, but just out of Anna's reach. "Do you remember the first time we made love?"

"It was over the phone," Anna said.

"That's right." Lily cupped her breasts and pushed them together. "Do you ever think about that night?"

"I do."

"I think about it all the time. You know why?" She licked her fingers and used them to pinch her nipple. "Because I like to picture you touching yourself."

Anna followed her cue and allowed her hand to drift to her breast. It wasn't unusual for either of them to "lend a helping hand" when they made love, but this was the first time they had done this solely for show.

"Show me what you were doing when you told me how wet you were." Lily dipped her own fingers between her legs and held them up. "Were you wet like this?"

Not taking her eyes from Lily, Anna opened her legs and delved into her center, coating her fingers the way Lily had.

"This is what I did, Anna . . . this is how I was touching myself when I told you what I wanted." Her eyes closed as she slid two fingers inside and began to pump. "Only I imagined it was you doing this."

35

"And you were doing this for me." Anna began to massage her clitoris.

"You were reaching deep . . . way up inside." Lily held one leg out to open herself more, using the fingers on her other hand to spread her labia. "Do you like this?"

Anna moaned her approval and increased the speed of her strokes. "I want to see you come."

Lily was breathing hard now, and she removed her fingers from her vagina to rub her clitoris. "I'll come for you"—she pointed to where Anna was touching herself—"but I want you to save that for me too."

With a groan of frustration, Anna slowed her hand, mesmerized by the smoldering look on Lily's face. It was all she could do not to climax when Lily suddenly dropped her lower jaw and drew in a deep breath.

"Is this what you wanted to see?" Still upright on the bed, Lily began to undulate, never dropping her gaze. She cried out in the rhythm of her thrusts, and suddenly drew her slickened hand from her own clitoris to slide it into Anna. "Now you."

Anna was way past ready, and in only moments, it was over.

Chapter 4

The whirlwind began on Sunday afternoon when Hal called to accept Anna's offer to come to work at Premier Motors. She named him vice president of finance and promised him a fat salary to go with it. By noon on Monday his accounting firm had shown him the door—not unusual, considering his company dealt with confidential client files—and he was on the lot first thing Tuesday morning. Eager to implement her vision for the dealership, Anna met with him behind closed doors all day, laying out her plan for growing the business and tasking him with working the numbers to get it done.

By Saturday afternoon, she had her new management team in place. Brad Stanley, Premier's longtime sales manager, was stepping up to vice president of operations, Anna's old job, minus the marketing responsibilities, which she kept for herself. Brad would handle day-to-day management, such as staffing and inventory control.

Holly Martin, last year's hire from San Diego, was a natural to take over Brad's post as sales manager. She knew more about the cars than any salesperson on the lot, and she had a real gift for closing the deal. Anna had taken advantage of the casual atmosphere at Premier to get to know Holly outside of their working relationship, and had begun to think of her as a friend. She would make a great addition to the team.

As expected, George had made himself scarce following his retirement announcement, taking the whole week off to pack for the cruise. He was oblivious to the major moves Anna had set in motion.

Even though her father was no longer running the business, she wanted to share with him her plans before he discovered them on his own. That meant catching him at home tonight before he and Martine left for Greece.

"Anna Kaklis, you have a call on line one. Anna Kaklis, line one."

Anna had been taking congratulatory calls from the business community all week after the press release in the *Times*. "This is Anna Kaklis."

The voice on the phone was deep and raspy. "What are you wearing?"

It took her only an instant to recognize Lily's mischief. "Funny you should ask. I can't remember putting underwear on this morning. I don't think I did."

"That's because I've stolen all your panties. I have a panty fetish, you know."

"That would explain why you're always taking them off me."

"I like to sniff them when you're not here."

Anna felt herself blushing at the intimacy, hoping no one at Premier accidentally picked up the wrong line. "What can I do for you, my little pervert?"

"You can come home. We just got an invitation to Sandy and Suzanne's for dinner. Sandy's fixing something that sounds French."

38

Anna checked her watch, then the pile of papers on her desk. "That sounds great, but I need to talk to Dad about Sweeney before they head out tomorrow. I was thinking about going by after work." She waited, hoping Lily wouldn't be too upset about yet another late night. "Why don't you go? I'll finish up here and head over to Mom and Dad's. Then I'll see you at home later."

"I don't have to go. I can come by and pick you up. We can grab a bite somewhere and then stop by so you can talk to George."

It was bad enough Anna had worked late every night this week. She wasn't about to wreck a night out with friends for Lily. "No, I don't want you to do that. You've worked hard this week. You've earned a night out, and you should go."

"By myself?"

"Yeah, go and have fun. Tell them both I said hi, and we'll have them over soon. Okay?"

"If you're sure . . ."

"I am." Anna felt her guilt recede. At least Lily would have a good time tonight. "I should be home by nine."

"Okay, I'll see you then."

Anna hung up and leaned back in her chair. Her first week as CEO had been hectic, but it was almost behind her. If she came in early tomorrow, she could take Sunday afternoon off to relax. Maybe she and Lily could pull out their calendars and find a few days to get away. Memorial Weekend in Hawaii was looking better all the time.

Lily pulled in behind Sandy's small sedan, excited about seeing her friends. To be truthful, she would have been excited to see total strangers after a full week of being on her own. She and Anna hadn't had a meal together all week, with Anna leaving for the dealership at six thirty each morning and returning in time to fall into bed exhausted. But it was only temporary . . . at least that's what Anna had promised.

39

She picked up the two bottles of wine—one white, one red—on her front seat and headed up the stairs to her friends' ranch-style home.

Sandy met her at the front door before she could even ring the bell. "What's this? Two bottles of wine?"

Lily greeted her with a hug, clicking the bottles behind Sandy's back. "I have no idea what tarti . . . whatever is."

"Tartiflette. It's a potato pie with cheese and bacon."

Lily held up the wine. "And that's best with what?"

Sandy took the chardonnay and left Lily holding the cabernet sauvignon. "Let me chill this."

"Fine. We can drink this one before dinner."

"Right . . . and pass out with our faces in our plates."

Lily followed her into the kitchen, where Suzanne was putting the finishing touches on the table.

"Hey, where's your pretty half?" Suzanne made no secret of her opinion that Anna was gorgeous—except that first time they all shared a nude soak in the hot tub. She had lost her tongue that night.

"She's working late," she answered with a mock snarl.

"On a Saturday night?"

"Yeah, I've hardly seen her all week."

"I guess she has a lot to do now that her father is retiring."

"He says he's going to work part-time. But now that Anna's in charge, she's making some big changes." Lily worked the corkscrew until it popped. Then she poured three glasses of red wine. "Don't tell anybody this, but she's getting ready to make an offer for the Volkswagen dealership in West Hollywood."

"Who would we tell?" Sandy asked.

"Nobody, silly. But she wants to keep things low-key so they can get things done without somebody else jumping in to bid."

Sandy led the way into the living room and offered Lily a bowl of cocktail nuts. "Eat these so I won't."

"Gladly."

"So how long is this working around the clock going to

last?"

"It better not be much longer, or I'm trading her in for a new girlfriend." Lily took a gulp of her wine and set the glass on the coffee table. "At least she's hired a new management team. Maybe she can start taking weekends off."

"Wouldn't that be nice?"

"It really would. We could have a normal life."

Suzanne came in and refilled Lily's glass before scooping up a handful of nuts. "There's no such thing as a normal life. Just ask Sandy."

Sandy shook her head. "Isn't that the truth! Try living with an ER nurse who works double shifts three times a week."

"No, thanks. Anna and I made a deal that we weren't going to let work take over our lives."

"So where is she?" Suzanne asked haughtily.

Lily realized her grousing about Anna's late hours had led her friend to pile on out of sympathy. "It's only for a little while longer. She was just saying a couple of weeks ago that she wanted to start doing more things with our friends."

"How did your camping trip go?" Sandy asked.

"We had a ball." Lily finished her second glass of wine as she described the weekend at Yosemite—meeting Anna's friends, the hike to the base of the falls, and how Anna adapted to the outdoors. "Their dog was so funny. He wouldn't leave Anna alone."

The oven chimed and Sandy herded them back into the kitchen to eat.

Lily smiled to herself as Suzanne poured chardonnay for the table. One more glass of wine and she would be spilling her guts about what they had done in their tent. But it was the weekend, time to relax. "Anna's friends had some cool news. They're having a baby."

"Aw, how sweet," Sandy said.

Suzanne shuddered visibly. "Rugrats."

Lily smacked Suzanne's forearm. "It is sweet. They're

excited."

"I bet," Sandy said, ignoring her partner's petulance. "Suzanne won't even let me have a cat."

"The coolest part is that Vicki's the one having the baby, but they did in vitro using Carolyn's eggs."

"Wonder how a court in Virginia would sort that out?" Suzanne grumbled.

It was Sandy's turn to deliver a smack. "Quit being so mean." She turned back to Lily. "So did that give you and Anna any ideas?"

Lily almost choked on her wine. "Hardly. I think Anna's given up on the idea. She used to say she thought she wanted a baby, but now . . . I don't know, maybe it's different because she isn't married anymore." It was disappointing that Anna had dismissed the idea of having a child now, especially after having been so keen on it with Scott.

"You could always have one," Sandy said.

"Oh, no. I don't think I even have a biological clock."

Suzanne dug into the dish and served herself an extra portion. "Kids are a huge commitment. I bet half the lesbian couples that jump through all the hoops to get kids don't even stay together to raise them."

Sandy wrinkled her nose at the grim assessment. "Yeah, but just because they don't stay committed to each other doesn't mean they aren't committed to their kids. Lily and I work with lots of kids who'd be better off if their parents never saw each other again."

"Suzanne's right." Lily sighed and pushed her half-empty plate away, her appetite gone. "If people aren't sure they're going to stay together, they shouldn't have kids. I wouldn't be surprised if that's why Anna's changed her mind."

Sandy set down her fork and gave Lily a serious look. "Is something wrong, Lily?"

"No . . . it's nothing. I just . . ." She realized she wanted to talk, but she didn't want to make Anna look bad to her friends.

"Everything's fine, but sometimes I feel like we're doomed all because Anna screwed up when she got married."

"You don't think you'll stay together?"

"I don't know what to think. It's not like there's anything wrong. It's just that we live day to day."

"That's all any of us do," Suzanne said.

"No, it isn't," she said, her voice harsh. It bugged her that Suzanne always tried to be contrary. "You guys go to sleep every night knowing you're going to be together tomorrow and the day after that and the day after that. I go to sleep wondering how long Anna's going to live like this before she decides she wants something else."

Suzanne gave her an annoying, dismissive shrug and got up to clear the table.

"Oh, that's great, Suzanne. Just be smug and superior." Lily tossed her napkin on the table and pushed away from the table. Immediately, she felt embarrassed by the childish display. Too much wine sometimes soured her mood.

"Whoa!" Sandy said. "Calm down, Lily. Nobody's trying to be smug."

Suzanne sat back down and gave her an apologetic look. "All I was saying was that none of us know what's around the corner. Some of us kid ourselves, but anything can happen."

Sandy sighed. "Please forgive my girlfriend, the fatalist. She isn't always this depressing. I think I get what you're saying, Lily."

"People want what they think is going to make them happy," Suzanne added. "For me, that's Sandy. And for you, it's Anna."

"But I don't know what it is for Anna."

"Have you talked with her about this?" Sandy asked gently.

"You mean like I did with Beverly just before she showed me the door?" Lily shuddered at the memory of how her ex-girlfriend had freaked out about the idea of making a commitment together. Their relationship went from comfortable to tenuous to hostile in a matter of only weeks.

43

"Beverly was a psycho bitch. Anna isn't," Suzanne said.

"She's right. Beverly had control issues. She wasn't going to let herself be held accountable for anything. Anna isn't like that at all."

For Lily, the possibilities were even worse. "No, Anna wouldn't turn into a bitch. She'd probably bend over backward to let me down easy and make sure I was okay. Then she'd go off and marry some guy."

"Lily, why are you torturing yourself with these awful scenarios? Is something going on?"

"No!" So why was she consumed with morbid thoughts? "I just love her so much. I couldn't stand it if she ever left me."

Sandy patted her arm. "You guys have been together for what? A year?"

"Yeah, a little longer."

"And it's all been great, hasn't it?"

Lily nodded.

"Then it looks to me like you're on a perfectly normal course. These things don't happen overnight, and that's a good thing. The ones that do are usually the ones that fall apart."

Sandy's arguments made logical sense, but that did little to quell the anxiety Lily had been feeding on for the past couple of weeks. Carolyn and Vicki had shown Anna the kind of committed love two women could have, but it hadn't impressed her at all. If anything, she seemed to be moving in the other direction, distancing herself from a desire to have children and mocking the very idea of having another wedding.

And if that wasn't enough, she worked too much.

Anna pulled into the driveway, readying her apology for working so late. Despite her promise to be home by nine, it was almost eleven. The main thing she wanted Lily to know was that she expected things to be back to normal soon, and if people stepped up into their jobs, it would allow her to take more

44

weekends off.

She was surprised to find an empty garage, though it assuaged her guilt to realize Lily was still with her friends. At least she hadn't been waiting at home all this time.

The briefcase beside her, packed ambitiously to get a jump on tomorrow, held printouts from Hal on Premier's finances. Anna left it on the seat and climbed out of her sports car, suddenly overwhelmed by both mental and physical fatigue. All she wanted was a long soak in a swirling tub. Her usual choice was the hot tub out by the pool, but with Lily gone, she would use the smaller one in the master suite.

She passed through the kitchen, staring for a moment at the contents of the refrigerator before settling on her usual. This was her third late-night peanut butter sandwich this week. Since Lily wasn't around to keep her company in the kitchen, she dragged herself up the stairs to draw a bath.

A ringing phone stopped her just as she was about to step into the tub.

"Hello."

"Anna, we missed you tonight."

"Hi, Sandy. I'm sorry I couldn't make it. Did you guys have a good time?"

"We did. But I'm afraid we're not all having a good time now."

"What?" Her stomach dropped. It hadn't even occurred to her to worry about why Lily wasn't home. "Is everything all right?"

"It's fine, but Lily's not in any shape to drive home. Do you want to come get her, or should we tuck her in?"

Anna remembered the fun they'd had last weekend when they returned from the dinner at Empyre's, and was momentarily tempted by the possibility of a repeat performance. "What does Lily have to say about it?"

"She can't talk right now. She's in the bathroom losing an excellent tartiflette."

"She's sick?"

"It's nothing to worry about. Just one glass too many. We were talking all through dinner and I think it snuck up on her."

That was how Lily had described it last time, losing count of her drinks at dinner before realizing she was tipsy. This sounded more than tipsy. "Maybe she ought to stay with you guys. What do you think?"

"I think that's probably best, but I wanted you to make the call."

Lily would probably prefer to come home tonight and sleep it off, but selfishly, Anna wanted to collapse in the tub. Besides, if she drove out to Sherman Oaks tonight to pick her up, she would have to make another trip tomorrow for the X3, and by then her whole morning would be shot. Having her stay the night with Sandy and Suzanne definitely made more practical sense. "No, you should keep her for the night. I'm beat. I was just about to get in the tub. Would that be all right?"

"Of course. I'll have her call you in the morning."

"Maybe she'll sleep late."

"She isn't going to wake up happy. I can promise you that."

Though initially irritated to find Anna's car gone yet again, Lily calmed down and admitted to herself she was actually relieved. Suzanne had busted her chops this morning for losing her dinner, and Lily didn't want to hear more of the same from Anna. Besides, she needed a shower to steam out the remnants of a headache.

She felt a little guilty for her whining last night, complaining to her friends about Anna's reluctance to commit. Their relationship was fine, moving along at a normal pace, just as Sandy had said. As long as both of them were happy, there wasn't any reason to look ahead with dread.

She parked and started into the house, struck by the sudden thought of how lucky she was. Two years ago, she would never have imagined herself living in such a beautiful home in a neighborhood like Brentwood, or even driving a luxury car like the X3. With Anna taking charge of their home finances, Lily now had plenty of money to buy the things she wanted, and to build a healthy retirement account. Her new lifestyle was a generous gift, and Anna never made her feel as though any of it was tenuous or given with expectations.

But the fact remained, if anything happened to Anna, all of it would vanish. There was plenty of love and joy in her life, but not much in the way of security. And as quickly as her emotions had swung earlier to being relieved Anna wasn't home, they shifted again. It wasn't irritation this time, but anxiety.

With one eye on the clock, she showered and dressed, purposely choosing the comfortable sweats she had worn last weekend when they lounged the whole afternoon on the couch. She and Anna deserved another day like that, especially after the horrendous work week Anna had put in.

From the master bedroom window, she checked the driveway each time she heard a car on the street. Anna usually didn't work on Sundays, so it was likely she would be home soon. In fact, Lily realized, she might not be working at all. This was the day George and Martine left for the trip, and Anna might have taken them to the airport.

After more than an hour, Lily gave in to the temptation to call. After four rings, her cell phone went to voicemail and Lily hung up. If she wasn't answering her cell phone, she was almost certainly at work, either on the lot, in the showroom or in the garage.

With growing frustration, Lily paced from the family room to the kitchen and back, the phone still in her hand. For Anna to be at work yet again after a whole week of late nights—and on the only day they could enjoy being together—was beyond ridiculous. When she was sure her temper wouldn't get the best of her, she dialed the number for the dealership. It didn't help that she was placed on hold for almost three minutes before Anna finally came to the phone.

"This is Anna Kaklis."

"Hello, stranger."

"Hey, baby. I was going to call you. How's your head?"

"It's okay. It wasn't that bad. I think I just ate something that didn't sit right."

"So you're feeling better? And you slept okay?"

"I slept fine." Except alone. "But I'd feel a lot better if you came home before I forgot what you looked like."

"God, I wish I could."

"Last I heard, you were the boss. You can walk out that door whenever you want."

"Not today, honey. I've been meeting all day with Hal and—"

"You're making your poor brother-in-law work on a Sunday?"

"We have to, baby. This offer has to go to the attorneys by tomorrow morning if we're going to get it out this week."

Lily bit her lip. It wasn't as if Anna routinely worked all hours of the day and night. This was a special circumstance, one that deserved support and understanding. She almost hated to ask what sort of day Anna was looking at. "Do you think you'll make it home for dinner?"

"Oh, absolutely. I haven't had a decent meal all week."

"Then I'll roast a chicken . . . that Italian recipe you like."

"Sounds fantastic."

"And after that, I'm going to take you upstairs and massage your body from head to toe."

Anna moaned.

"And then I'm going to have my way with you."

". . . six o'clock. What else do they need?" Anna cradled the phone to her ear and jotted notes on her desk blotter. Another week had flown by. Premier's attorney, Walter Kaplan, had gotten a reply from Sweeney Volkswagen and wanted to discuss the next step in their negotiations. "I want Hal there too . . . Right. See you then."

She hung up and walked the twenty feet to her brother-in-law's office. She was thrilled to have him on board. After only two weeks on the job, it was clear he was a natural fit in her plans for growing the dealership.

"I just heard from Walter. Sweeney wants to set up the audit. We're supposed to be over there at six."

"Tonight?"

"Tonight. We need to meet after the sales staff leaves to keep this under wraps."

"His sales staff is gone by six?"

"Yeah. Now you know why I see so much potential over there."

Hal sighed and looked at his phone. "Your sister is going to be pissed."

"I know." Anna would have to cancel her plans to go with Lily to a bridal shower for the woman marrying her boss. "But the sooner we get this wrapped up, the sooner we get our lives back." She returned to her office and closed the door. Lily wasn't going to like the news either, but she would understand. She dialed the direct number to Lily's desk.

"Lilian Stewart."

"Hey, sweetheart. You having a good day?"

"Not bad. We're all trying to hurry so we can grab dinner before the shower. You want to meet me at the house at five thirty?"

"Uh . . . that's why I was calling. Something's come up here. I need to be at Sweeney's at six o'clock for a meeting. It's probably going to last a couple of hours, so I don't think I'll make it to the shower."

"You're meeting tonight? Can't you do this during normal working hours?"

Anna picked up on the irritation in Lily's voice, and hoped she could lighten things up with a joke. "You know how you sneaky

49

lawyer types are. It's the only way we can meet without everyone finding out about it."

Lily didn't answer at all.

"Seriously, honey . . . this is a good thing. Once we get the audits going, it's just a matter of agreeing on a price. Then Walter takes over with the paperwork."

Lily sighed. "And it has to be tonight?"

"Sweeney's ready now. I can't give him too much time to think this over, or he'll start making a list of conditions."

"Fine."

It didn't sound fine. "Honey, please. I'm sorry, but I really need to do this."

"I know. I'm just whining. We haven't been out together for a couple of weeks and I was looking forward to it."

"I will make it up to you in ways you can't imagine." Like Maui.

"Okay, I'll go with Lauren and Pauline. But I'm holding you to that making-it-up-to-me part. You'd better not plan on working tomorrow night."

A Friday night at home sounded great. "You've got a deal. Have a good time."

"I'll see you at home."

"I love you." She smiled at how nicely all of her plans were coming together. As soon as she hung up, she would call a travel agent to help her shop around for a nice Hawaiian getaway.

Lily walked out of her office and into the hallway. "Pauline, can you come to Lauren's office for a minute?"

The secretary joined her and they continued down the hall, where fellow attorney Lauren Miller was working on her computer. "What's up, guys?"

"I wondered if you two wanted to ride together to the bridal shower tonight. Anna just called and she's tied up at work. You can leave your cars at my house and we won't have to worry about parking."

They kept their voices low so that Tony wouldn't overhear. In two days, their boss would cease being one of LA's most eligible bachelors. Colleen Turner, a young widow with two small children, had applied for an internship at the firm last fall, hoping to get some hands-on experience with the social services system. She was fresh out of law school, but hadn't yet taken the bar exam. In a matter of only a few months, she had swept Tony off his feet.

Lauren and Pauline followed her home after work as planned, and they rode in Lauren's car to Colleen's sister's home.

"Are these people movie stars?" Pauline asked, obviously awed at the Brentwood mansion.

"Not exactly," Lauren said. She and Colleen had become friends, so she knew a bit about the family. "I think Colleen's brother-in-law is a big shot at one of the major recording companies."

The house was only slightly larger than the "big house," which is what Anna and her sister called their parents' home in Beverly Hills. But George and Martine didn't have uniformed servants, like the one who greeted them at the door.

They were led to the main room of the house, where a lively party was already underway, complete with piano music and an open bar. No fewer than a hundred women filled the room, the chatter spilling over onto the patio. Lily spotted Colleen and they weaved their way through the room to say hello.

Pauline ventured to the bar for their drinks, but came back empty-handed. "They don't have any red wine. He said the caterer forgot to stock it. What's your second choice?"

"I don't care," said Lauren. "I don't like sweet drinks."

Lily made a face. "Me neither."

"I had a vodka martini once. It was pretty good, and it wasn't sweet."

"I'll try it," Lauren shrugged.

"Me too."

Lily had never been much of a liquor drinker, but found the chilled drink surprisingly refreshing. What wasn't much of a surprise was the buzz she felt after the second. But why shouldn't she celebrate on such a happy occasion?

"This is a great party," Lauren said. "Too bad Anna couldn't come."

"Yeah . . . too bad. Anna can't do anything but work," she said, aware that her words weren't coming out clearly.

"Uh-oh," Lauren said. "How many of these have you had?"

Lily slammed back the drink in her hand, her fourth, and started again for the bar. "Not enough."

"Hold on." Lauren caught her arm, but Lily shook free and continued, stumbling against the back of a sofa.

She set her glass on the bar and motioned for one more just as Lauren caught up with her.

"Your girlfriend's going to kick my ass."

"She won't even be home," Lily scowled. She wasn't sure what transpired over the next few minutes, but she found herself in the front seat of Lauren's car.

"Crack your window," Lauren told her sternly. "No getting sick in my car."

Vaguely aware that Pauline was getting into the backseat, Lily contemplated the need to throw up and decided against it. The ride home was a blur, until the moment they pulled into the driveway and saw the dark house. Anna was making a night of it at her office. "Fuck."

Chapter 5

Anna brushed the powder on her cheeks and checked her look. She was thrilled to finally have a chance to go out, and Tony's wedding was a great occasion. She and Lily needed time together in the worst way.

Things were going better at the dealership, but she found that her strategy sessions with Hal were consuming the day, and all the paperwork was waiting for her when the doors closed and the sales staff went home. Holly was doing a great job managing the inventory and getting cars out the door, but Anna was growing more and more frustrated with the unexpected errors in her paperwork. She had finally called her in on Friday night to talk about it, and Holly told her of her problems with dyslexia. There were ways to get around it, she said, and if Anna would be patient, she would come up with a new sales form by the end of next week. In the meantime, Anna had no choice but to check all of her contracts.

"You'd better not be thinking about work, Amazon. You're mine tonight." Lily smiled accusingly at their reflection in the long bathroom mirror as they dressed for the festive occasion. "You got it, sweetheart." Her cheeks reddened slightly at Lily's seeming ability to read her mind. She didn't dare confirm that her thoughts were still on her work, or that she was silently wishing she could spend just a few hours there tomorrow to catch up on the sales contracts.

"Zip me?" Lily offered her back.

Anna seized the moment to kiss her exposed neck and shoulder. "This is my favorite dress. I remember the first time I saw this dress." Lily had worn it to dinner at Empyre's that night after they ran into each other at the courthouse.

"That was the first time I wore it. I bought it that afternoon because I didn't have anything to wear to a fancy place like Empyre's."

"You wore it like it was made for you."

"Off the rack at Bloomingdale's in Sherman Oaks. Sandy and I both cut out of work that afternoon so she could help me find something. In fact, I had something scratching me in the rib all night, and when I got home, I found the tag still in it." She chuckled at the memory. "I think I started falling in love with you that night."

Anna spun her around and kissed her deeply, wishing she could peel off the dress and lead Lily back into their bedroom. They hadn't made love since last Sunday. "Let's go get your boss married so we can come back here and get reacquainted."

"Our table is number eighteen," Lily said, taking Anna by the hand to lead her through the maze. "Colleen put all of us from the office together, and I got her to add Sandy and Suzanne."

"That'll be fun. Colleen made a beautiful bride. I loved her dress."

Lily pulled out two chairs and they sat. "One of these days,

I'm going to make you show me your wedding pictures."

Anna groaned.

"Because I can't imagine a more beautiful bride than you."

During Tony and Colleen's vows, she had caught a glimpse of Anna wiping a tear. "Did something bother you during the ceremony?"

"Not really. I just thought it was very sweet."

Lily gently stroked Anna's forearm and ducked lower to make eye contact. "Sure that's all?"

Anna covered her hand and squeezed. "I was listening to what they were saying to each other . . . and thinking about the big mistake I made with Scott."

"You need to let that go, sweetheart. It's all in the past."

"I know. Especially since I've got the greatest partner I could ever have right here with me."

Lily's heart surged at Anna's sweet words. She looked around at the growing crowd in the ballroom. "Okay, people," she said, her voice too low for others to hear. "Sit down and eat so we can wrap this up. I have to take this woman home and make love to her all night."

Suzanne pulled out the chair next to Lily. "That was great. Where's the food?"

Sandy joined them. "You should have heard Suzanne's stomach growl right in the middle of the prayer."

"I haven't eaten since midnight."

"That's because you slept all day."

"That's because I worked all night."

Anna stood. "I'm going to the bar. Anyone want a glass of wine?"

"I'll take one," Sandy answered.

Lily had been thinking she might not drink tonight. Yesterday's hangover from the bridal shower had lasted till mid-afternoon. But she could get something to sip. "Maybe just a merlot."

She polished off her wine before hitting the buffet line, and washed down her meal with sparkling water. When they finished,

55

she volunteered for the next bar run, deciding after all that the festive occasion warranted kicking back again and having a good time.

"I guess I'll have another," Anna said, polishing off her first glass of wine.

Lily picked up their empties and made her way through the crowd to the bar.

"Lily! How are you?"

"Andrew, hi. Don't you clean up well!" Andrew Shively was a sergeant with the LAPD, and a frequent volunteer for Kidz Kamp, the group that treated foster children to weekend outings in the great outdoors.

"You're one to talk. That's a great dress."

"Thank you."

"Are you and Anna doing any Kidz Kamp trips this summer?"

"I think we're down for August, but I'm not sure." She placed the empty glasses on a tray and turned toward the bar. "I'd like two glasses of merlot . . . on second thought, make that one merlot and one vodka martini."

"Would you like that with an olive or a lime?" the tuxedoed woman asked.

"Lime sounds good."

"You should try a kamikaze," Andrew suggested.

"What's that?"

"It's vodka, triple sec and lime juice. You can get it on the rocks or as a shooter. Go ahead, try one. I'm buying."

"Okay, I'll try a shooter."

"Make it two." The bartender expertly poured the two liquors and added a splash of lime juice. Lifting his shot glass, Andrew offered a toast. "To Tony."

"To Tony." Lily threw her head back and slammed the shooter, not prepared for the clenching sensation in her chest as the drink reached its mark. "Wow! That was good." Turning back to the bartender, she amended her order yet again. "Okay, make it one merlot and one kamikaze on the rocks." As Andrew walked away, she ordered one more shooter and downed it at the bar.

By the time she returned to the table, Tony and Colleen had taken to the dance floor for the ceremonial first dance. Gradually, couples joined them on the floor, but Lily held back.

"Are we going to dance?" Anna asked, looping her elbow through Lily's and giving her a tug.

"I don't know. Maybe I should ask Tony if it's all right. I don't want to freak his mother out."

Sandy stood up and pulled Suzanne from her chair. "It is. He told me earlier he expected to see us out there on the dance floor."

"In that case . . ." Lily got up and steered Anna toward the crowd, vaguely aware she was feeling the effects of her drinks. "I don't get this chance very often."

Anna folded into an embrace on the dance floor. "No, the only other time we've done this was the Christmas party at Premier."

"I remember. And then you took me home and fucked my brains out."

Anna's eyebrows went up in evident surprise at her brash statement. "Yes, I did."

"Are you going to do that again tonight?"

"Absolutely."

Lily turned her face into Anna's neck and began to kiss her. "Good. Can we leave yet?"

"I think it might be a little early." Anna reached behind her and stilled Lily's wandering hands. "But we'll definitely go before we scandalize Tony's wedding."

The music stopped and they parted, sharing a look of heated desire. "Are you ready for another glass of wine?"

"I don't think so."

"Okay, I'll be there in a second."

Lily returned to the bar yet again, downing a shooter before heading back to the table with a cocktail on ice.

"What is that you're drinking?" Anna asked.

"It's called a kamikaze. Andrew Shively told me about it. It's got vodka . . . lime . . . and something else. I forget what. Want one?"

"No, thank you. I'll stick to my wine."

Anna turned in her seat to converse with Lauren and her husband, but Lily had other ideas. She leaned over Anna's shoulder and whispered, "I want my tongue inside you when you come." She followed that with a wet flick to the ear.

Anna suddenly stood. "I think Lily and I need to be going. We've both got a lot to do tomorrow to get ready for the week."

As excuses went, that one sounded pretty lame, but Lily didn't care. All she wanted was to get home as soon as possible.

Anna took the wheel of the sports car and Lily stretched across the console to press a hand underneath her dress.

"If you don't stop that, I'm going to kill us both," she said, retrieving Lily's hand from her crotch.

"But what a way to go." She could see the streetlights going past, and fought a wave of nausea as the car spun around a corner. "I have to pee."

"We're almost home."

She heard the garage go up and struggled to sit upright. Twice she tried to open the door as Anna was disengaging the lock and it stuck. When it finally sprang free, she got out and made a beeline for the side door, impatient for Anna to unlock it. Once inside, she dashed into the closest bathroom, the one between the family room and the kitchen.

"I'll lock up," Anna called.

Lily finished and started up the stairs to their bedroom, kicking off her heels halfway up. By the time she reached the top, she had wriggled out of her dress and dropped it in a heap on the landing. She turned the corner and stumbled to the bed, stripping off the last of her clothes. Lovemaking . . . that would have to wait until tomorrow.

• • •

Anna folded the sports page to read the story on last night's Dodgers game. It would be great to get to the ballpark one of these days, she thought, but that didn't look possible anytime soon, not with the extra duties at work.

From her seat by the pool she saw movement in the kitchen, and almost wished she had gone on to her office after breakfast. Her irritation about last night might have subsided if she hadn't sat and stewed about it all morning while Lily slept in. But they needed to talk, and it wasn't going to be pretty.

Lily emerged from the French doors onto the patio, a mug of coffee in her hand. She was barefoot, dressed in one of Anna's button-down collar shirts, its long tail hanging to the top of her thighs. Her wet hair was slicked straight back, evidence she had tried to wash away the remnants of last night's celebration.

Under other circumstances, Anna would have smiled and said something flirtatious.

"Hi," Lily said, planting a kiss on the top of her head.

"Good morning," Anna responded coolly. "Sleep well?"

"Yeah, how about you?"

"All right, I suppose."

"Are you ready for a refill?" Lily gestured at Anna's empty mug.

"No, thank you," she answered formally, not sure of how to broach her displeasure.

Lily rummaged through the paper for the main news section. "Listen to this. 'In a sixteen-hour procedure, a team of surgeons in Johannesburg successfully separated eight-week-old Sudanese twins joined at the hip and thigh. The infants, in critical but stable condition, were rejoined with their parents in the Sudan.'"

Anna had seen the story, but realized Lily was playing it for laughs. She wasn't in the mood for it.

"Get it? Siamese twins rejoined with their parents?"

She still wouldn't answer.

"Like, what's the point of separating them from each other if you're just going to rejoin them to someone else?"

59

"I get it," Anna said sharply. "I guess I don't find it funny."

Lily laid the paper down and looked at her. "Okay, what's wrong?"

From behind the sports page, Anna answered matter-of-factly. "You fell asleep on me last night."

"And I'm getting the cold shoulder for that?"

Anna sighed. "It hurt my feelings, Lily. I finally got some time off for us to be together and we wasted it."

Lily tossed the paper back onto the stack. "Your work schedule isn't my fault. I'm sorry I fell asleep. I guess I partied too much. But if you want more of me, you could always spend more time at home."

"You know how busy things are at work right now. I don't want to be gone so much, but I have to be, at least until things are running smoothly. And you said you understood that."

"I do. But that doesn't mean we do everything on your schedule."

Last night wasn't the only problem, but it was symptomatic of something else that had begun to cause Anna concern. "Lily, you've been partying a lot lately. You got tipsy at Empyre's a couple of weeks ago, then last weekend you couldn't drive home from Sandy and Suzanne's." There was also the night of the bridal shower, when Anna had found Lily asleep by nine thirty, and smelling strongly of alcohol.

"Are you suggesting I have a drinking problem?" Her defensive tone was unmistakable.

"No, but it isn't like you to drink as much as you have lately. I guess I don't want it to turn into a problem."

"It won't, Anna. But don't expect me just to jump in your lap whenever you snap your fingers and say, 'Hey, I've got a minute.'"

The ring of the kitchen phone ended the conversation abruptly, and Lily walked briskly back into the house.

Anna felt awful. All she had wanted was a chance to express her concerns, and instead, she had practically accused Lily of being an alcoholic. On top of that, she had gotten a loud and clear message that her workload was the reason they hadn't been connecting recently. At that moment, she made the decision not to go to her office after all. She didn't like feeling as if there was something between them.

When she heard Lily hang up the phone, she got up and followed her into the kitchen. "Who was that?" she asked, trying to sound more cheerful than before.

"That was Mom. She wanted to remind us that she and Bill are coming next weekend. He's got that oncology conference in Long Beach."

"It'll be great to see her again. So what's the story with Bill?" Last Anna had heard, Eleanor and Bill were dating, but tentative.

"I get the feeling that fizzled. She doesn't talk about it anymore. They're obviously still friends, but he's going to stay at the conference hotel, and she's going to stay here."

Anna stepped behind Lily, slipping her hand under the shirttail to stroke the flat stomach. "So how would I go about getting on your dance card today?"

Anna sank wearily into her chair and picked up the blinking line. "This is Anna Kaklis."

"Anna, it's Ted Kimble. How are you?"

"Doing great." Ted owned the BMW and Volkswagen dealerships in Palm Springs, and his success was proof that Premier could benefit from expanding their line to include another German brand. Premier and Kimble often swapped BMWs when customers wanted a certain color or package not in inventory. Soon, they could do that with VWs too. "What can I do for you?"

"I heard a rumor you guys were interested in Volkswagens."

Anna stiffened. "I'm not at liberty to talk about my interests, Ted." And she was steamed that someone at Sweeney had

61

apparently violated their confidentiality clause. If Kimble jumped into the mix, the price would surely go up.

"I know, but I'm not calling about Sweeney. I'm calling to give you a heads-up in case you're interested in bidding on Desert Import Motors."

"Are you getting out of the business?"

"Let's just say your father was very lucky to have someone like you who wanted to step into his shoes. My youngest just followed her brother to medical school on the East Coast, so there's no point in trying to build a legacy dealership out here in the desert."

This was exactly what Anna had envisioned for Premier, though her business plan called for further expansion in three years. Still, it was a golden opportunity to acquire two top-notch dealerships in the same region. "Where are you in the process?"

"We're opening the books to auditors."

Anna blew out a breath. If Kimble's books were as solid as she expected, financing the deal wouldn't be a problem. The bigger roadblock would be paperwork, most of which Hal would have to handle.

"I can send a team down on Monday morning. Is that soon enough?"

"That works. I've had some interest from one of the national investor groups, but I'll tell you up front that price isn't my only concern. I've worked with this staff a long time, and I'd hate to see them pushed out for someone else's people."

Anna would feel the same way if she were selling Premier, but she couldn't do a deal that tied her hands with staffing. "You realize an acquisition only works for me if I can bring it under one management umbrella."

"Yes, but that doesn't have to mean mass layoffs. My people could help you."

"I'll keep that in mind."

"I'll be looking for you next Monday then."

"Thanks for your call, Ted."

62

"You're welcome. I've always enjoyed my dealings with Premier."

"We feel the same about Desert Imports."

She hung up and twirled around in her seat. The financials were already set for the Sweeney acquisition, so Hal could easily shift his focus to Kimble. The downside was she had been looking forward to an easing of her workload once the Sweeney deal closed, but this would keep things in high gear for at least another two or three months. If she wanted time away with Lily, it had to be soon.

She picked up the phone again and dialed the familiar number. "Pauline, it's Anna Kaklis. I need to ask a favor. Do you have Lily's calendar handy?"

Hard at work on a brief, Lily slapped absently at the button for her speakerphone. "Lilian Stewart."

"Raw fish?"

She smiled at once, recognizing Anna's typically disjointed greeting. "I'm fine, sweetheart. Thanks for asking. Are you inviting me for sushi, or was that a reference to something else?"

"The former, actually. But I wouldn't rule anything out."

Things were smooth again between them after their flare-up over the weekend. They had spent all of Sunday afternoon in loving pursuits, and she had vowed to herself not to drink at all until Anna was comfortable it wasn't a problem. "That sounds promising. What time will you be home?"

"How about seven?"

"I'll be ready."

"Oh, and I have a surprise for you . . . two, actually."

Lily changed into jeans as soon as she got home, anticipating Anna would do the same. But Anna never came inside, honking the horn from the driveway at ten till seven.

"You're early."

63

"I couldn't wait," Anna said. "I got a call today from Ted Kimble. He owns the BMW and VW dealerships in Palm Springs, and he's looking for a buyer."

"Are you . . . ?"

"We're salivating. Our assets more than cover the risk."

"But I thought this was your long-range plan."

"It was, but these dealerships don't come on the market all that often, especially with the investor groups buying up everything."

Lily listened as Anna excitedly described her new plan, including the likelihood they would keep the Palm Springs staff intact. The best news for Lily was that Anna didn't expect it to put a strain on company resources, including her time. It was a profitable, turnkey operation, just like Premier Motors, she said.

They reached their neighborhood sushi restaurant and went in, snagging a table for two in the center of the room. The waitress recognized them and hurried to take their order.

"How about a dragon roll, a spicy tuna roll, a spider roll, four pieces of unagi, two salads with ginger dressing, two hot teas and edamame." Lily looked over the menu at Anna. "You want anything?"

Anna rolled her eyes and waved the waitress away. "One of these days I'm going to order a bento box and watch you try to eat all of that by yourself."

Lily stretched her hands across the small table and grasped Anna's. "You said you had two surprises. What's the other one?"

"Oh yeah. I promised you another surprise, didn't I?" She reached into her purse for a folder of documents, which she passed across the table.

Lily recognized the papers as a travel portfolio and eagerly looked to see where they were going. "Maui! We're going to Maui!" Her excited shouts turned the heads of several adjacent tables. "When?"

"Next weekend. We leave Friday night at seven fifteen and

come back on the redeye in time for work on Tuesday morning. I wanted it to be longer, but Pauline said you had a court date on Tuesday afternoon."

"You already called Pauline?"

"I had to make sure you could go. I thought we could use some time away together."

Lily couldn't contain her glee. It didn't get any better than Maui with Anna. "You're the best, you know."

"Yes, I know." Anna winked. "I'm sorry I've been working so much lately. We'll be wrapping up the Sweeney deal soon and things should calm down."

"Oh, believe me. This makes all of that worth it. I'm going to have you all to myself for three whole days on a beach and I'm not even going to let you think about cars."

Lily set out three mugs and poured coffee. She was glad to have her mother visiting, especially after Anna explained she needed to work most of the weekend.

"It's great you could come down with Bill. Where is his conference?"

"He's staying at one of the downtown hotels. But I saw his golf clubs in the trunk, so I don't expect much conferencing."

Lily chuckled and eyed her mother's basset hound, who watched her every move in the kitchen. "Did you feed Chester already?"

"Yes, but he thinks if he looks sad enough, you'll fry him some bacon."

"I doubt we even have any." She addressed the dog. "Anna would go get you some, because she spoils you rotten."

"I do what?" Anna asked, sweeping into the kitchen and dropping her blazer on the counter. "I can't believe you guys are up already. You were still talking after midnight."

Chester's toenails clacked on the tile as he danced excitedly at seeing Anna. She responded by squatting and scratching his chin.

"Mom hasn't slept past six for as long as I've known her."

"Boy, it's easy to tell you're adopted," Anna said, dodging Lily's swat.

"I think you ought to play hooky and come with us. We're going up Strawberry Peak."

"I can't." Anna gulped her coffee and set the mug down. "I gave Brad the weekend off so he'd cover for me next weekend."

Lily turned to her mom. "Did I tell you we're going to Maui?"

"That sounds wonderful."

Anna put on her blazer and picked up her car keys. "I hope you have a good time today."

"Don't forget, Amazon. We're going to your mom and dad's for dinner at six, so I expect to see your smiling face by five thirty."

"I'll be here." Their plans set, Anna stole a quick peck on the lips and disappeared out the door.

"I like her," Eleanor declared, as if saying it for the first time. In fact, it was something she said often, a regular affirmation that she approved of Lily's choice.

"I like her too, Mom." Lily finished making sandwiches, and filled sealable plastic bags with carrots, trail mix and orange sections. She then filled her two-liter Camelback water bladder, adding three one-liter bottles of water, and lifted the pack. It was heavier than what she usually carried, but not more than she could manage. "Are you ready?"

"Do you have room for my camera in your daypack?"

"Sure."

"I'll take my turn carrying that thing, you know. Tell you what, you carry it until lunch then I'll carry it the rest of the day."

Lily frowned. "But after lunch, it will be practically empty."

"Yes, I know," her mom deadpanned, walking out the door.

Lily had picked a moderately challenging ten-mile hike for their outing. That would get them home by three, in plenty of time to rest a bit and get ready for dinner at the Kaklis home. She was looking forward to finally introducing her mother to Martine and George—especially George. Lily had the feeling her mother would handle him perfectly.

They parked the SUV at the trailhead and gathered their things. Lily strapped on the pack, which her mother lightened immediately by removing a bottle of water.

"Mom, can I ask you a personal question?"

"I bet you want to know what's up with Bill."

"Yeah. You used to talk about him all the time, but I get the impression you guys are cooling off."

Her mother chuckled. "I'm not sure you could say we ever heated up. I think he still misses Liz more than he's willing to admit."

"They were married a long time, weren't they?"

"Twenty-eight years."

"It's so ironic, an oncologist losing his wife to cancer."

"He says he felt helpless."

"That's really sad." Lily thought of Anna's mother, and how difficult such a loss must have been for George. "Anna's father married again four years after her mom died."

"Some people can do that. Others move on, but they go to a different place. Bill's like that."

"But you still enjoy each other's company?"

"Very much. I think we're both getting what we need."

Saddened by the melancholy in her mother's voice, Lily hooked their arms as they trudged up the wide shaded path.

Two and a half hours later, they were standing at the pinnacle of Strawberry Peak. From this vantage point, they could see the Pacific Ocean to the west, Mount Baldy to the east, and the entire LA basin. Or at least, they could have seen it, had it not been blanketed in smog. Still, it was beautiful and sunny where they stood.

The peak was a stopping point for dozens of hikers and bikers, and Lily couldn't resist asking another hiker to snap a picture of her with her mother, here in one of her favorite places. "I don't think we've had our picture taken together since I graduated from law school."

"Then we should get copies made, so we can both have one."

"One of these days you're going to have to break down and get a digital camera."

"But this one's more fun," her mother said, replacing the lens cap and dropping it inside the backpack. True to her word, she strapped on the pack for the return trip.

"This has been such a great day. Hiking with you on the weekends is the thing I miss most about leaving home. I wish you could get down here more often."

"And you could come home too, you know."

"Yeah, maybe I will. Anna's been so busy with work, and it's probably going to pick up again for a while if she buys the dealerships in Palm Springs. Maybe I'll come up in a couple of weeks and we'll do the Priest Rock Trail."

As they descended in comfortable silence, Lily acknowledged her attitude about Anna working so much recently had softened considerably since the Maui surprise. She appreciated that Anna had recognized her frustration and done something about it. And Lily knew she had to respond in kind, by being more patient and understanding about the long hours. This was a short-term issue, and Anna needed her support.

Anna's slightly late arrival had her rushing to get ready, but by six, she was piling into the X3 with Lily, Eleanor and Bill for the short ride to her parents' home. "What about Chester?"

"He'll be fine," Eleanor said from the backseat.

"Let's bring him along," she said, hopping back out before anyone could object. Chester was still near the front door, and she quickly clipped his leash in place and led him out to the car. "It'll be fun to see how Jonah reacts. That's my nephew," she explained. "He hasn't been around many dogs that I know of."

"How old is he?" Bill asked.

"Ten months. He's walking already."

When they arrived at the Kaklis home, Anna led them through the house to the patio, where everyone was gathered by the pool to watch Jonah splash in the water with his dad. She wanted to join them, but tonight was really about her parents meeting Eleanor.

She put her arm around Lily's mother and led her to the umbrella table, where her parents suddenly stood. "Eleanor Stewart, I'd like you to meet my mother, Martine, and my father, George."

"How do you do?"

Martine addressed her warmly. "We're very pleased to meet you, and so glad you could come. We think the world of your daughter."

"She feels the same way about you two." Her eyes twinkled at George. "And she's particularly fond of you."

Anna chuckled at her father's obvious surprise. "And this is her friend, Bill Mueller. He drives a Mercedes," she hissed.

"We can fix that," George said, extending his hand. "Just have Hal hold his head under water until he sees the light."

Bill laughed amiably. "Actually, my lease is up this month, and I thought I'd like to drive something different. The 750Li is one of the three cars that I've been studying."

"What are the other two?" Anna and George asked their question in perfect synchrony.

"Well, I was looking at the Jaguar."

"They're alien droppings," George said, shaking his head.

"What he means," Anna interjected diplomatically, "is that you don't see very many older Jaguars out there. They don't exactly have a reputation for being well-built. What's the other one?" It was the usual good guy-bad guy routine, but Bill didn't seem to recognize it.

"The other is the Cadillac."

"Ah, the Cadillac," George remarked. "Well, there's one good thing about driving a Cadillac."

"What's that?"

"Tell him, Anna."

"If you're driving it, you can't see how ugly it is."

Bill threw up his hands in surrender, laughing. "I suppose BMWs are the only cars anyone here recommends."

"Bill, if you really are considering the seven fifty, I can set you up tomorrow morning," Anna offered. "Just tell me what color you want and I'll have it ready to go by early afternoon. No pressure, but you can have the family discount—what I'd pay myself if I were buying it. You won't get a deal like that anywhere."

"White."

"Purchase or lease?"

"Lease."

"Three years or five?"

"You pick."

"Three. That way, I get it back sooner to sell again."

"Then I guess I'll have to turn in the Mercedes at the local dealer first thing tomorrow."

"Oh, no. We'll deliver it for you. That's our favorite part."

With business out of the way, Anna left Bill and her father to chat about the Greek Isles. Eleanor and Martine were off exploring the garden, and Lily was sitting with Kim by the pool. Suddenly aware of how tired she was, she stretched out in a lounge chair to relax. Chester nuzzled her hand before hopping up into her lap. It was idyllic, and striking in its contrast to how hectic things had been at the dealership since her father had stepped down.

Chapter 6

At noon on Sunday, Lily drove her mother and Chester to Premier Motors to meet Bill so they could get underway back to San Jose. Anna was waiting for them beside the new vehicle, beaming with obvious pride.

"Drive carefully, Bill. When Lily got her X-three, I couldn't keep her under eighty. And then there was that time out of Tahoe—"

"Hush, Amazon! Are you trying to give my mom a heart attack?" Shaking her head, Lily turned to reassure her mother. "I'm a very careful driver."

"I know you are. So are you coming up in a couple of weeks like we talked about?"

Lily looked back at Anna to indicate they would discuss her plans later. "Yeah, I'm going to try to get up soon. I really enjoyed our hike yesterday."

"Me too, sweetie." Eleanor wrapped her in a mighty hug. Next, she broke up the lovefest in the parking lot between Anna and Chester in order to extricate her hound.

"You can leave Chester with us, Eleanor. We'll bring him back one of these days."

"You can't have my baby," she said.

Bill guided Chester into his crate, which he had strapped to the backseat. Immediately content, the dog settled down with his rawhide chew.

After one last hug for Anna and Lily, Eleanor got in and rolled down the window. "Love you both."

"Love you too," they shouted as they watched the sparkling BMW pull out.

"You and your mom really had a good visit, didn't you?"

"Yeah, it was too short though. But our hike yesterday was really special. We talked a lot. It was like the old days."

Anna put her arm around Lily's shoulder as they walked back into the showroom. "I wish I could come home with you right now."

"You're still the boss, aren't you?"

"Yeah, but I need to stick around. I can't leave Holly on her own just yet. She needs a little more management experience."

Lily knew Anna thought a lot of her new sales manager, but that Holly had trouble with paperwork. In fact, she and Holly had been working late together quite often to resolve errors.

"What time do you think you'll be home?"

"I promise not to work too late. As soon as we get everyone off the lot, I'll pack it in."

"I'll make it worth your while, Amazon."

"Of that, I have no doubt."

Lily was relieved to hear that things had calmed down at Premier Motors, though Anna said it was only temporary. She was holding off on the offer for the dealerships in Palm Springs until they completed negotiations with Sweeney. But for at least a couple of weeks, it meant they had a home life again. Anna was sleeping in until six thirty and getting home in time to eat dinner together. Or, as was the case tonight, to have dinner with Kim and Hal at their home.

"Don't go dashing after Jonah the second you get in the door," she told Anna.

"Thanks for reminding me. I felt so bad when Hal said she was feeling neglected."

"It's easy to do. Babies are irresistible, especially when they're as cute as Jonah."

Kim greeted them at the door.

"Hiya, sister," Anna said, delivering a warm hug.

Lily followed with one of her own and presented Kim with a gift bag of gourmet coffee. She couldn't help but smile at Anna's obvious struggle not to track down her nephew.

"Hi, yourself. It's good to see you guys again. We didn't get much of a chance to talk on Saturday." She turned back toward the kitchen with the coffee. "Hal's got Jonah upstairs if you want to see him."

"We'll see him later," Anna said. "Something smells great."

"It's Cornish hen. I got the recipe from one of the women I walk with." Kim had become the quintessential stay-at-home mom since Jonah was born, putting her real estate career on hold. Anna said they were hoping to have another baby soon.

Hal walked in with Jonah in his arms, fully expecting to give the little guy up to his aunt. "There's your auntie, Jonah."

Lily intercepted the handoff and hurried off into the living room, out of earshot of Anna and Kim. "No, no. I get to play with Jonah tonight so Anna can talk with her sister."

"Kim will like that," Hal said. "She's been going nuts lately because I've been working late so much."

"I can relate to that. I've hardly seen Anna since George stepped down." She paced the living room with a wide-eyed Jonah taking in every detail.

"I've never seen anyone work like her, Lily. She's on top of absolutely every detail. She knows my job, Brad's job, Holly's job

". . . and I'm sure she could do anything in the garage."

"That's because she loves it, Hal. Every bit of it."

"I can tell." He took his squirming son from her arms and helped him stand. "Can you walk to Lily?"

She got down on all fours to coax his lumbering steps. "Mom wanted to kidnap Jonah. Could you tell?"

"Your mom's such a sweetheart. I bet she wouldn't mind one bit if you and Anna had a family."

Lily made a noise somewhere between a snort and a chuckle, but was saved from having to respond by a call to dinner. She followed Hal into the dining room, where he placed Jonah in a playpen on the floor beside his mother. Anna gestured for Lily to take the other seat next to the playpen, while she sat across from Hal.

"Did Anna tell you we're going to Maui on Friday night after work?"

Kim shook a fork at Anna. "You better not be making my husband work overtime."

"I'm not. In fact, I was thinking when we got back, you and Hal could go while Lily and I kept Jonah."

"Oh, right. Which one of you is going to breast-feed?"

Anna and Lily pointed at each other.

"Hal and I don't get to do fun stuff anymore. Jonah's a full-time gig."

Hal had opened a bottle of chardonnay for dinner and began to pour for the table.

"None for me," Lily said, covering her wineglass. "I'll just have the Perrier."

Anna gave her a curious look, as if noticing for the first time that she wasn't drinking alcohol. In fact, Lily hadn't had a drink since Tony's wedding, when Anna had made such a big deal about it.

Anna took a sip. "You should have some of this. It's very nice."

Lily was confused. She thought for certain Anna would be

74

pleased, but she was acting as if she didn't care. "The . . . the water's fine."

"You really ought to try this," Anna said, passing her glass to Hal, who emptied the last of the bottle.

Lily couldn't help but feel that Anna was encouraging her, as if to acknowledge that she understood and accepted what Lily had said—that her drinking recently wasn't anything to worry about. She sipped the wine. It was crisp and dry—just the way she liked her chardonnay—and she was glad Anna had pressed her into trying it. Still, she was self-conscious about drinking too much or too fast, enough that she deliberately paced herself through dinner, careful not to finish hers first.

On the drive home, Anna seemed out of sorts. "Something wrong?"

Anna drummed her fingers on the steering wheel and looked away. "Kim's having a hard time."

"With Jonah?"

"No, with Hal. Actually, with me, if you get right down to it."

"What does that mean?"

"Just that I've been working him so much . . . and Kim's been home by herself with Jonah. She said . . ." She pounded the wheel with her fist. "God, I feel like shit. She told me that for the first time in thirteen years of marriage, they're actually fighting."

Lily knew exactly where Kim's frustration was coming from, but Anna didn't need a "me too" to go with the guilt she was already feeling. "You've both been working very hard, Anna. But it's like you said. It won't always be this busy."

"I'm not going to break up my sister's marriage by turning her husband into an asshole who doesn't come home from work. I'll have to hire another accountant to help him out."

"That'll make it easier on all of you, won't it?"

"Yeah, I guess. I can get somebody from Morty's firm to lend a hand for a while."

Lily was tempted to teasingly suggest she find a temporary

75

CEO to share her load, but Anna wasn't in the mood for jokes tonight. When they reached their home, she offered to lock up so Anna could go on upstairs and get ready for bed.

When Anna's footsteps grew faint on the staircase, Lily walked into the kitchen and opened the refrigerator. She was glad to see she had remembered correctly, that the bottle of chardonnay they had opened almost two weeks ago was corked. Hurriedly, she opened it and poured the rest into a water glass. It wasn't as crisp as the vintage Hal had served, but it hit the spot—just enough to polish off her meal.

"Lily, I'm going on to bed. Will you be up soon?" Anna called from the top of the stairs. She always had trouble falling asleep if Lily was still up and wandering the house.

Lily wanted a few minutes to unwind, and to finish her wine downstairs. "I need to look over the mail. I didn't get a chance before we left."

"Can't it wait until tomorrow?"

"I guess." Lily turned up the glass and drained it in three gulps. Then she detoured into the downstairs bathroom to touch a bit of toothpaste onto her tongue before heading upstairs to Anna.

Anna sat in the conference room at Premier Motors, drumming her fingers as she reviewed the agenda, waiting for her senior staff to arrive. She smiled as her mind drifted back to the spontaneous lovemaking with Lily the night before. Their long weekend in Maui would change their lives forever. Of course, all of that hinged on Lily's answer. Was she ready to take this step? It certainly seemed that way to Anna, but it was possible she might want a little more time. Lily had been hurt before by lovers who pulled the rug out from under her just as she began to feel they were ready for commitment.

"I called the wholesaler this morning to come by for the two Hondas." Brad startled her as he took a seat across from her at the conference table. One of the first changes she had implemented was to move the weekly senior staff meeting from Monday at eight thirty to Thursday at ten. By meeting later in the week, they could better plan for the weekend rush, she reasoned. The change to ten was to allow Holly to come in later, since she worked the lot until closing on Thursday nights.

Hal walked in and took the chair next to Anna. Holly sat directly across from him. The seat at the head of the table had remained empty ever since George left. Even as new CEO, Anna felt funny about moving to that chair after all these years. Besides, her father had an open invitation to attend the senior staff meetings, and the way she saw it, that was still his chair.

"Okay, we're all here. The first bit of news I have for all of you is that I got a call from Walter this morning." Walter was the attorney who was handling their offer for Sweeney Volkswagen. "Gordon Sweeney signed off on the deal, and he wants to close on Tuesday afternoon. Hal, if you have the offer ready for Ted Kimble—"

Carmen, Premier's receptionist, broke in over the room's intercom. She rarely interrupted these meetings, but over the years she had developed a sense of which calls should be put through. "Anna, Bill Mueller's on line one."

"Uh, oh," Holly said. "I hope his new car's okay."

"Me too, or I'll never hear the end of it." With a grin, Anna spun in her chair and picked up the blinking line. "Hi, Bill. What can I do for you?"

It took her a moment to understand the purpose of his call. "Oh, dear God."

Lily leaned over and whispered her thoughts to Tony, her boss, who was in the midst of jury selection for a case involving an Asian man charged with trespassing because he refused to vacate his rented home to make room for a new Hispanic tenant. In her opinion, this potential juror had too much in common with the landlady at the center of the case.

"Your honor, the defense would like to thank and excuse this juror, Mrs. Pedroso." With his fourth peremptory strike, they were left with two possibilities, both of whom were acceptable for their case.

"It's a good mix," she whispered. She loved it when her schedule allowed her to sit in with Tony, especially for jury selection.

People had been coming and going in the courtroom all day as they readied for the trial, but something made Lily turn to see the latest arrival. She was startled to find Anna and Hal taking seats near the door. Meeting their eyes, a panic gripped her deep inside. Anna had never come to the courthouse to see her before. "Tony, I need a recess."

He looked down at her hand, which was digging into his forearm. Without hesitation, he stood. "Your honor, the plaintiff requests a short recess."

"Would counsel approach the bench?" Notorious for his no-nonsense demeanor, Judge Anston seemed to bristle at the request. "What's going on, counsel?"

As Tony explained the situation to the judge, Lily glanced back over her shoulder at Anna. Something was undeniably wrong, and it was all she could do not to bolt toward the door.

The gavel pounded and Judge Anston addressed her directly. "Ms. Stewart, I don't appreciate these disruptions."

"I understand, Your Honor. I won't make a habit of it. And thank you."

Lily walked through the gate and followed Anna and Hal into the hallway. "What's going on, Anna? Why are you here?" Their solemn faces terrified her.

Anna took her hands and squeezed, obviously fighting tears. "Something awful has happened, Lily. It's your mother."

"Mom?" Lily's knees went weak and she gripped Anna tightly for support. "Then we need to go. I have to be with her."

Anna pulled her into a tight hug as Hal's hand came to rest on her shoulder. "I'm so sorry, baby."

Chapter 7

Anna intertwined her fingers with Lily's as they boarded the plane to San Jose. Lily was clearly in shock, nearly overwhelmed by the swarming crowd and the details that had become a staple of air travel. She guided Lily into her seat by the window in first class, and hoisted their suitcases into an overhead bin. Seeing her shiver in near-shock, Anna took a blanket and laid it across her lap. "Do you want anything else? A pillow?"

Lily shook her head.

Anna too was devastated by Eleanor's unexpected death, but knew she would have to pull herself together in order to help Lily get through these next few days. As they had packed, she dutifully relayed the information she had gotten from Bill. When Eleanor failed to arrive at school that morning, the school secretary called her home. Getting no answer, she called Bill, knowing that the two were close. Bill agreed to stop by Eleanor's house after his hospital rounds. He and Eleanor had exchanged keys for emergencies, so he let himself in after knocking for several minutes. He found her on the floor in the hallway upstairs. From his physician training, he surmised that she had died late last night of something catastrophic, such as a stroke or an aneurysm. Since she died alone, a coroner would conduct an autopsy, the results of which would be known sometime on Friday.

Landing in San Jose one hour later, Anna collected their bags and guided Lily through the narrow concourse to the baggage claim area. Bill had arranged for one of Eleanor's neighbors to pick the women up.

"Lily!" A gray-haired woman of about sixty-five called out.

"It's Charlotte Beck. She lives next door," Lily said. She stiffly acknowledged the woman with a nod as they pushed through the crowd of people fighting for their luggage. "Charlotte, hi. Thank you for coming."

The woman pulled Lily into a hug. "Your mother was such a friend to me, Lily. I'm so sorry."

"Thank you." She turned and held out her arm to Anna. "This is my friend, Anna Kaklis."

"Charlotte," Anna said, shaking her hand.

The woman led them quickly to the parking garage where they piled into a small station wagon for the ride to Eleanor's house. "Just to let you know, Ernie and I have Chester for the time being. We'll keep him as long as you want."

Lily nodded absently then suddenly turned toward Anna in the backseat. "I need my car, Anna. I have to bring Chester home," she said with urgency.

Anna's heart broke to see Lily's brimming tears. "I know. I'll take care of everything." They had talked this out already, but it was clear Lily couldn't keep her thoughts straight.

When they reached the small Victorian home, Lily thanked Charlotte while Anna handled their bags. Lily stopped before opening the front door, no doubt dreading the sensory assault that awaited their entry. Once inside, Anna stood silently in the foyer as Lily slowly ascended the stairs. After a few moments, she followed, knowing the sight would break her heart. She found Lily crumpled in the hallway, sobbing as she ran her hands along the hardwood floor as though feeling for her mother's touch.

Anna had secured rooms for her family and their friends at the Fairmont Hotel in downtown San Jose, only a few blocks from Eleanor's Naglee Park home. Sandy and Suzanne were the first to arrive, getting in early Friday evening.

"Thanks for coming. I'm sure it will mean a lot to Lily to have you guys here." Anna led them into Eleanor's small sitting room.

"How's she holding up?" Sandy asked.

"It's hard for her. We got the results from the coroner this afternoon. It was an aortic aneurysm. He said it happened very quickly, and that was some comfort, I think."

Suzanne slumped onto the love seat. "Has she worked out the funeral arrangements?"

Anna wasn't surprised to see Suzanne near tears. Though she usually tried to come off as tough and emotionless, she had a sensitive side she couldn't hide. "Eleanor made her own arrangements years ago. We're holding the service on Sunday afternoon to give her old boss time to get here from Maryland."

"Eleanor really did everyone a big favor by taking care of all that herself," Suzanne said.

Anna nodded numbly. "There's still a lot to do. Lily met with the funeral director first thing this morning and he gave her a list to go through . . . things like moving the utilities into her name until the house is sold, canceling credit cards . . . that sort of thing."

"I'm sure it's overwhelming," Sandy said. "Is there anything we can do?"

She shook her head. "Lily will be glad you're here, though. She was sleeping earlier, but I heard her moving around in the bathroom just a few minutes before you got here."

"I don't want to get in her space, Anna." As Lily's best friend, Sandy was well aware of Lily's penchant for trying to deal with difficult things alone. "Why don't Suzanne and I go pick up something for dinner and bring it back?"

"That's a great idea. She might even eat a bit with you guys here." Anna gave them directions to a nearby Chinese restaurant.

When they left, she collapsed on the love seat, near exhaustion. She had lain awake with Lily most of the night, giving comfort as needed. With the help of a sleep aid delivered this morning by Bill Mueller, who also was grief-stricken, Lily had finally taken a much-needed nap. That gave Anna the opportunity to call her family and enlist their help. Hal volunteered to drive Lily's car to San Jose tomorrow. Kim and Martine offered to watch over things in the kitchen, especially since people would probably start bringing food tomorrow. Anna had hesitantly asked her father to fill in for her at the dealership next week, and was genuinely touched to hear he had been on the lot since yesterday afternoon when Anna left.

Tired though she was, she went back upstairs to check on Lily. Finding the guest room empty, she continued down the hall to Eleanor's room. Lily was there, sitting in the bedside armchair, examining the contents of the nightstand. Anna leaned into the doorjamb, overwhelmed with sadness for Lily's loss. The clock on the nightstand showed seven p.m., which meant their plane was leaving LAX for Maui without them. She wanted to tell Lily what she had planned, but it seemed out of place in the midst of their grief. Besides, she never wanted Lily to think her sentiments came from pity, or a need to comfort.

Like Lily, her mother had been adopted as a child, but by an older couple who had died when Eleanor was in her twenties. That left Lily as her only surviving relative.

She walked solemnly alongside Anna from the limo to the

gravesite, thinking she knew now what it really meant to "go through the motions." Over two hundred people had packed the small sanctuary for the funeral, including the entire staff of the elementary school where Eleanor had been principal, but only a few close friends had followed to the cemetery.

For the next twenty minutes, the minister celebrated her mother's too-short life, praising her as an adoptive parent, a lifelong educator and a friend to everyone who knew her. Then he came close to share a few private words, words Lily barely understood in a context so surreal. All she could comprehend was that she had lost the one person who had always been there for her, the only constant in her life.

"She saved me, Anna," she whispered, fighting back tears.

"I know. And I'll be grateful to her for as long as I live." Anna gave her a firm hug before steering her toward the departing mourners, each of whom wanted one more moment with her to convey their sympathy.

As the crowd dwindled, Lily looked back at her mother's casket. Bill Mueller stood beside it, his head hanging and his hands in his pockets. She walked up beside him and looped her arm through his, willing the lump in her throat to relax. "You were so dear to her, Bill."

He nodded sadly. "She was dear to me too. After Liz died I didn't want to let anyone else close again. But how could you not want someone like Eleanor Stewart in your life?" He broke down in sobs.

Lily's heart went out to him. He had buried his wife, and now was losing another close companion. They stood together, arm in arm, staring at the casket in sorrow.

"You were everything in the world to her, Lily. She was so proud of you."

"I wouldn't have made it if she hadn't taken me into her home. None of the good things in my life would have happened." Certainly nothing that would have set her on the course to meet Anna.

83

They broke apart and she turned to see the others. Sandy and Suzanne were huddled with the people from the Braxton Street Legal Aid Clinic.

"You guys are the best friends a person could have," she said, making teary eye contact with each of them.

"Don't worry about things at work," Tony said. "Colleen hasn't heard back from her bar exam, but she can do some of the grunt stuff. Lauren and I will cover for you in court."

"I appreciate that." She sent each one off with a warm hug.

Finally, the Kaklis family was all who remained. Lily thanked Martine and Kim for all they had done to help. "You were perfect, Jonah," she said, placing a kiss on his forehead. "Mom would have been glad you were here."

Hal and George were standing together a few feet away, and Lily was struck by how lucky she was to know them. A few of her lesbian friends shied away from having men as close friends. Obviously, they knew no men like these, especially Hal.

"Hal, thank you for everything you've done. It's been a real comfort to have you here."

"You can count on us for anything, Lily. Kim and I both really liked your mom." He leaned down and kissed her on the cheek, and then walked over to join his wife.

Lily turned to face a nervous-looking George. They had barely spoken to one another since he had arrived yesterday, but she appreciated his support for Anna more than she could say. "I'm really glad you came, George. Thank you."

He surprised her with a fatherly hug. After a long moment, he tearfully whispered so that only she could hear, "Don't worry about a thing, Lily. We're going to be your family now."

"Then tell him to fuck off!" Anna growled, slamming down the phone in Eleanor's kitchen. Not usually one to lose her temper, she couldn't imagine what sort of asshole wouldn't care that she was in the middle of a family emergency.

84

"What's up, honey?" Lily appeared suddenly in the doorway, which made Anna realize she had been shouting into the phone.

"Sweeney's being an ass. He wants the deal done tomorrow or he's going to shop his dealership on the open market."

"So what's the problem? Aren't you guys ready to go to final?"

Anna looked at her feet. The last thing she wanted to do was make Lily feel bad. "Yeah, it's just that I would have to be there, and I want to be here with you."

"That's crazy, Amazon. This is all you've been working on for a month."

"I don't give a shit about Sweeney Volkswagen. I'd rather stay here."

"That's ridiculous. You got me through the hardest part. All that's left is to sort through Mom's things and meet with the lawyer, and I really don't need you for that. I know it's going to be emotional, but I feel like it gives me one more chance to be with her. I can handle it."

"Lily, I—"

"Seriously, Anna. I can do this. Go home."

Anna looked at her dubiously. It was true that Lily usually preferred to work out tough things on her own, and she was probably craving her solitude.

"Go!"

"It won't take that long to wrap this deal up. I can come back when I finish."

"You don't have to. You're as worn out as I am. Get your work done and get some rest."

Anna hugged her close, realizing in a convoluted way that her leaving was exactly what Lily needed right now.

Lily watched sadly through the window as the post hole digger planted the For Sale sign in the front yard. The agent had assured her that the home would sell very quickly and for top dollar, as it had been renovated throughout and was situated in an ideal neighborhood. No matter how much money it brought, it would never equal those intangibles it had provided over the years—comfort, security and love.

The week she had expected to be in San Jose had turned into two. It was a formidable task to close out someone's life, even though her mother had kept things in order. Lily talked with Anna by phone every day, assuring her that it was fine for her to remain in LA.

Eleanor's lawyer had called the second Monday, asking Lily to stop by for the reading of the will. As expected, her mother had left her everything, even setting aside a sum for the care of Chester should her daughter choose not to adopt the dog. How could her mother have thought she wouldn't want Chester?

She strolled slowly through the house. It seemed barren, all the books and trinkets packed in boxes in the foyer. The truck from the women's shelter was due soon to pick up her mother's clothing, kitchenware and linens. She had encountered few surprises among the personal effects, but was overwhelmed with how much of her own life her mother had preserved. Besides the standard refrigerator decorations from her art classes, Lily found her old report cards, a few high school papers, cards from every occasion and photographs. Lots of photographs. She packed them into a box and placed it in her X3, along with most of her mother's hiking gear, and a favorite sweater.

She then turned her attention again to the paper bag containing the contents of her mother's safety deposit box, readying herself for the emotional onslaught of carefully reviewing each item. From the inventory she had taken with the bank officer, she already knew what was there—a life insurance policy worth a quarter of a million dollars, certificates of deposit totaling almost that much, and a packet containing Lily's original birth certificate and all of her adoption papers. The piece that had jolted her was the Mother's Day card, one she had fashioned from blue construction paper and decorated with glitter and glue when she was only seven years old. That was before her adoption was finalized, and she had written inside, "To Miss Stewart, love, Lily Parker."

Lily closed the card and held it to her heart, tears suddenly filling her eyes. That her mother had safeguarded such a silly thing for twenty-five years . . . Lily had always thought of her adoption in terms of how she had been saved, never truly understanding the gift of love she had given her mother in return. Bill had tried to tell her this at the gravesite, and now for the first time, Lily was able to see it for herself.

Anna sifted through the stack of contracts, immensely pleased with the new format, which left practically no room for the types of transposition errors Holly was prone to make.

"You wanted to see me, Boss Lady?" Holly appeared in her doorway, a knowing grin on her face.

"Congratulations. Not one error in the bunch."

"I told you we'd fix it." Holly had worked all last week with a business form consultant to design the new contract. "I've been dealing with this dyslexia thing all my life. I knew there was a way around it. I just had to explain it to somebody who could help."

"The new layout is perfect. We should have done this years ago."

Holly sauntered in and took one of the armchairs across from Anna's desk. "I believe the saying is that necessity is the mother of invention."

"So it would seem. This is going to solve a lot of problems."

Holly crossed her leg, resting her ankle on her knee, an almost masculine pose. She had a lithe, athletic build, and her golden tan and bleached curls offered further evidence of her self-described surfing addiction. "But is it going to get you out the door at a decent hour?"

Anna glanced at the wall clock—ten after seven—and shook

her head. "I had a message earlier from Lily. She was planning to leave San Jose around four, so there's no point in me going home to an empty house."

"Even on a Sunday night?"

Sundays with Lily were sacrosanct. "Especially on a Sunday."

"How's she doing?"

"It's hard for her, but she's a survivor."

"And she has you, which is a big plus."

"Yeah." Since promoting Holly to management, Anna had noticed a shift in their relationship. They had always enjoyed chatting, but with working late together so often, they had begun talking a bit about their personal lives and interests. Anna found her easy to relate to, especially since they shared an obsession with the car industry. "I hope we can reschedule our Maui trip soon, but this deal with Kimble is going to gum up the works for a while."

"Not to mention taking over things at Sweeney."

"That starts tomorrow morning. I'll probably be over there all week."

Holly drummed her fingers on the arms of a chair pensively.

"Something on your mind?"

"May I ask you a personal question?"

Anna shrugged, unable to imagine where this was leading.

"I just wondered if you ran into any problems with your family about Lily, and how you handled it."

"Are you . . . ?" Was Holly saying she was a lesbian too?

"I have a potential situation with my folks. I know they're going to be disappointed, but I hate having secrets. You know what I mean?"

Anna listened with fascination as Holly described the challenges she faced. Their situations were remarkably similar, and Holly was equally determined to make her own choices.

"I kept things from Dad for a while. It was nerve wracking." Anna went on to describe her father's misgivings, and the playful way Lily had broken him down. "You should have heard him at her mom's funeral. He told her she was part of our family now."

"Let's hope things go that well at my house."

"Speaking of houses, I should probably get on home. The way Lily drives, she could make a five-hour trip in four." As she packed up her things to head out, she acknowledged with disappointment that the next few weeks would bring more long hours. Finding time to get away would be nearly impossible.

"I'm so sorry, baby," Anna said, spooning tightly from behind.

"It's okay," Lily said. She had come home from San Jose to an empty house because Anna had misunderstood her garbled cell phone message, expecting her to leave at four instead of to arrive. All the while Lily had moped about being alone, Anna had been in her office killing time. "Where is he now?"

"Still on his bed, I think," Anna said with a groan. She had tried first to have Chester sleep downstairs in the family room, placing his familiar flannel beanbag in the corner by the door. After thirty minutes of whimpering and scratching, Anna caved and brought the dog and his bed to their bedroom. Chester had climbed onto their bed twice, seeking comfort at Anna's feet. But each time, she had gotten up and marched him back to his own bed. The third time, she even stretched out beside him on the floor, petting him until he began to softly snore.

"He misses her," Lily said sadly. "And he always slept at the foot of her bed."

Anna squeezed her shoulder and planted a soft kiss. "I promise I'll show him a lot of attention."

Lily chuckled softly. "I told Mom's lawyer that he should give you the money she set aside for taking care of Chester."

"I'm glad we have him, especially since she loved him so much."

"You know, I can't believe how much money Mom left me, especially once the house sells."

"Mmm . . . you want me to get you an appointment with my financial planner? It might be good to have the same person managing both of us so we'll know everything is taken care of."

Lily felt a swell of love inside. Anna probably had no idea such a simple statement would carry so much weight, but the idea that she thought they should plan their finances together was, to Lily, a giant step toward the commitment she sought.

Chapter 8

Lily leaned into the office cubicle Tony had put together for his wife. "I hear congratulations are in order."

Colleen jumped up from her desk. "Lily, welcome back." She gave her a small hug. "Yeah, I just got the news that I passed. Now all I need is a real job."

Lily remembered the excitement she had felt when she was admitted to the bar almost seven years ago. "You applied at the public defender's office, right?"

"Yes, but they said they have a backlog of applicants."

"I wouldn't worry about that. Their turnover rate's astronomical. That's hard work, and underappreciated."

"I know, but . . ."

Lily understood the calling to public service, but steered clear of criminal court when she could. Family court was much more rewarding. "By the way, thanks for taking care of all these cases for me. It was a real comfort not to have to worry about it while

I was gone."

"I'm really glad I could help. You know, Tony thought the world of your mom. I really wish I could have known her."

"Thanks, Colleen. She was special."

"Lily, you have a delivery," Pauline called down the narrow hallway.

"Great. Everybody in the conference room, now!" Tony, Colleen, Lauren and Pauline obediently made their way to the meeting room, curious about the aromatic box at the front door. Lily paid the young man and carried the box down the hall, unloading its contents in the center of the table. "Let's see, we have double cheeseburgers for the carnivores, a veggie burger for Pauline, french fries, onion rings, sodas and three flavors of milk shakes."

Lauren inhaled deeply and smiled. "How wonderfully decadent!"

"I wanted to show you guys how much you've meant to me these last couple of weeks." Lily's voice cracked slightly. "I couldn't work with a better bunch of people."

"Well, it's mutual," Lauren said. "Now pass the food."

She laughed, grateful for Lauren's deflection, and dug into the feast with everyone else, eating more at one sitting than she had eaten in any day since her mother died. Then sated, she returned to her office to sort out her client files for the week.

For the next two hours, she brought herself up to speed on the status of eight cases whose proceedings were already underway. Pauline had updated her calendar to include court appearances tomorrow morning, and again on Thursday afternoon. Two new case files sat in her inbox, one involving a divorce, the other dealing with a child endangerment defendant. She grimaced to see the criminal case. Fortunately, she didn't get them often.

By the time she got her caseload organized, it was a few minutes after three—too early to consider packing it in for the day. But Lily was distracted, unmotivated to plunge into the details of her clients and their legal troubles. After spending so much time alone in San Jose, she craved her solitude. And she wondered what Chester was doing on his first day alone in a new house.

The telephone interrupted her thoughts, its digital display announcing a call from Premier Motors. "If this is about my car payment, I'm going to send the payoff in later this week."

Anna chuckled at the greeting. "Hi, darling. How's your day?"

Lily smiled at hearing the sweet voice. "It's going fine. It's all still . . . I don't know . . . It just washes over me every now and then, and I have to pull myself together."

"How about we both slip out early and I'll take you to dinner somewhere nice?"

Lily's stomach churned. "I just ate enough cholesterol to seal the Lincoln Tunnel. I can't possibly think about food right now."

"So how about a walk on the beach?"

The surprise gesture was so sweet that Lily had to fight to stop the tears from spilling out. "That'd be great, Amazon."

Two hours later, she and Anna—and one very happy basset hound—were romping in the sand at Leo Carrillo State Beach in Malibu. Watching Anna and Chester play fetch was just the ticket for lifting her spirits. Eventually, Chester tired of that game and Anna hooked a thirty-foot leash to his red leather collar. The hound continued his amusing antics, chasing the receding waves, then running like mad when they rushed ashore.

"I've always loved this beach. This was such a good idea," Lily said, looping her arm through Anna's as they walked along the shore. The mid-June sun was still relatively high, but at nearly six, the heat of the day was past, giving way to a cool wind blowing in from the sea.

"It's good to have you back home, sweetheart," Anna said tenderly. "I couldn't stop thinking about you all day, just sitting in your office not ten miles away."

"For what it's worth, I like playing hooky. We should do this more often."

"We'll do it every chance we get," Anna said, squeezing her arm. "I was especially glad to do it today, because it looks like I'm going to be busy again for a few weeks. With the Sweeney deal sewn up, we've started negotiations for the two dealerships in Palm Springs. I'm probably going to have to go down there tomorrow afternoon, maybe stay for a couple of days."

Lily had known this was part of Anna's business plan for Premier Motors, but she wished it wasn't all happening now. "I don't suppose there's any way you could put this off for a couple of weeks, is there?"

"I wish. But Ted's sort of anxious about it. I think he's getting some pressure from one of the investment groups, and he'd really rather sell to us." Anna stared down at the sand while she talked, her mind obviously miles away in her office. "Now that we've started the process, I'm worried that any delay could get us into a bidding war with somebody else, and we won't be able to go much higher."

Lily couldn't blame Anna for the timing of this deal. Nor could she fault the way Anna had dropped everything to be at her side when she needed it most. "It'll be all right. I've got a couple of appearances in court this week and preliminary motions on the docket for Monday. I won't have any time for you anyway," she said haughtily.

"I promise I'll wrap things up as quickly as I can. I was supposed to be down at Sweeney all morning, but negotiations heated up quicker than I thought."

Lily shook her head and smiled. "You and your empire."

"Almost empire," Anna said. "Oh, I meant to tell you. I collected your mail. It's on your desk, but I pulled out everything that looked like a bill and paid it so you wouldn't get late charges."

"Well, aren't you handy to have around?"

Anna made a silly pouting face. "You just love me for my money."

"Don't be silly. I have money now. I love you for your body."

The saga of Maria and Miguel Esperanza was never-ending. Over the past three years, the Braxton Street Clinic had handled two restraining orders, a divorce, and six different custody hearings for the couple's children, Sofia and Roberto. Today's motion was a request to return the children from their Aunt Serena to their mother, as Maria and Miguel were making plans to remarry. As she watched the once again happy couple leave the courtroom, Lily couldn't help but think the reconciliation would only start the destructive cycle again.

"Lily!" She stopped as she heard her name.

Turning from the elevator, she saw Sandy approaching. "Go ahead, I'll get the next one," she said to the man holding the doors. "Hi."

"I wasn't sure you were back."

"Yeah, I got back on Sunday. Sorry I didn't call."

"That's okay. I know you've been busy."

"Just trying to get caught up and back into the swing of things." That and she had gotten very mellow the night before on a nine-dollar bottle of cabernet while Anna was in Palm Springs. "I know I said it already, but I really appreciated you and Suzanne coming up for the funeral. It meant a lot to me to have my friends there."

"We were glad to come." Sandy wrapped an arm around her shoulder. "Now that you're back, why don't you and Anna come over for dinner? I've got to stop at the store and get some fish to grill. It's just as easy to get four fillets as two."

"Thanks, but Anna's down in Palm Springs on business, and I still have a lot of work to catch up on." Lily loved her friends, but she didn't really want to be with anyone right now. "How about a rain check?"

"You've got it."

Lily noted her disappointed look. "It may take me a little

95

while, but I promise we'll be back into things again soon."

Sandy gave her a quick hug as the next elevator arrived. "We'll be ready."

Chester barked suddenly, a sign to Lily that Anna had finally returned from Palm Springs. The projected two days had turned to four, but at least she was back in time to enjoy the weekend. Excitedly, Lily bounded downstairs, anticipating the commotion that always ensued when Anna greeted Chester. "You better save some of that for me, Amazon."

Anna jumped up from the floor and grabbed her around the waist. With Lily secured in a one-arm hold, she used her free hand to playfully scratch Lily's stomach. "Is this what you want?"

Lily screamed with laughter and tried to wriggle free. "Stop it!"

Instead, the scratching turned to merciless tickling, and Lily dissolved into a heap on the floor. Chester immediately jumped on her, licking her face with excitement. Lily dragged Anna down by her shirttail, which was more than Chester's poor bladder could stand. What might have been a simple hello was now all-out mayhem.

"Ewwww! Look what your dog did!" Lily shrieked.

"My dog?"

"He's your dog right now."

Chester seemed to know he was the object of their disgust and he sulked away, obviously ashamed of his loss of control.

"Look, you've hurt his feelings."

"He peed in my lap!"

"He's upset."

"I'm upset!" Despite her hysterics, Lily couldn't keep a straight face. "Come here, Chester. It's okay, boy."

The hound put on his best pitiful look and ambled back to Lily's lap for a scratch.

"I'll clean this up," Anna said, extricating her long limbs from the pile on the floor. "You need a shower."

Lily chuckled to herself as she climbed the stairs. It was great to finally have Anna home.

She got an extra treat when the shower door opened and Anna joined her. They took turns with back scrubbing, and then Anna stepped out. Lily took a few more minutes to savor the warm water. Once out, she hastily dried and slipped nude between the sheets . . . where she found Anna sound asleep.

"You can't be serious. You've been gone all week," Lily said.

Anna had known this wouldn't go over well, but she was a week behind in making her presence known at the Volkswagen dealership. "That's the problem, sweetheart, that I've been gone all week. I need to go meet the staff at Sweeney today." She didn't dare add that she also needed to spend tomorrow in her office at the BMW dealership.

In a surprising display of frustration, Lily slammed her dresser drawer and spun angrily into the bathroom.

"Honey, I'm sorry." This wasn't like Lily, but then Anna understood that she was still under a lot of stress. "You usually go hiking on Saturdays."

"You mean like I did with Mom, only by myself?" She kicked the bathroom door shut.

Anna was jarred by the hurtful words, but knew she needed to change her plans. "I'm sorry. I'll call them and reschedule for Monday," she said, leaning into the closed door.

A few moments later, the door opened a crack. Lily, looking contrite, scrunched her nose. "PMS?"

Anna reached out and pulled her into a hug. "I'm a selfish, insensitive jerk."

"No, you aren't." Lily shook her head. "I'm just being a baby. It isn't as if you working on Saturday is anything new. At least you'll be home tomorrow."

In her head, Anna dismissed any notion she had of going to work on Sunday. Lily needed her at home, and it would be good for them to have some relaxing time together. "Want to come with me today and watch me kick some ass?"

Lily chuckled softly. "That's a pretty tempting offer. But I think I'll pass. I've still got that mail to go through."

"You sure?"

Lily nodded. "Beat it. Get your work done so you can hurry back home."

Anna kissed her and pulled away, glancing at Chester, who was sitting at her feet. "You be a good boy, Chester. No peeing on your mother."

Anna flipped through a stack of folders in the conference room of Sweeney Volkswagen, soon to be Premier Volkswagen. Her mood, already sullied by the guilty exchange with Lily, took a further tumble when she stepped out of her Z8 and heard a series of wolf whistles emanating from the sales offices. Between that and the aroma of cigarette smoke in the showroom, the anemic sales figures weren't all that surprising.

She seethed at the conversation underway on the other side of the corkboard wall. The voices were unnecessarily loud, as though the entire scene was being staged for her benefit.

"I don't care who she is. I've been working here fourteen years and I don't need her telling me how to be a sales manager." That voice belonged to Tommy Russell, she noted.

"I hear she's done a pretty good job over at Premier," offered another voice. Judging from something he had said earlier, she guessed it was Ben Dunlap, the fleet manager. "I'm sort of looking forward to the change. We've only hit quotas once in the last two years." Anna smirked at his apparent dig at the sales manager.

"That was her old man that kept everything running over there," Tommy said. She could practically hear his sneer. "She's nothing more than a pretty face."

"She's certainly got that." One of the salesmen. "And pretty lots of other things too. I wouldn't mind having me a—" Someone wisely cut that crude sentiment short. Otherwise, she might have walked around the corner and cleaned house.

Anna picked up the phone and dialed the receptionist. "Would you page Tommy Russell to the conference room, please?"

She stewed for twenty minutes as Russell stalled. When he finally made it to the conference room, he took a seat at the far end of the long table. Tommy Russell was going to be a genuine pain in the ass.

"Mr. Russell, I'm so very glad you could make it," she began. "I have a number of charts I'd like to go over with you this morning. Please move to this end of the table so we can look at these together." Her tone was firm, but polite.

As he took the seat to her right, she was overwhelmed by the stench of stale cigarette smoke that seemed to radiate from his pores.

"I'll get right to the point. One of the reasons I wanted to buy this dealership is because I believed I could improve the sales performance and the service revenues. Your sales staff has been missing quotas for much of the last two years. New car sales have fallen thirty-one percent. Obviously, used car sales are off too, since you don't bring as many cars in on trade when you miss your quotas."

She glanced through the picture window as a boom truck began disassembling the tacky yellow and green Sweeney Volkswagen marker. A nearby truck held the new beacon, a black and white sign touting this dealership as Premier Volkswagen.

Tommy shifted in his chair. "We haven't had much support. A couple of years ago, Gordon pulled his advertising out of the paper and started putting it into cable TV. The only people that come in here are ones who watch those weird infomercials at three o'clock in the morning."

Anna was mildly impressed that Tommy Russell had connected those particular dots, but he was conveniently forgetting his role in the dismal picture. "I'm going to spend some money here to sell Volkswagens. I can build the traffic on this lot, but I'll expect to see a sizable increase in closings, and in used car activity."

"You get people on the lot here, we'll sell them cars," he said boastfully.

"I have a small problem accepting that at face value, Mr. Russell. Your closing rate is much lower than the industry average, unusually low for cars of this caliber. Your sales staff is writing fifteen contracts a week that don't close. That's something I'll expect you to fix. I can send you for training, or I can get a trainer to come in here and pump up the whole staff. But I'm going to expect results, and pretty quickly."

"We don't need no trainer. We know how to sell cars. All we need is the traffic. The boys are chomping at the bit to have people walking onto the lot."

"Why don't we come back to that issue in a moment? You've just brought up another point I want to address. I've noticed from my personnel review that there is not one single female on your sales staff. I'd like to see that change."

Tommy was obviously flustered. "I wouldn't mind hiring a woman if I had one show up who knew the first thing about cars. All due respect, our customers would rather deal with men. They trust men more."

"Unfortunately, there just isn't much evidence of that here. Besides, we're going to try to broaden the customer base, so maybe we'll find a few buyers out there who aren't so narrow-minded." Her implication was unmistakable. "You know, three of the top five sellers at Premier last year were women. I'm sure once we get a little diversity in the sales staff we'll see the numbers go up."

He was grinding his teeth. "So which one of us is going to be in charge of hiring the sales staff? That's always been a part of my job." He reached into his pocket for a cigarette.

"Don't light that," she said sharply. "Hiring of the sales staff will still be your responsibility. But I'll expect you to do it according to my guidelines. In fact, Mr. Russell, I'm going to expect everything at Premier Volkswagen to be done according to my guidelines."

"Is there more?" He gripped the arms of the chair as if to stand.

"Yes, there's much more, but I want to make sure I get the chance to talk with all of the senior staff today, so we can schedule another time next week to go over specifics. But there is one more thing I'd like to take care of this morning." She looked at her watch. "Effective at nine thirty a.m. today, there is to be no smoking anywhere on the property by any of the staff."

"You can't be serious. Not even outside?"

"No, not even outside. It's my prerogative as owner to keep the workplace smoke-free for everyone. I don't want our staff and customers exposed to secondhand smoke. Furthermore, those on the sales staff who smoke will no longer be allowed to get inside the cars for any reason. Not for a test drive, not to show the features, not even to wipe the dashboard. One of the best things about a new car, Mr. Russell, is the way it smells, and I want to leverage that asset."

He spun out the door without responding, his ears beet red with apparent anger.

Anna picked up the phone and dialed the receptionist. "Would you ask Ben Dunlap to report to the conference room?"

The day ended with a general meeting of all staff. Not surprisingly, Tommy Russell failed to show, and Anna sent her fleet manager to find him. When they returned together, she began.

"Thank you all for coming. I'm not going to keep you long. I know you're all eager to get home to your families. I want to thank those of you who welcomed me today, and assure you that I'm really glad to be here. As I told many of you, you're going to see some changes here over the next few months as we complete the transition of ownership. I'm excited about our opportunities, and I'm confident that if we can work together as a team, we'll all share in the rewards." Applause broke out at that overture. She knew from the personnel records that salaries had been stagnant for two years.

"At this time, I'd like to meet briefly with all of the senior staff in the conference room. Good night to the rest of you, and I'll see you next week."

Anna followed the senior staff—all men—to the conference room and took her position at the head of the table. "Gentlemen, today was a good day for me because I saw just how much potential there is for this dealership. However, the reason for that potential, I'm afraid, is your current poor performance." She paused and made eye contact with all but Tommy Russell, who had found something more interesting under the table. "Please understand that I am not dependent upon you to make this company successful. I am dependent on the competency of a sales manager, a fleet manager, a service manager and a finance manager. Who actually holds those positions is irrelevant to me. I will work with each of you as necessary to turn this dealership around, but I expect nothing short of your complete cooperation."

Tommy blurted, "Look, I don't care if you do own the place. Threatening us with our jobs isn't what I'd call a brilliant motivating technique. We could all walk out the door right now and leave you here to pick up the pieces."

Anna stared back coolly, sweating him just a moment for effect. "Mr. Russell, let me tell you a little bit about management theory. I do own the place, and it is therefore not necessary for me to prove my abilities to you or to justify my means. You're the one in the grace period right now. If you believe yourself to be incapable of working as a productive part of this management team, I've already got two strong candidates on my other lot."

"Then you should call one of them, because I quit. I can find a job at any dealership in the state." He lit a cigarette and calmly walked out of the room.

● ● ●

Driving down Wilshire Boulevard, Anna was at a crossroads—literally. A right at the next light would take her to Premier BMW, and a left would take her home. She had been away from her desk for five days, and judging from the backlog of paperwork she had found upon returning from Eleanor's funeral, the mountain awaiting her attention would be high. But she had promised Lily she wouldn't work on Sunday, no matter what.

Ten minutes later, she pulled into her driveway, noticing immediately that only the side door porch light was on. Lily's car was in the garage, which piqued Anna's curiosity about why the house would be dark. She entered the family room, where Chester greeted her enthusiastically.

"Honey?" Anna played with the dog as she waited for Lily to answer. "Lily?" she called, louder this time. She walked through the lower level, turning on lights as she went, finally spotting the unlocked patio door off the kitchen.

She walked out onto the patio, where the underwater lights illuminated the perimeter of the pool. She finally spotted Lily in a chaise lounge at the far end. "Hi, babe. Everything okay?" Approaching the chair, she warily eyed the contents of the adjacent table—an ice bucket, a bowl of cut-up limes and a bottle of vodka, which was more than half empty. Lily was wrapped in a blanket, holding a glass in her lap.

"How nice of you to drop by, Anna." Despite the sarcastic words, her tone was low and flat.

Anna was instantly filled with guilt. This was her fault for leaving Lily on her own all week. "I'm sorry. I stayed a little later tonight so I wouldn't have to go in tomorrow." She sat down on the chaise and took Lily's icy hand.

"Good. We can pretend to be a couple."

The words stung, but Anna didn't respond. From this new vantage point, she could see that Lily was very drunk, her eyes closed and her chin dipping to her chest. She had no idea what she was saying. "Have you eaten yet?"

"Not hungry."

Probably just as well. As it was, Lily was going to spend plenty of time hanging over the porcelain bowl. "Why don't we go upstairs then?" She stood and helped Lily slowly to her feet, and then took the position closest to pool so Lily wouldn't accidentally stumble and fall in.

Chester bounded about their feet as Anna walked Lily up the stairs. "I'll take you out in a minute, boy." He seemed to understand her, at least the O-U-T word, and ran back to the family room where his leash was kept. She helped Lily undress and climb into bed, where she instantly passed out.

Anna was exhausted, but had several things to do before turning in. First on her list was something to eat. She wolfed down a peanut butter sandwich while walking the dog on the median in front of their house. "Eating dinner with you was a bad idea," she grumbled to Chester as she scooped up his business in the plastic bag.

Next, Anna went out to the pool to gather up Lily's carnage, and stored the vodka on a high shelf above the refrigerator. She was astonished to see two unopened bottles in the back. They never kept that much liquor in the house.

When she turned off the lights in the family room, she noticed a light under the door to the office. Lily's desk was disheveled, an obvious sign she had been going through the stack of mail that had arrived while she was gone. As Anna reached across the desk to pull the chain on the green-globed banker's light, a manila envelope caught her eye.

Photos. Please do not bend.

Anna noted the return address in San Jose. "I can't believe I missed this," she whispered to herself as she picked up the card. A photo fell out as Anna opened it, the bright smiling faces of Lily and her mom in their hiking clothes. Lily was perched upon a rock, both arms around the shoulders of her mother, who stood in front. Anna realized instantly that the picture had been taken only four days before Eleanor died.

Chapter 9

Lily paged through the file and read her notes, the ones she had scrawled on Saturday afternoon after finding the photo of her with her mom. Work had been a poor distraction for the overwhelming sadness, but she had fixed it in her head that this case was prepped. It was not.

"Counselor, would you like to make a statement?" the judge asked.

"Yes, Your Honor." Lily went to the podium, continuing to flip through the file. Her client watched nervously, obviously reeling from the charges of neglect laid out by the attorney for social services. "My client would like to express her regrets for the conditions that led to the removal of her children from the home, and she—"

"Excuse me, I'm a bit confused," the judge interjected. "Are there more children involved in this incident? My report mentions only a four-year-old, Rene Flores."

"Yes . . . yes, that's correct," Lily stammered. "And in light of Mrs. Flores's recent work to . . ." She scanned her notes to find what corrective action she had recommended for her client, but the information wasn't there. "In light of her recent efforts, we're asking that the child be returned to her mother."

"Ms. Stewart, are you certain you have the right case in front of you?"

Lily shuddered at the possibility she had made a major gaffe. She glanced quickly at her client, then back at her notes, confirming for herself that this was Silvia Flores, whose daughter had been removed from the home because a daycare worker had reported her being soiled and hungry. "Yes, Your Honor."

The judge shook her head and looked at the opposing counsel. "Is Rene Flores a boy or a girl?"

"Rene is a boy, Your Honor."

Lily felt her face heat up. "Yes, of course. I apologize. I believe I may have confused this case with another." She introduced her client and allowed her to summarize for the court her success in a parenting class.

The judge took the information under advisement and scheduled a second hearing for the following week. All in all, it was a good outcome, Lily thought. Her confusion about the case hadn't affected the judge's obvious satisfaction that Silvia Flores was taking all the right steps toward getting her child back.

Anna had juggled her work schedule all week so she could be at home with Lily in the evenings, though it meant leaving the house each day by six thirty a.m., and bringing work home at night. Lily's time in San Jose had put her behind at work as well, so she too made use of their evenings at home to catch up, though both vowed not to let this become routine. Anna missed their relaxing times together, and enjoyed being close enough in the family room to talk and trade occasional touches. Just being together again made Anna feel as though their ship had righted,

that the rift her extra hours had created was behind them.
The one thing that still seemed out of sorts was their intimacy.
They hadn't made love since the day they went to the beach,
their only time since Eleanor died over a month ago. Lily's kisses
were sweet and loving, but she turned away onto her side soon
after they went to bed.

"You okay, hon?" Anna asked, gently stroking Lily's bare
shoulder from behind.

"Yeah." Lily seemed surprised by the question and rolled
onto her back. "I'm almost caught up from being gone. How
about you?"

"I may never catch up. But I promise to get back on a
reasonable schedule soon. I think I'm going to hire someone to
manage the VW dealership. I just can't be in two places at once.
Thank goodness the dealerships in Palm Springs are stable."

"How's that going?"

Though details of the desert deal had consumed her for the
past two weeks, Anna hadn't talked about it at home, not wanting
to make an already bad situation worse. "They have our offer.
We should know something next week."

Lily sighed softly and snuggled closer. "It's amazing to think
how much has happened in just the last couple of months, isn't
it?"

"It is." And it was amazing how Lily had turned her question
about how she was doing into an inventory of the state of Premier
Motors. "Are we okay?"

"Of course we are. Why wouldn't we be?"

They hadn't talked at all about the hurtful things Lily had
said when Anna found her drunk by the pool, but it was likely she
hadn't remembered much about that night. "I was just thinking
maybe you were still mad at me for working so much. We haven't
. . ." She floundered for the right phrase, long enough that Lily
spared her the search.

"We haven't made love. That's my fault." Lily turned toward
her, but buried her face beneath Anna's chin. "It isn't you, Anna.

I just feel guilty about it right now . . . having fun, I mean. It'll be okay. I just need a little more time."

Anna's heart broke to hear the sadness in Lily's voice. It was more than losing her mom. It was the sudden nature of how it had happened, and the overwhelming sense of being alone. Anna rose up on her elbow, forcing Lily onto her back so she could look her in the eye. "Take all the time you need. I'm going to be here for you when you're ready. You aren't alone, and whether you think you deserve it or not, we're going to make some time to get away together."

Lily sniffed, prompting Anna to hug her tightly.

"I love you so much, Lily."

"I know you do, and I love you too. I've been a little crazy, but things are getting better. We'll be back to normal soon. I promise."

Not normal, Anna thought. They would be better and stronger as a couple for having gone through this together, ready to face anything.

Lily pressed the button on the speakerphone. "This is Lilian Stewart." She had forwarded her calls to the conference room, where she had spread out index cards outlining the prosecutor's case against her client.

"My little auto empire has officially doubled," Anna said triumphantly.

"You heard from Kimble?"

"Just now. They've accepted our first offer, so we don't have to go through all that same crap we had to do with Sweeney."

"That's fantastic." She knew the Sweeney negotiations had taken a toll on Anna and her senior staff, so it was nice to hear they wouldn't have to go through that again. "That means a celebration is in order. I might have to take you out to dinner, Amazon." If she hustled, she could get the whole family together tonight at Empyre's.

"I've got a better idea. How would you like to ride down to Palm Springs with me tonight? I want to be there tomorrow when they make the announcement to their staff."

Getting away—even if just for a Friday night—sounded like a great idea, the perfect antidote for all the nights they had worked at home. "Do I get to watch?"

"Of course." Lily could practically hear the smile in Anna's voice. "You'll see me in sucking-up mode. I really need to win their support so they'll stick around. Otherwise, I'll have to replace people, and that would mean having to spend a lot of time down there, which I don't want to do."

"Nor do I want you to," Lily groaned. "I think I'll stand in the back of the room and make faces. Is that okay?"

"Absolutely. And maybe when we're done, we'll go have some fun. Joshua Tree isn't far. Have you ever been there?"

Lily was jolted by her memories, but recovered quickly. "Yeah, Mom and I went there a few years ago . . . but I'd love to see it with you. It's beautiful."

Anna's tone went serious. "We need to make some memories of our own, don't we?"

"Definitely."

"I'll meet you at home, then. How soon can you get there?"

"Are we playing hooky again?"

"You bet."

"Give me an hour. What about Chester?"

"I bet I can get Holly to keep him."

Lily's mind worked for a second to place who Holly was. Then it dawned on her. She was the new sales manager, the one from San Diego whom Anna had hired last year, the one who had the problem with filling out the contracts. "Don't tell her how spoiled he is."

"It's too late. Chester stories are more popular than Jonah stories now."

• • •

109

The drive across the desert was the most relaxing two hours Anna could recall in recent weeks. As they drove out of the city, they traded stories about the Kimble deal and Lily's current case, but then their conversation drifted away from work. Anna was pleasantly surprised by Lily's wandering hands and flirtatious banter.

They checked into the Viceroy and carried their overnight bags to a room on the third floor.

"There are plenty of restaurants in walking distance," Anna said. "Whatever you want is fine with me."

Lily kicked off her shoes and dropped across the bed. "I was thinking more along the lines of room service . . . much later." She patted the bed.

Anna grinned and fell alongside her, wasting no time in claiming the position on top. "You're so damn sexy. You were driving me crazy in the car."

Lily tried to answer, but Anna covered her mouth with a hungry kiss. As their tongues danced together, she reached into Lily's collar to tickle the warm, smooth skin at the base of her neck. One button . . . then a second gave way and her fingers deftly released the clasp of Lily's front-hook bra. As she fondled the supple breast, Lily's hands wandered over her back.

Fearing she would lose her dominant position once Lily heated up, Anna continued beyond the shirt's button to Lily's waist, where she worked to unfasten her slacks. As she slid them over Lily's hips, she caught the familiar scent of sexual arousal. Unable to resist, she buried her face into its source, eliciting a loud moan.

"I love that," Lily murmured. One of her hands twisted through Anna's hair, pulling her closer. The other teased her own nipple, left bare by the open shirt.

Anna savored the salty taste, dragging her tongue slowly along the slippery lips to tease the swollen clitoris. As she read Lily's mounting excitement in the pulsating tugs of her hair, she quickened her strokes.

Suddenly, Lily gasped and began to writhe beneath her. "You're making me come."

Anna zeroed in on the hardened nub and drew out the orgasm until Lily pulled away. Then she followed to share the taste with a kiss. "I'm so lucky I get to do that," she whispered.

So lucky for everything, she realized, wrapping Lily into a strong embrace.

Lily walked with Anna toward the revolving doors of the Viceroy, getting her first good look at the art deco-style décor of the historic hotel. She had barely noticed her surroundings last night, she was so intent on getting to their room and ripping off Anna's clothes. Their weekend couldn't be off to a better start.

The desert heat slapped her in the face the moment she exited. Anna's convertible—top down—was already waiting.

"Think you'll want the air conditioner?" Anna asked wryly as she walked around to the driver's seat.

Lily tucked their bag into the small trunk as Anna raised the top. She was looking forward to seeing Anna in action today at the dealerships. Watching her work at home or behind her desk at Premier was one thing, but seeing her in executive mode with her staff was a whole other experience.

After brief introductions to Ted Kimble and his senior staff, Lily busied herself checking out the new X3 in the showroom, politely waving off an offer of assistance from a saleswoman. She had adamantly refused Anna's suggestion to trade hers in when the new models came out, vowing to drive it for at least five or six years. That's when Anna said she would maximize her trade-in value.

An announcement over the intercom called all available staff to the showroom, and Lily watched as Anna took her place on the stairway to the second floor offices. It was impossible not to admire her confidence and authority when it came to the dealership, but this business persona was only one facet of the total package.

There was also the family Anna, the happy "girl next door." This Anna would do anything for her family members, or for the families of her close friends and coworkers. She was there for all of them, especially her sister, and she paraded Jonah around as if he were her own. Lily smiled as she recognized that it was the family girl in Anna who loved Chester so much.

Then there was the grease monkey, the one who donned the grimy jumpsuit to get her hands dirty under the hood of a classic car. Lily found this Anna totally irresistible. It wasn't just the stark contrast from the runway model chic that most people got to see. It was more that the grease monkey symbolized Anna's fascination with all things mechanical. She loved knowing how things worked and couldn't care less about the mess she made of herself. And she had no idea this look was so sexy.

Next, there was Anna the friend, one of the nicest, warmest people she had ever met. It was this Anna whom Lily had fallen in love with, the friend who had gone for help when they were trapped underground, and returned at her own peril. As a friend, Anna had helped out at Kidz Kamp, and spotted her a hell of a deal on the X3 when her resources were tight. It was also the friend who had been a constant source of strength throughout the ordeal of saying good-bye to her mother.

Anna as a lover was the most beautiful experience Lily had ever known. Never could she have imagined connecting so deeply with another person.

And now, she was getting her first real glimpse of Anna the executive, a woman with vision and drive, and the know-how to reach her goal. No doubt it was these qualities that had first attracted Scott Rutherford, the business professor at Southern Cal. Lily too found the CEO Anna quite seductive.

Anna was perfection, she thought, everything she could ever want in a partner. Except they still hadn't talked about the kind of permanent partnership Lily wanted, and it seemed as if it wasn't even on Anna's radar—certainly not when these business dealings were occupying nearly all of her time. Maybe this weekend would be the turnaround they needed, a time they could start to negotiate the path of their future together.

"I'm very excited about this new opportunity here in Palm Springs," Anna said. "Over the next few weeks, you'll see some unfamiliar faces in here, going over the books and procedures, meeting with people, generally being disruptive and annoying." Most of the people chuckled, but a few seemed to be reserving judgment. Lily knew Anna would win them over eventually. "Please forgive them, and get to know them if you can. I promise you they're good people, and I've asked them to get all of the Premier dealerships in sync. We'll probably make a few changes here, but given your success, we're just as likely to adopt some of your practices for the dealerships in LA."

Lily could tell that Anna was trying to make eye contact with as many people as possible as she worked the crowd. When their eyes met and Anna smiled, she was startled by a tingling and knew she had begun to blush.

"Finally, I want everyone to know that at this time, I have no plans to make any personnel changes. Your positions and salaries will not be impacted, and with more employees now in our workforce, we expect to negotiate a better benefits package for all of you. Your hard work has brought about this company's success, and I sincerely hope that each of you will plan to stay on through the transition. Thank you very much. I'll try to meet each of you personally before I leave today. Right now, I'd like to see the senior staff in the conference room."

Lily gave her a wink and slipped out the side door. Anna would be tied up here for several hours, enough time for her to tour The Living Desert, a nearby nature attraction. When she reached the car, she was annoyed to see a man leaning on the hood, smoking. "Can I help you with something?"

"I was just admiring your car," he said. "I saw one just like it not long ago in LA. I used to work there. I've been here about a month."

Lily read his nametag: *Tommy Russell*. He worked next door at the Volkswagen dealership. "It isn't mine. It belongs to your new boss. She just bought these two dealerships."

His face fell and he tossed the cigarette onto the pavement and ground it out. She could have sworn he uttered an obscenity as he stomped back to the VW lot.

Anna pulled into the garage and turned off the engine. As far as she was concerned, it had been the perfect weekend, and that had nothing to do with taking over the dealerships in Palm Springs. She and Lily had finally reconnected, talking intimately again of their feelings for one another for the first time since the weekend in Yosemite. More than once, Anna had been tempted to spring her big question, but Lily deserved her own getaway for that, not an add-on from a business trip.

"That was fun, Amazon. Remind me to think up a nice way to thank you for asking me along."

"I'm sure you'll come up with something," Anna said, hoisting their bag over her shoulder.

"Right now, I'm thinking something involving the pool."

"Sounds good to me." They had driven to Barker Dam inside the national park at Joshua Tree, and then hiked three more miles to visit the oasis. It was certainly beautiful, but difficult to enjoy in the overbearing heat.

Lily opened the side door. "It's weird coming in and not being bowled over by Chester. I got used to him in a hurry."

"How will we ever sleep without him?"

"I plan to wear you out."

Anna grinned and followed her upstairs, where they discarded their clothes and put on their robes. Minutes later, they dropped them on the chaise lounge and slipped nude into the heated pool.

"It seems like a year since the last time we did this," Lily said as she glided through the water on her back.

114

Anna swam faster to catch up, and hooked Lily underneath her breasts. "We have a lot to catch up on. This weekend has been a nice start."

Lily spun in Anna's arms and they sank beneath the water as they kissed. "I'm drowning in you, Amazon," she sputtered when they came up for air.

"Let's get in the hot tub." That was Anna's favorite way to relax. She settled into the warm churning water and pulled Lily's feet into her lap. "I've missed this."

"Is the worst of it over?"

"I probably won't have to work the long hours anymore, but it's going to take months to make sense of the mess Gordon Sweeney left. And I can't hire someone to manage it until I get it all straightened out."

"And Palm Springs?"

"I can pop in there a couple of times a month to check on things. Maybe we'll look for a condo down there. Would you like that?" She shuddered as Lily slipped a hand between her legs.

"If all our weekends in Palm Springs are going to be like this one, that's an offer I won't be able to refuse."

"Winters could be nice. Summers we'd spend inside . . . in our air-conditioned bedroom."

"Now you're talking."

Anna moaned as Lily's fingers went inside her. No doubt about it—she and Lily were home again.

"We find the defendant not guilty, Your Honor."

Lily had performed her job nicely, getting her client acquitted of charges of reckless endangerment of a child. She felt like shit. She had demonstrated to the jury probable doubt that Mr. Thuy was aware that his children had access to his gun. The family had narrowly avoided a tragedy when their four-year-old son fired the gun into their mattress as he rushed to place it back under the bed. She wanted to take Mr. Thuy down to the morgue, where on any given day he could see firsthand the damage a gun can do. Then perhaps he would trouble himself to get a gun lock, or better still, get rid of the goddamned thing.

She spoke briefly with the prosecutor, accepting his congratulations and assuring him that she had already taken steps to educate her client on gun safety and children. Both were hopeful they had seen the last of this careless father.

Lily trudged back to her office and closed the door. She hated criminal trials, but Tony had assigned her this one when he and Lauren had gotten behind in their own work, having split her workload while she was gone. With the trial over quickly, she could get back into the divorces, adoption filings and custody hearings that comprised the majority of her cases.

There was a light knock, and her door was opened a crack. "Lily, you got a minute?"

She looked up to see Tony in her doorway, unusual for this late on a Friday afternoon. "Of course. Anytime." She gestured to a chair across from her desk.

Tony stepped into her office and closed the door. He looked nervous. "So how are you doing, my friend?"

"It's hard sometimes, Tony." She turned and picked up the newly framed picture from Strawberry Peak. "I still miss her. I guess I always will." She knew her eyes were misting, but she held the tears in check.

"I'm sorry, Lily. If we can help you with anything, you'll let us know?"

Lily nodded. After a few quiet moments, she asked, "Is there something else?"

He shifted his feet from back to front and leaned forward in the chair, as if reluctant to continue. "I wanted to ask you about your workload. I was wondering if maybe we've pushed you back into things too quickly."

"I don't think so. Is there a problem with my work?" she asked testily.

"I've gotten a couple of calls. Silvia Flores said you didn't seem like you were prepared for her custody hearing last week, and she asked for another attorney."

"She got her son back yesterday. What more does she want?"

He looked across the desk at her, but she wouldn't meet his eye. "It's not like you to go into court unprepared, Lily."

"It was the Thuy trial, Tony, which by the way, ended this afternoon with an acquittal. You know how I hate criminal stuff. It just takes me longer to slog through it all."

Tony nodded in apparent understanding. "Okay, Lil. But if you need any help, you've got to let me know. Colleen still hasn't heard anything from the PD's office, so she's available to lend a hand."

Lily bit her tongue to keep from blurting out a sarcastic reply about Tony's flagrant suggestion that his wife could do her job. Instead, she answered crisply, "If I need any help, Tony, I'll be sure to ask."

Tony returned to his office, leaving Lily to stew. The clock by the door read only a few minutes after four. Quitting time.

The headaches at Premier Volkswagen continued to grow. Less than a month after the takeover, only Ben Dunlap remained. The service and finance managers were dismissed for failing to follow Anna's new guidelines. While Ben was loyal and easy to work with, he wasn't the sharpest knife in the drawer, which meant Anna had to look elsewhere for management help. She had replaced Tommy Russell with Marco Gonzalez, a thirty-one-year-old dynamo who loved Volkswagens. She desperately needed Hal's help with the books, but was reluctant to add to his workload, especially since he was already spending two days a week in Palm Springs. So here she was on a Friday night, poring over printouts in the conference room, trying to reconcile the inventory with the revenue.

Realizing she wouldn't make it home for dinner, she called

Lily with a plan. "Hey, sweetheart. How was your day?"

"Well, I won my case, but all things being equal, I'd rather have seen my client do a little jail time," Lily said cynically.

"So, I guess it's too bad you're so good at what you do." Lily sounded genuinely dismal, and Anna hoped she would like her idea. "I'm going to be stuck here at the VW place for awhile. I was wondering if maybe you'd . . . pretty please . . . pick up a pizza and come by." She listened hopefully for Lily's response.

"Hmm . . . That actually sounds better than cooking. Do you have a nice tip in mind?"

"Definitely."

An hour later, Anna saw the X3 pull onto the lot, slipping into the space beside her Z8. She was happy to see Chester hop out from his crate in the backseat. Anna met them at the side door, taking the leash and the pizza box as Lily returned to the car for their drinks. Once they were all inside, she threw the deadbolt to lock them in.

Alone in the dark showroom, she quickly stole a kiss. As their lips met, she was immediately aware of the overpowering taste and smell of alcohol, and of the breath mints Lily had obviously used to cover it up. The realization that Lily had been drinking alone so early on a Friday night set off a few alarms. First and foremost was Anna's worry that something had happened again to trigger her depression about losing her mother. She was even more concerned that Lily had driven herself to the dealership when she likely had no business driving. Bringing that up would probably set off a fight, but stopping Lily from driving drunk was too important to dance around.

As they ate and played with the dog, Anna watched for any of the telltale signs that Lily was drunk. She seemed to be in complete control, but the smell of alcohol was pronounced on her breath, even as she masked it with the pizza and soda. There was no way around the awkward exchange.

"You know, I don't feel like working anymore tonight. Why don't we head home?"

118

"Good call, Amazon. Come on, Chester!"

"Whoa!" Anna grabbed her arm. "Why don't we ride home together? Would you bring me back in the morning?"

"That's silly. Can't you just follow me?"

Anna sighed. "Lily, I'm sure you're fine to drive, but I can smell the alcohol on your breath from all the way over here."

Lily bristled. "Yes, I had a drink this afternoon when I got home from work. No, I am not drunk."

"I know you're not. It's just that—"

"So if you know I'm not drunk, then what's the problem?" Lily stood up and began to pace around the conference room. "I worked hard this week. What's the big deal about me having a drink to relax?"

"It isn't a big deal. But—"

"How many times have you driven home from Empyre's after a glass of wine? Once? Twice? More like fifty times, I bet."

Anna hated Lily's angry tone, but she wasn't going to be pushed around on this. Even though Lily didn't seem drunk, she smelled strongly of liquor. "Sweetheart, anything could happen, and if it does, you'd be the one in trouble, no matter whose fault it was. It's just silly to take a chance when we both have our cars here."

Her eyes dark and piercing, Lily finally tossed her keys on the table and they noisily slid across. "Fine. Let's just go." She snatched Chester's leash and walked quickly down to the showroom, leaving Anna to tidy up their mess.

Despite Anna's chipper attitude, Lily remained irritated about their confrontation at the dealership, especially when she realized she would have to drive Anna to work. Her first instinct had been to rip into her for working on a Saturday in the first place. She had said she would try to do that less, and if she had stayed later last night instead of insisting on playing babysitter, she might have finished her work. But that didn't matter today, because

Lily was in no mood for company—at least not Anna's company. She didn't feel like having to defend something as insignificant as an after-work drink, and she wasn't going to be dictated to as if Anna were her boss.

Instead, she was heading out with Kim, who had called earlier to invite her along for a walk today through Topanga Park. She wasn't emotionally ready to take on the rugged hiking trails again, but she missed being outside in the fresh air.

With amazing energy, Kim pushed the three-wheeled stroller up the steep path. "I'm sure you're getting tired of this question, but how are you doing, Lily?"

Lily was tired of the question, but she hadn't seen Kim at all since the funeral, so it was fair. She lowered her sunglasses from her forehead to cover any tears that might spring up and looked out across the hills. "I'm doing okay, most of the time. It's hard sometimes though, like putting on these boots today. The last time I went out, it was with Mom."

"I'm glad you came with me. I know how much you like hiking. You're welcome to join Jonah and me any weekend. The other ladies don't walk with me then, because their husbands have normal jobs." She sneered as she said the word "normal," as if knowing Lily would understand.

"I hear you. I get to watch Anna come home in time to fall into bed exhausted, and she's going out the door again when I get up."

"That's exactly like Hal, and now he's gone one night a week to Palm Springs. How do you deal with it?"

By pouting, Lily thought. "I don't always deal with it. Sometimes it gets to be frustrating, and the next thing I know, we're fighting about it." Lily wasn't sure she should be confiding their problems to Anna's sister, but she thought it would be nice to hear from someone who at least understood what she was going through.

"Hal and I had a few fights at first. But you know, I shouldn't complain. He's really happy with this new job and all the responsibility. And he's pushing himself to do a good job for Anna."

"Anna's pushing herself too." She didn't add that Anna was working even harder to keep from asking more from Hal. "But she loves it."

"So does Hal. Not like Anna—she's a fanatic. But he's happy working there, and I wouldn't want to take that away from him. I guess I expect him to be some sort of 'super dad,' home every night to take over with Jonah and help with the dishes. That's just a fantasy. But I have to admit, he's holding up his share. And with him working at Premier, we don't even miss my income."

"Anna says it's going to calm down soon. What do you think?"

"It'll calm down for Hal when he gets through the books in Palm Springs. But I think my sister will work herself to death to take the load off everyone else. I hope you're making her come home sometimes and relax a little."

Kim's words gave Lily a fresh perspective. Anna wasn't just working because she was obsessed. Her long hours meant others could have a more normal life, and it was typical of Anna to put her employees first. "We do the best we can. I catch myself making little comments every now and then to make her feel guilty about being gone so much, but I always apologize. I can't deny it's there, though."

"Believe me, I understand. Just call me if you get lonely in that big old house. Jonah doesn't have a pool, you know."

These days, it seemed to Lily that she was lonely all the time. The loss of her mother had left her feeling like a family of one. And her irritation at the extra hours Anna was putting in at work was probably only a symptom. She needed more from Anna than just her presence. She needed to know now what Anna saw for their future. Otherwise, there might be no end to the sadness she felt.

• • •

Lily smiled to herself as Chester dashed off to greet Anna in the family room. After studying her feelings all afternoon, her mood was a hundred and eighty degrees from where she had been this morning. Fresh from her shower, she was barefoot and wearing one of Anna's large gray BMW polo shirts over long baggy shorts.

Anna entered the kitchen with obvious apprehension. "Did you and Kim have a good walk?"

"It was nice. I'm glad she called." Lily set aside the salad she had been tossing. "Come here, Amazon." She held her arms open.

Anna grinned broadly and stepped into the hug, returning it with ferocity. "I love you, Lily."

"I love you back. I'm sorry I was a jerk."

"Me too."

Walking with Kim today, Lily had reached an understanding about why she had felt so much anger of late . . . and why she expressed it by drinking more than Anna thought she should. Now more than ever, she needed a constant in her life. The love she shared with Anna was strong and still growing, but Lily wanted a promise. She wanted to dream, to look ahead as she grew old, and to know that Anna would always be by her side.

Eleanor Stewart was the only person on earth who had ever made such a promise to her, and that vow of love and commitment had always been her anchor. If Anna couldn't do this, Lily would have to plant her own stake in the ground. Her heart knew that Anna would be her last chance.

But today wasn't the day to press the issue. She certainly didn't want Anna having doubts just because she had been such a brat lately. They needed some time away from all the things that pulled at them, time just for one another.

"Sweetheart, whatever happened with the Maui thing? Did we lose that or can we reschedule for another time?"

"I've still got the tickets," Anna said. "I think all we'd have to do is call the travel agent and try to pick another time we could go." She reached past Lily and snatched a cherry tomato from the salad. "What if we tried for Labor Day?"

That was more than six weeks away. Lily feared she would be a basket case by then. "Any chance we could go before that? I could really use a getaway," she asked hopefully.

"I don't know. The VW place is a mess. Everything else is running fine, thank God, but every time I put a fire out over there, another one breaks out. If we don't stop hemorrhaging money in the next two months, we're going to lose our shirts." Anna had slipped seamlessly into her CEO persona.

"Okay, let's shoot for Labor Day."

Lily wheeled the X3 into the narrow driveway of the simple house in Hispanic East LA. Maria Esperanza's old neighborhood, she remembered, thinking of the night she had rushed out to protect her client from her violent ex-husband, now her loving current husband.

Beside her in the front seat was thirteen-year-old Marga Alvarez, a foster child who had deeply touched Lily's heart. Inside the house, Marga's young mother lay dying, in the final stages of liver cancer. Too soon, Marga Alvarez would be all alone. Sandy had called last week asking Lily to represent the Alvarez family, and she had agreed to serve as both the executor of Mrs. Alvarez' estate and as guardian *ad litem* for Marga.

As guardian *ad litem*, Lily made the decisions about Marga's placement. It was a tough assignment, especially after losing her own mother, but she couldn't say no to Sandy. Lily had comforted the girl about her ordeal, even talking about her own loss, as Anna had when she reached out to Lateisha, the Kidz Kamp girl whose mother had died.

The teenager jumped from the car almost before it had stopped, running eagerly into the house to see her mother. Marga had been in foster care since last week, when Lily had reluctantly deemed the home situation unsafe. The only adult present was now almost fully incapacitated, and the house teemed with home health care workers, whose job duties did not include caring for a thirteen-year-old. Fortunately, Mrs. Alvarez had relatives in Chicago, and Marga was welcome in their home. But for these last few days, Lily stood by the girl's decision to stay close to her mother.

Lily carried her briefcase into the house, thinking she might get some work done in the kitchen while Marga visited with her mother in the back bedroom. Just as she settled down with her files, the front screen door squeaked, announcing a new arrival.

"Mrs. Alvarez?"

That voice.

"Mrs. Alvarez? It's Bev Adams, from HHC."

Beverly. Lily tasted her lunch in the back of her throat. She had not seen her ex-lover in over six years, since the day she had packed her few belongings and left their home, hurt and bewildered about how things had gone so horribly wrong. And she did not want to see her today.

Lily heard Beverly's voice in the bedroom, and knew that Marga would soon give her presence away. Quickly, she ducked into the small bathroom off the living room and locked the door. She was perfectly content to ride out Beverly's visit counting the small octagonal floor tiles as she sat on the covered toilet seat.

It was not to be. "Are you okay in there?" Beverly asked.

Of all the home health care professionals in LA, Beverly Adams had to be the one seeing Mrs. Alvarez. "Fine," Lily answered, lifting her voice an octave in disguise. "Just something I ate, I guess." She rolled her eyes at how disgusting that sounded.

"Look, I'm a nurse. I've got something that will settle your stomach."

"No, thanks. I'm sure I'll be fine. I just need to sit here awhile." The situation couldn't possibly be more humiliating.

"Okay, but let me know when you're out. I need to get something from the cabinet in there."

Fuck!

Lily cracked the door and waited until she was certain Beverly was talking to the sick woman. The she slipped out of the bathroom and made a beeline back to the kitchen to gather her things. She was shoving them in her briefcase when Beverly suddenly appeared in the doorway.

"Lily?"

"Oh, my goodness. Look who it is." Beverly had let herself go, gaining at least thirty pounds in the past six years.

"I thought there was something familiar about that voice."

"How are you, Bev? And how's Josh? What is he now, eleven years old?" Josh was Beverly's son, whom Lily had adored.

"I'm fine. We're both fine. How about you?"

"Mostly okay, I guess. I lost my mom a couple of months ago. That was hard." Eleanor had always treated Beverly warmly, though she confessed later to Lily that they hadn't really seemed a good match.

"I'm really sorry to hear that. I always liked Eleanor."

"Thanks."

Beverly held up her hand, which sported a band of hammered gold. "I got married again. Josh needed a daddy."

"Congratulations." Lily almost choked on the word.

"It isn't ideal . . . obviously. But it's nice to know someone is going to be there for us, you know?"

Lily felt like throwing up. "I'm happy for you, Beverly." Especially happy to know she was stuck in a relationship that wasn't "ideal."

"And you? Are you with someone?"

She had no interest in trading personal information with Beverly. "No."

"Aw, I'm sorry to hear that. I know that's always been important to you. But the right one will come along someday, Lily."

Lily twisted to avoid Beverly's hand on her shoulder. "Marga, I'll be in the car," she shouted. "Tell Josh I said hello." With that, she pushed past Beverly and went to wait out Marga's visit in the X3.

A sense of panic gripped Anna as she pulled into the driveway. Lily's car was gone, and the house was dark, save for the outside light by the side door, which came on when it detected her presence in the drive. She had been calling the house off and on all evening, but assumed that Lily was working late also. It was when she failed to reach Lily on her cell phone that she became concerned.

A rude surprise awaited her in the kitchen, where Chester huddled against the back door, anxious about her reaction to what he had done. The puddle in the floor confirmed that Lily hadn't been home at all.

"It's okay, boy. Not your fault." She turned him out into the side yard, not wanting to stray from the phone in case Lily called. On her cell phone, she dialed Sandy, who had no clue where Lily was. Next, she retrieved voicemail from every possible source. Then she wandered the house in search of a note. Finally, the phone rang.

"Anna, I need you to come get me."

"Where are you? Are you all right?"

"I'm fine. I'm at the jail downtown."

It wasn't unusual for Lily to be at the jail. Sometimes, her clients got into trouble and she had to bail them out. But Lily's sullen tone told her this time was different. "Where's your car? Should I send someone to pick it up?"

Lily sighed audibly. "It's impounded, Anna. I got caught driving drunk."

At first, she was stunned by the news. Then as it sank in, she found herself shaking with fury. "I can't believe—"

"Save it. Just come and get me. Please."

Forty minutes later, Anna pulled to the curb where Lily was waiting.

"Thanks for coming. I . . . I'm sorry."

Anna didn't answer, her eyes straight ahead as the excess

126

adrenaline from her unchanneled anger caused her to push the tachometer higher than usual. The sports car responded with power, lurching as she cycled through the gears.

"Take it easy, now. It wouldn't do for both of us to get arrested on the same night."

"Please don't talk, Lily."

For the remainder of the trip, Anna bit her tongue, not wanting to lash out and make things worse. If Lily was still drunk, she probably wouldn't remember the conversation tomorrow anyway. Lily made the rest of evening easy by going to bed as soon as she got home.

Though relieved that Lily was all right, Anna was still furious. This was exactly what she had warned her about the night they ate pizza at the VW dealership. How could Lily have been so careless? And why was she out drinking anyway? It was the middle of the week.

Entering their bedroom, Anna wasn't at all surprised to find Lily already asleep. For a fleeting moment she considered staying the night in the guest room. But that single act had been the beginning of the end of her marriage to Scott. She wouldn't do that again, not with Lily. Foregoing their usual intimacy, Anna followed Lily's lead and donned a nightshirt. Taking her place in the bed, she slowly let her hand drift across the bed, coming to rest on Lily's hip.

Lily needed to stop drinking. And Anna knew her long nights at work had to end.

Chapter 10

Lily checked her watch, noting that it was nearly nine. Anna was still in her nightshirt by the pool, eating a leisurely breakfast as she read the paper. That was normal for a Sunday, but not for a Saturday.

"If you're worried about me needing to go somewhere while you're at work, I don't. I have some reading to do," Lily said as she refilled their coffee mugs. They had barely spoken since her arrest, but Anna didn't seem to be angry anymore.

"I thought I'd stay home today."

"Fine. But if you're doing it in case I need something, it isn't necessary."

Anna lowered her paper and reached across the table to take her hand. "I'm worried about you. I know this has been an awful time, and I haven't exactly been very supportive."

"That's ridiculous. You've been perfect." It was ironic how Anna's words were meant to soothe, but instead carried such bite. On top of the misery Lily already felt about her spiraling loss of control, Anna was adding guilt by taking part of the blame herself. "I . . . I don't know what's gotten in to me. I never used to be like this." Briefly, she considered telling Anna about her humiliating meeting with Beverly, but she knew it would sound as if she was making an excuse for drinking and driving.

"Honey, you lost your mother," Anna said softly. "And it hasn't helped things that I've been gone so much. I know if I were in your shoes, I wouldn't want to be left by myself all the time, or wondering how late you were going to be every night." She stood and walked around the table, her arms encircling Lily's head against her stomach. "I'm going to try very hard not to work so much. I've already called this morning and offered Brad and Holly extra incentives to work the weekends so I don't have to. We'll get through this, baby."

Lily thought she might cry. "I'm so sorry I've been such a pain in the ass."

"I love you so much. But you have to promise me . . ."

"Anything, Anna."

"I need to know you'll talk to me when things are bothering you . . . that you won't let these walls grow up between us."

"I will." She sniffed. "I just don't want you to think I'm making excuses. This was my fault."

"It doesn't matter, Lily. You have to let me in there, and don't ever be afraid to tell me what you need from me."

Lily nodded, clinging to Anna's arms as if they were a lifeline.

Lily knew she was very fortunate to have landed in Judge Anston's court, as he remembered her recent loss. Lauren had represented her at the arraignment, where she pleaded no contest in exchange for a 120-day suspension of her driving privileges. Since it was her first offense, she was able to negotiate an exception for any driving related to her work, so only her home, social and recreational activities would be impacted.

She shifted in the chair to tuck a leg underneath her. It was almost ten o'clock on a Tuesday night, and here she was, prepping a case in Anna's office at the BMW dealership, while Anna methodically processed the work in her inbox. Chester lay under the desk, sound asleep. Lily hadn't wanted to stay home alone. Something inside her was disjointed, and it was amplified when she was by herself.

Lily looked around the office. True to her word, Anna had thrown out her father's cherry desk, along with those hideous green wingback chairs, replacing everything with a Scandinavian motif. Her numerous awards and plaques from BMW and the business community hung hidden behind her door, which was closed to keep Chester from wandering around. He had recently developed a very bad habit regarding their tile floors. And he hadn't yet acclimated to the new doggie door at home.

Besides the numerous model cars that dotted the room, two framed photographs were the only obvious personal touches. One was Jonah at six months, smiling and posed in his infant BMW wear. The other was of Anna with Lily, the one taken at the base of Yosemite Falls. Lily had that photo on her desk too. Happier times.

"Are you about ready to call it a night?" Anna's voice startled her.

"Whenever you are." Without a driver's license for the next five months, Lily was completely at Anna's mercy. "Thanks for coming to get me."

"I liked you being here. And the best news is I'm totally caught up, which means I won't even have to stop by here tomorrow."

"That's good." Lily tried to sound enthusiastic, but the reality was that it didn't matter much whether they were together at home or here. The atmosphere was the same, with Anna being supportive and Lily feeling guilty about it. She felt as if she were falling into a dark, bottomless hole.

• • •

Dressed in her black suit for the somber occasion, Lily directed Marga Alvarez to the front row of the church, where she would sit with her mother's cousin during the service. Taking a seat at the side several rows back, she noted with relief that Beverly was not among the mourners.

Marga was a remarkable young woman. Watching the girl absorb the priest's parting words, she marveled at the teenager's maturity and poise in the face of her loss. She couldn't help but wonder where a thirteen-year-old got that kind of strength. Lily had come apart when her mother died. And now, a painful lump formed in her throat as she looked upon this child and saw herself sitting with Anna in the front pew of the church in San Jose. Had it already been two months?

Lily had signed all the paperwork earlier this morning to transfer custody of Marga to her relatives in Chicago. The girl was packed and ready, and would leave first thing tomorrow to start her new life. As they walked down the steps from the church, Lily sought out her youthful charge one last time to say good-bye.

"Good luck to you, sweetheart. I'll be thinking about you." The hug they shared was meant to soothe Marga, but Lily found it comforting for herself.

"Good luck to you too, Miss Stewart. I bet our moms are watching over both of us right now."

That did it for Lily. She turned quickly toward her car as the tears burst forth. After all these weeks, why was it still so raw?

She composed herself in the car for more than twenty minutes before starting back to her office. As she mindlessly navigated traffic, she called Anna's direct line. More than ever, she needed a friendly voice.

"Hi, sweetheart. How did it go?" Anna asked.

"It was sad. I just needed to hear your voice."

"You want to have lunch with me? I'll come downtown."

Lily would have loved that, but she didn't feel right about

131

asking Anna to drop everything and rush down, especially since she had been coming home early in the evenings. "No, that's okay. Thanks though. I'll probably just grab something at the deli and eat at my desk."

"You sound down, sweetheart. Is everything all right?"

Lily didn't want to get into the business about the funeral over the phone. She had only just gotten her emotions under control. "Yeah, it's fine. It'll be okay when I get home and can see you."

"I was going to call you this afternoon. Something's come up at the BMW lot in Palm Springs. Hal found a couple of irregularities in their accounting, and he needs me to come down tonight and take a look."

"Can't you just fax some things, or send the documents by e-mail?" Lily was trying desperately not to sound whiny, but she really didn't want to be alone tonight.

"I would, but this is really sensitive. Hal's found a six-figure discrepancy, and we really don't know if it's just a mistake or an intentional cover-up." Her voice was hushed in case others in the hallway might be listening. "I have to leave right after lunch, but I should only be gone overnight."

Lily could hear from Anna's tone that she was very worried about the situation in Palm Springs. It was childish to expect Anna to stay in LA when something that serious loomed at her business. "Sounds like you really need to take care of that. I'll be okay."

"Why don't you go with me? I bet we can be back by noon tomorrow."

"I can't. I have to be in court at eight thirty."

"I wish I didn't have to go."

She hated that Anna was again feeling guilty over something that wasn't at all her fault. "It's okay. I'm a big girl."

"I love you."

"I love you too."

• • •

Not at all eager to head home to the empty house, Lily worked on her cases until after six, calling clients to get status reports and to schedule appointments. Only her obligation to Chester, who needed a regular walk in the early evening, propelled her from her office. She dreaded the dark and lonely house.

The realization that Anna wouldn't be home played over and over in her head. On impulse, Lily detoured slightly from her direct route, stopping less than a mile from her home to purchase a supply of vodka. She knew she shouldn't, but the idea of being home alone tonight was too much. A few drinks would take the edge off, numb the ache she felt in her bones and bring her merciful sleep. She and Anna had never actually had the "not drinking anymore" conversation, so it wasn't like she was breaking a promise or anything, and she wasn't going to drive anywhere. Beside, Anna would never know.

At six thirty that evening, Hal found it—the evidence that the errors they were looking at were not the result of deception. A simple programming glitch in the way their contract forms had computed sales tax meant Kimble Motors owed the IRS and the state of California more than $100,000 before the deal could be finalized. Ted Kimble apologized profusely and assured Anna he would take care of it immediately.

With the matter now settled, Anna and Hal caravanned back to their LA homes. Anna tried to call Lily from the car to let her know she was en route, but the satellite network was apparently down in their area. Rather than waste time by stopping to find a pay phone, she decided to push ahead and get home as quickly as she could, maybe even before Lily had gone to bed.

She was startled by an excited Chester as soon as she stepped out of her car. "Hey, boy. What are you doing out?" She looked around, expecting to see Lily nearby. On her way to the side door, she found the back gate standing open, which explained why Chester was running around loose. "Get in here," she said, closing the gate behind her.

As she approached the kitchen, she was taken aback by the sight. Lily was standing at the counter, calmly pouring a drink. A flood of emotions—anger, frustration, despair—surged through her as she watched Lily drink from the glass and fill it again.

She flung the French door open wide. "Hello, Lily," she announced herself brusquely.

Lily jumped at the sound of her voice, but recovered quickly, leaning against the counter with infuriating nonchalance. "You're back early."

"What the hell are you doing?"

"What the hell does it look like?"

"Goddamn it, Lily! It looks like you couldn't wait to have me out of your hair for a night so you could get drunk again." She was angrier at the apparent deception than at the act itself.

"And you were more than happy to oblige," Lily shot back, her words slurred.

Anna grabbed the bottle and began pouring its contents down the sink.

"Goddamn it, that's mine!" Lily screamed, lunging across the counter.

The next few moments second to pass in slow motion. Anna jerked back, sloshing the vodka over herself and the floor as Lily grabbed for the bottle. A nervous Chester had positioned himself behind Anna's feet, and she tumbled backward and hit the floor. The bottled shattered on the tile and she cried out as blood spurted instantly from a deep gash across her palm.

"Oh, my God, Anna!" Lily hurried to the drawer for a clean dish towel.

Anna looked in shock at her injured hand, suddenly pulling it away from Lily's view as she snatched the towel and began to wrap the wound.

"You need stitches. We have to go to the hospital." Lily tugged at her arm to see the wound.

"No! I'm not going anywhere with you. You're drunk."

"Anna?" Lily was wide-eyed, clearly panicked. "At least let me ride with you. I'll keep the pressure on it." She reached out to hold the bandaged hand.

"I'll do it myself!"

"Please let me help," she whimpered, tears now pouring from eyes.

"Just . . . just see if you can manage to clean up this mess before Chester gets hurt." Pushing past her, Anna grabbed her keys again and stormed out.

Chapter 11

Anna flinched as the doctor efficiently tied off another stitch. It wasn't the pain—her right hand was loaded with a local anesthetic—but the sight of the open wound that unnerved her. More than two inches long, the gash had split the meaty part of her palm below the thumb. They were up to twenty-one now, not including the dissolvable stitches she had gotten deep inside to reconnect the tissue near the bone. Glass cuts were particularly nasty, the doctor said, leaving jagged tears in the skin that were tedious to close.

Her hand had throbbed all the way to the UCLA Medical Center, more so when she used it to change the gears on her Z8. She was certain it would throb tomorrow as well, and probably for several days after. The scarlet towel had drawn quick attention when she entered the emergency room, where a nurse immediately applied pressure to the wound to stop the profuse bleeding.

That nurse appeared again with bandages as the doctor was finishing. Tall and lanky with graying hair, she reminded Anna of Suzanne, who worked as an ER nurse at St. George. "Ms. Kaklis, are you sure there isn't someone we could call to come pick you up?"

"No, I can manage, thank you." Anna had no choice but to manage. She couldn't call Lily, and she wouldn't call anyone else. As far as she was concerned, the fewer people who knew about this night, the better.

The doctor spoke up. "If there's no one to call, I'm going to recommend that you rest here for a couple of hours. Your blood pressure dropped a bit from the loss of blood, so I don't think it would be wise for you to drive just yet."

"Whatever you think," Anna muttered. She hated not having choices.

"Just for a couple of hours," he assured. Before leaving, he prescribed a mild painkiller, but cautioned her to wait until she arrived home before taking it.

Anna sat alone in the curtained room, not wanting to believe that things had gone so bad. What misery Lily must feel to have all that anger and need for escape. Anna was running out of ideas for how she might fix it.

"I need to bandage that." The nurse said, taking a seat across from her.

Anna held out her hand.

"You were lucky this time, you know," the nurse said. Her tone was sympathetic, not accusatory.

"I beg your pardon?"

"You got some stitches in your hand. What'll it be next time? Broken teeth? A ruptured spleen?"

Anna was genuinely confused. "What on earth are you talking about?"

"Ms. Kaklis, I'm not trying to intrude. I know people like to keep things like this private. But we see this all the time in here, women coming in here after fights with their boyfriends and husbands." She wrapped neat figure eights around Anna's thumb and wrist. "If that's what's going on here, you should know that there's help available."

"It isn't what's going on." It horrified her that people might think such a thing.

The nurse sighed and nodded, as if accustomed to the denial. "Look, I can smell the alcohol on your clothes, but you don't seem like the one who's drunk. I figure there's a drinker in the house, and you're the punching bag."

"No, I'm not a punching bag. We were having a . . . disagreement and I tripped over the dog." She met the nurse's skeptical eye. It was important to defend Lily. "Really. It wasn't a fight. More like tug of war . . . over a vodka bottle," she conceded. "She'd . . ." Anna caught herself, wondering how much she should say. "She'd never hurt me."

If the nurse was surprised that the other party was a woman, she didn't let on. "Are you really sure of that? These things have a way of escalating."

"Yes, of course." Things already had escalated, Anna thought, but what had happened was an accident. Lily already felt awful about it, maybe enough to convince her once and for all that she shouldn't drink anymore. "She's been under a lot of stress lately."

"Have you talked to her about her drinking and how it hurts you?"

"We've talked. But it's hard for her right now. She lost her mother recently, and I've been too busy at work to be with her." The nurse's manner was disarming, and Anna loosened up a bit.

The woman finished wrapping the bandage, taping the ends securely around Anna's wrist. "You're going to need to change this bandage every couple of days, and keep it dry until the stitches come out." Placing her bandaging materials back in the plastic container, she added, "You know, there's somebody here at the hospital you could talk with, somebody who might be able to help."

"I . . . I don't know. I think we'll be able to work this out."

"I'm sure you're both trying very hard. But whatever it is you're doing right now isn't working. Not for you, and apparently not for her either." She patted Anna's forearm. "It happens this way sometimes. People lose control and they need a little help getting back on the right path. It's nothing to be ashamed about. But not doing everything you can to fix it would be a shame."

Something about the nurse's words brought tears to her eyes. The idea that Lily might be suffering with a problem she couldn't help was almost more than Anna could bear. "What can I do to help her?"

"Let me make a call. The doctor said you should stay here a couple of hours. I can have somebody here before then."

Her gentle smile was encouraging. Talking to someone was a very big step. "Okay."

Forty-five minutes passed before the hospital's on-call substance abuse counselor joined her in the examining room. Reluctantly, Anna told him all she could remember about Lily's drinking behavior and the things that had been going on in her life. She also related the things she had done to help ease Lily's sorrow, like trying to be with her more. She even mentioned the trip to Maui they now had planned for Labor Day weekend.

The counselor took a long look at his notes before leaning back and folding his arms across his chest. "I'm pretty sure you won't like what I'm about to tell you. It sounds as if your—may I call her your partner?"

Anna nodded.

"From what you tell me, I'd say your partner is showing the classic signs of alcoholism."

"But she's never had a problem with drinking before. This is all because her mom died, and . . . because of me. She just feels so lonely. It's like the bottle is her companion because no one else is there for her."

He nodded and sighed. "I'm sure it must seem like that, Anna. But alcoholics don't drink because they're sad or lonely. They

139

drink because they're alcoholics."

"That sounds like a circular argument."

"Not really. Do you get drunk whenever you're sad and lonely? Do you drive? Do you sneak around and try to do it behind people's back? No. Lily does these things because she's an alcoholic. She understands that her drinking has detrimental effects, but she can't resist the urge. There are millions of people like her, but lots of success stories."

"So all I have to do is convince her to get help. Right?"

"It's probably not going to be that simple, especially since you've already established an enabling pattern."

"A what?"

"You've been an enabler, Anna. You shoulder part of the blame for Lily's behavior. You try to adjust your life to accommodate hers, and you accept what happened to her mother as a valid excuse for getting drunk."

"But what happened tonight was an accident. What am I supposed to do?"

"Lily needs to stop drinking. But she isn't going to do that until she truly has to face the consequences of her actions. And you have the hardest job of all, which is to sit back and do nothing while someone you love falls all the way to the bottom. Only then will Lily realize that she has to be the one to pick herself up."

"I can't do that. Lily already feels abandoned by everyone who ever mattered—her birth mother, her adoptive mother." She stopped short of mentioning the lovers that had broken things off.

"That's why yours is the hardest job," he explained. "It's painful to see loved ones struggle, especially when we think we can help. But she doesn't need your help right now. She needs your support, but only to help her fight this, not to help her keep it up."

Anna couldn't believe what he was asking of her. Tears filled her eyes as she thought of how hurt Lily would be to face yet another abandonment in her life. "I don't know if I can do that."

"Anna, I don't mean to trivialize your relationship with Lily. I'm sure you both love each other very much. But it isn't what's important here. Lily's in a battle for her soul. Stepping back may very well cost you her love. Not stepping back may cost you both everything."

The crimson blood on the white tile floor stunned Lily into sobriety. What had she done? Shaking uncontrollably, she scrubbed the floor as best she could, shooing away a clearly confused Chester to protect him from the broken glass. The blood had stained the grout, leaving the awful image for all to see.

Over an hour had gone by since Anna left for the hospital. Lily had wanted to follow in her car, but knew Anna would be furious with her for driving.

Anna had every right to be angry. Lily could only hope she hadn't gone too far this time. She had been nothing but a pain in the ass for weeks—always depressed, losing her driver's license, and making digs about how much time Anna spent at the dealership. And now this.

But Anna wouldn't stay angry long. She was far too kind, far too generous, far too forgiving. In fact, she had already taken much of the blame for being gone so much. But Lily knew there was more to it that was under the surface, things Anna didn't even know. Lily hadn't told her about the trouble at work, or about seeing Beverly the other day. Or about getting smashed at Colleen's bridal shower, or the two bottles of vodka hidden in the garage, behind their camping gear on the second shelf.

Anna would just come home and not say anything. She would be angry for a day or two, and then everything would be back to normal. She would probably try harder not to work late, and even try to smooth everything over. Then in a few weeks, they would go to Maui and spend three days together acting as if nothing had happened. Anna might still have her stitches.

And when they got home, Lily knew she would screw up again.

Adamant that she was no longer under the alcohol's influence, her reasoning seemed perfect. She needed to leave. Anna wouldn't want her to, and would ask her to stay. That's why she needed to be gone when Anna got back. She couldn't risk another incident like this. What if it got worse?

She retrieved the suitcases from the hall closet and hurriedly packed. Underwear, shoes, belts, jeans, shorts, T-shirts and nightshirts, all were crammed haphazardly into the roller bag. Cosmetics went in the smaller bag, and all of her essential papers and books were stuffed into her briefcase. Once these were loaded in the X3, she made three trips to her closet, collecting several suits and tops for work over the next few days while Anna cooled off. These she laid across the back of the SUV. Finally, she jammed as much of her hiking gear as would fit in her backpack and threw it onto the backseat.

"Chester!" She couldn't take him. She had no idea yet where she was going. "You be a good boy, you hear? Anna needs you to be a good boy."

As she turned on her headlights to pull out of the garage, she remembered the vodka behind the camping gear. She hastily stowed it under the seat and backed out of the driveway, vowing to herself that she would never hurt Anna again.

"Here are the invoices you asked for, Anna." Marco Gonzalez, her VW sales manager, startled her as he dropped the papers on the conference table. "You know, we'll find you an office if you want. You don't have to work in here every time you come."

"If you really want to make me happy, find out where these six cars went," Anna snapped.

Marco sheepishly took the list and stepped back. "I'll see what I can do."

142

"Marco, wait." She sighed and looked away, ashamed of her behavior. "I didn't mean to snap at you. You're doing a great job, and I really appreciate it."

"Thanks, Anna. I'll get on this now."

Anna pressed her fingers against her brow, nursing a small headache that had loomed for the last two days and threatened to become a full-blown migraine. Since Wednesday night. Since Lily left. She hadn't heard from her at all, and had no idea where she had gone.

The intercom beeped, and a voice followed. "Anna, there's a call for you on three."

"This is Anna Kaklis." Her stomach knotted as the silence told her that Lily was on the other end of the line.

"Hi."

"Hello." Anna was so relieved to hear her voice that she was tempted just to forgive her immediately. Surely they could work through this. But the counselor's warning stopped her. Lily's soul was at stake, he said. She needed to step back and let Lily be responsible for herself. And as he said, it was hard, but it was the only way.

"Anna, I'm so sorry about the other night. Is . . . is your hand okay?"

"It's fine," Anna lied. It hurt like hell. She had bumped or strained her sore appendage repeatedly. It was amazing to her to realize how many times a day she used her dominant hand.

"I thought maybe we should talk. You know, sort of clear the air about the other night." Lily sounded so sad. "Anna, I can't believe I acted like that. I feel awful about it, especially you getting hurt because of me. I'd give anything if I could take it all back."

"It's okay, Lily. It was an accident."

Lily sniffed, a sure sign she was crying. "I'm sorry I left. I just thought it would be easier if you didn't have to put up with me for a couple of days."

"I understand." Anna fought her own tears and the crack in

143

her voice. "It probably helped us both to have a little space."

After a long silence, Lily said, "Is it all right for me to come back, or do you need a few more days?"

Anna took a moment to compose herself, afraid she might dissolve in tears. Lily didn't need that, and neither did she. They needed reason to guide them, not emotion. Her instructions had been clear: Give no support for anything other than getting Lily help. "We can't go back to the way things were, Lily. You have to get some help for your drinking problem. I'll do anything I can to help you, but you have to be the one to do it."

"It's not that bad, Anna. I've just been having a hard time lately and I let it get out of hand. I have a grip on it now, and it won't be a problem anymore."

Anna had practically memorized the pamphlet the counselor had given her, and she knew she had to stick to her message in the face of Lily's promises. "Sweetheart, your drinking has become a problem for me. We argue. We hurt each other's feelings. We never used to do that. When I can't be home, I feel guilty. And I worry about you and whether or not you're out driving drunk."

"Anna, if you feel guilty about not being home, maybe you should—" Whatever she had intended to say, she swallowed it. "It's not like I drink every day."

Determined to get her message through, Anna spoke in a calm, even tone. "Honey, there are all kinds of programs and services out there for alcoholism. Even if it's just going to AA meetings. I'll help you in any way I can to find whatever works, but you have to do something."

"So now I'm an alcoholic, am I?" Anna could hear her getting worked up. "Fine. If you want me to stop, say the word. I won't ever drink again. I swear it."

Anna desperately wanted to believe her, but there was too much at stake. She simply couldn't risk a broken promise, and another incident like the last one might rip them apart forever. Lily needed to make this decision for herself, not as a promise to Anna. "A promise to me isn't enough. You have to get some help.

I'll support you to get help, but not to keep drinking."

"Support me? Oh, I like that. Where would I ever be without you?" she asked, her voice thick with sarcasm.

"You know that's not what I—"

"I'm perfectly capable of quitting on my own, Anna. I don't need some goddamned treatment program!" Lily's pleas had turned to anger. "Do you really think I belong in a roomful of people with the shakes, guys who come home drunk and beat the hell out of their wives and kids? Is that the kind of person you think I am?"

Anna had known Lily would resist, especially if it meant having to talk with strangers about things that bothered her. Her style was to work through things on her own, but this clearly was too big for her. "Sweetheart, I'll help you look for the right kind of program, something for people like you."

"And just what kind of people are people like me, Anna?" She was shouting now. "God, am I some kind of monster?"

Anna had expected a battle, but not one so hostile. "Honey, you're a normal person who has gone through difficult times." She recalled the nurse's words. "You don't have to feel ashamed about it. People shouldn't be embarrassed about needing help."

"I can't believe you're doing this to me."

"Lily, please—" She heard a click, and then a dial tone. Staring at the now silent phone, Anna pressed her throbbing hand to her throbbing temple. She had never felt more helpless in all her life. After all the words they had exchanged, she sadly realized that she hadn't even told Lily she loved her.

And she still had no idea where Lily was, and if she was all right. Foregoing the intercom, she dialed the receptionist's extension. "Wanda? It's Anna. Do we have a record of incoming calls? I need to know where that last one came from."

Only twelve miles from her Brentwood home in Playa del Rey, Lily put the last touches on her makeup beneath the dim

145

light in the small bathroom. The Waterways Lodge wasn't fancy, but it had everything she needed to be on her own for a few days—long enough to let things chill at home.

Ten miserable days had passed since she last talked with Anna. In that time, Lily had formulated her plan. Two days from now, she would call again and announce that she had gone two weeks without a drink. That should be enough to convince Anna that she had a grip on the situation, and if Anna still wanted her to get help, she would agree to talk to a counselor. In fact, these days alone had hardened her resolve to do whatever it took to make things right again, and to make up for the trouble she had caused these last few months.

She walked out of her second-floor room and closed the door firmly behind her, already dreading her return at the end of the day. A flurry of new clients and filings at work had kept her distracted from the anguish that consumed her during her evening hours alone. Even her long nightly walks along the beach had offered little solace, though the wind and cool air seemed to clear her head somewhat. The walks had grown longer each night, as she dreaded the sleeplessness and solitude that caused her to dwell on her misery.

This weekend was the Labor Day holiday. She wondered if they still had reservations for the Maui flight on Friday night at seven. And if Anna would still be willing to go.

As with every morning since leaving home, she reached her office well before everyone else. Soon after she arrived, she heard someone else enter.

"Lily, can we talk?" Tony came into her office and took a seat across from her.

"It's seven thirty on a Monday morning. I couldn't have done something wrong already," she joked nervously. She hoped Tony hadn't found out about her troubles with Anna. The fewer people that knew about that, the better.

"Lily, I don't know how to tell you this, so I'm just going to say it straight out. I'm pulling you off the Esperanza case. I'd like

146

for you to gather up all your files and notes and bring them to my office."

Surely she had heard wrong. "Tony, I've been working that case for more than two years. Why are you pulling it now?"

"I got a call from Mrs. Esperanza on Friday night. She feels that you're resisting her wishes."

"Goddamn right I am! You know as well as I do that it's all going to start all over again, and it's the kids who are going to pay."

"We aren't social workers, Lily," he said. "We're lawyers, and we're supposed to serve our clients."

"Who's serving the kids, Tony? Tell me that." She was fuming. "Two years, Tony! Two goddamn years! Those kids have been pulled out of their home four different times, twice because of their crazy father, and twice because of their careless mother. Neither one of them deserves to have those children."

"You're not the judge here. It isn't for you to decide. If they want their children back, it's our job to deliver the best legal services we possibly can. Not to throw roadblocks in their way."

She glared at him angrily, and he glared right back. Until this very moment, she had never questioned her decision to become a lawyer. But if she couldn't help protect kids like Sofia and Roberto, what was the point?

Tony stood, and in a calmer voice, said, "Try to have the files in my office by the end of the day."

For the next hour and a half, Lily meticulously extracted each file, each note, each record—every single scrap of paper or electronic data byte that documented the Esperanza saga. When she had gotten it all together, she boxed it and dropped it wordlessly on the corner of Tony's desk.

She spent the next two hours stewing, occasionally looking at the case she and Tony would handle first thing tomorrow morning, that of Lon Phan, a Vietnamese immigrant seeking a stay of deportation for her ailing mother. Immigration law was complicated, but Lily felt certain they could make their case.

Satisfied there was no more she could do in her office, Lily called their client to schedule one last briefing for this afternoon. She needed to get out of the office for a while, and could only take her car if it was work-related.

Passing Pauline's desk on the way out, she tersely said, "Would you let Tony know that I've gone to do a final briefing with Lon Phan?"

From the corner of her eye, she saw Colleen emerge from Tony's office carrying the Esperanza box. Anger roiled inside her as she realized Tony was handing off her case to his wife. "That certainly explains a lot," she muttered, flinging open then banging the door on the way out.

"I don't think she's walking tonight, boy. Maybe she's watching the Dodgers, eh?" Anna scratched Chester behind his ears as he peered over the dashboard. Every night since learning where Lily was staying, Anna and Chester had driven by, parking a half block away in hopes of catching a glimpse. Six times in the past ten days they had spotted Lily on her late-night stroll from the beach. From this far away, it was impossible to see her face, but Anna could tell from the hanging head and slumped shoulders that Lily was sad.

It wasn't the seediest motel in LA, but Anna worried about her nonetheless. Most of the guests appeared to be sports fishermen, arriving in the evening from the marina shuttle. Lily probably kept to herself, and she was smart enough to walk along a well-traveled street coming back from the beach.

Anna had resisted calling her at the legal clinic, but she worried every day that passed that the distance between them would become insurmountable. She wanted Lily to know that she loved her very much, and that she was there to offer whatever she needed, no matter what had transpired. "I can't stand this, Chester. I'm going to call her tomorrow. You think that's a good idea?"

He thumped his tail against her leather seat.

"Yeah, that's what I thought." She pulled out of the parking space and drove slowly by the motel, where Lily's X3 was parked at the bottom of the staircase leading up to the second level. "Sweet dreams."

Chapter 12

"Get out of the fucking way!" Lily screamed at the crawling line of cars in front of her. She had fallen asleep without setting the alarm, waking up only fifteen minutes before she was due in court. Luckily, Tony was co-chairing, but she knew he would be pissed at her for being late.

She lost another twenty minutes looking for a parking space, but finally found a surface lot three blocks from the courthouse. "Sorry I'm late. How are we doing?" she whispered to Tony as she slipped into the seat beside him.

Tony ignored her and continued taking notes. The government's immigration attorney was wrapping up his arguments about why Lon Phan's mother should be deported immediately, so at least she wasn't late for her opening presentation.

Tony stood to address the bench. "Your Honor, I'd like to request a short recess."

Lily followed him out of the courtroom with their client

and they headed for one of the small attorney-client conference rooms. "Mrs. Phan, I need a word with Ms. Stewart in private. Will you excuse us? You can go get something to drink if you want. Five minutes."

As he closed the door, Lily braced herself for a stern reprimand. "Sorry I was late. Traffic was awful today, and then I couldn't find a place to park."

"Lily, have a seat. We need to talk." He held her chair as she slowly sat. "We were lucky today, because both of us had planned to be here. I don't have to tell you what could have happened if this had been your case alone."

Their firm probably would have been fined by the court. She might have been disciplined by the bar. The worst-case scenario was that their client's case could have been tossed out and Lon Phan's ailing mother deported.

"Yes, I know. I'm really sorry. It was just one of those days. I appreciate you carrying the ball. Did it go okay?" She was anxious for him to get on with his reprimand.

"And you smell like liquor," he added softly.

Lily leaned back in her chair and looked away. She hadn't realized that others could tell. "I . . . I admit that I had a couple of drinks last night. Losing the Esperanza case to Colleen was kind of hard to swallow."

"Lily, I know you've been through a lot. And I know the Esperanza kids mean a lot to you. What you have to understand is that the Braxton Street Law Clinic means a lot to me. I won't have it tainted by shoddy work . . . or by a drunken attorney."

She absorbed his harsh words without meeting his eye.

"As of right now, I'm putting you on indefinite suspension. Go home and get your act together. I can't take a chance of letting this continue."

Stunned, she sat frozen in her chair as he picked up his briefcase and disappeared into the hallway.

● ● ●

Anna returned the phone to its cradle and slumped in her chair. Lily was in court today, Pauline had said. From the receptionist's cheery voice, she guessed that Lily had probably not told her coworkers about their troubles. Anna hoped they would be back together before anyone found out. She hadn't said anything at all to her family, declining invitations over the past two weeks so she could avoid having to explain where Lily was. She had done the same when things had started to fall apart with Scott. The difference here was that she wanted to work through this with Lily, no matter how difficult it was.

Marco appeared suddenly in the doorway of the conference room and dropped a folder on the table. "Remember those six cars you asked me about? I asked the LAPD to track the VINs, and you'll never guess what I found."

She listened with growing fury for the next ten minutes as her sales manager took her through his findings. The vehicle identification numbers had shown up in the state's database as registered vehicles, confirming they had been imported and delivered. The original invoices had been deliberately purged from the company's database, but the VINs had shown up on the annual aggregate report from VW. Since the Sweeney books had no records of their sales, the vehicles should still be on the lot. Marco had discovered that all six vehicles were at one time registered to the same person, a Sherilyn Richardson, identified by the longtime receptionist as Gordon Sweeney's youngest daughter. Mrs. Richardson—and probably someone else from within the company—had simply stolen six cars over the last two years. Anna directed Marco to turn the information over to their attorney for follow-up. Either Gordon Sweeney compensated Premier VW for the six vehicles, or his daughter was going to jail.

Marco's discovery was a tipping point for Anna. For the first time since she had taken over the business, she took stock of all the headaches and problems the ambitious moves had cost her and those she loved. And for what? Her vanity? More money than she could ever spend in a lifetime? Nothing she could possibly have gained from adding more dealerships to the Premier brand could be enough to make up for losing Lily . . . or for Lily losing herself.

She picked up the phone and called her brother-in-law at his desk at the BMW dealership. "Hal? Something big just came up over here in VW Land. I need for you and Kim and Jonah to get on a plane Thursday night and fly to Maui."

"Anna, you're not making any sense . . . but that doesn't mean I'm going to argue with you."

"There's nothing to make sense of. Lily and I had reservations, but I can't go. I want you and Kim to go, and for both of you to relax on the beach for three days. I'll see you Tuesday afternoon." She hung up without waiting for an answer.

That night, she and Chester watched from their vantage point up the street as Lily walked toward the Waterways Lodge. If possible, she appeared even sadder than she ever had before.

Consumed with guilt from her realizations earlier that day, Anna made a move to exit the car and go to her. Then she saw the tall brown bag in Lily's hand and stopped. The counselor had told her it might take a few weeks for Lily to hit bottom, and only then would she realize there was no way to go but up. Lily wasn't ready to help herself yet, and bringing her home now was just asking for things to get worse.

Lily sat up in bed and banged her head three times against the wall in frustration. Her anonymous neighbor answered back with a pounding of his own.

"Sorry," she yelled.

She was more miserable than she had ever been in her life, saddened by what she had gone through and disgusted with herself for getting drunk again two nights ago. But things were different this morning. Something had struck her last night when the clerk handed her the tall bottle of tonic water in the brown bag and told her to drink one for him. She had come back to her room and emptied both bottles of vodka down the sink. Then she had donned her mother's heavy sweater and returned to the beach, where she sat watching the planes roar over the ocean until the wee hours of the morning.

As she had left her room, she glimpsed a car like Anna's as it rounded the corner and spun out of sight. There were only a handful of Z8s in LA, but Anna wouldn't have been in this neighborhood.

Lily burrowed deep into the bed and pulled the covers over her head. The "Do not disturb" sign would ward off the housekeeper, and she had nowhere to be—and no way to get there, she realized. Since she wasn't going to work anymore, she wasn't allowed to drive at all.

Her misery growing worse by the minute, she got up and dressed. The beach was too crowded for her tastes in the daytime, so she opted instead to kill the time until it thinned out by finally going through the box she had brought from her mother's house after the funeral. For reasons she couldn't explain, her birth mother, Karen Parker, had been on her mind a lot these last few days. Perhaps it was the solitude she felt, as though she wasn't connected to a living soul.

Her adoption file was moderately thick, since Eleanor had saved the court report in which Katharine Fortier had itemized the reasons the child should not be returned to her birth mother. Lily sat transfixed as she pored over the testimony and arguments. Growing up, she had talked with Eleanor from time to time about her fleeting memories of living with her mother. She vaguely recalled parties, with smoking and drinking, and even seeing naked people walking around. More vividly, she remembered the nasty taste and smell of beer on the breath of one of her mother's boyfriends who had kissed her on the mouth. To this day, she hated beer.

Reading the file today gave her a much fuller picture of the person her biological mother really was. She had always known the tale of how she had come to be declared a permanent ward of the state. There was the shoplifting arrest, then the time when Karen had left her by herself in the car for so long, and the final incident, in which her mother had hit a woman with a bottle and stolen her car. But Lily hadn't known the extent of her mother's encounters with law enforcement. There among the charges related to her neglect were several others for forgery and writing bad checks, and skipping out on restaurant and hotel charges. But the thing that shocked her most was the discovery of three arrests on public drunkenness.

I am like her.

Lily rummaged through her briefcase for her digital organizer, scanning the directory for Andrew Shively, the police sergeant from Kidz Kamp who had introduced her to kamikazes. She needed a favor from someone with access to a statewide database.

Anna spun in her chair to grab the phone. "Anna Kaklis."

"Have I told you lately that I love you?"

She smiled at her sister's voice. "I thought you might be rather fond of me today. Are you packed?"

"I am, and I've called a limo for the airport to come at four thirty. I was wondering if you've turned my husband loose yet."

"He left about twenty minutes ago. He should be home any minute."

"Good. I'm really sorry you and Lily couldn't go. Actually, that's a lie. I'm thrilled. Hal and I need a few days together."

"I hope you have a great time."

"We will, and we want you guys to come to dinner next weekend."

Anna hesitated. "I don't know yet if we can. Things are crazy." Since seeing Lily two nights ago, Anna had swung back and forth on a pendulum. The logical part of her said she was doing the right thing by waiting for Lily to take a step out of her abyss. But the emotional part of her wanted to drive down to the Waterways Lodge, help Lily gather her things and bring her back home where she belonged.

"You two have to make time for each other. And for us. Where would we be without you?"

"Let me talk with Lily." She wasn't above making up an excuse out of thin air. "She's been swamped lately. She might just want to relax at home."

"You two have turned into hermits. We've seen you once since her mom died. Is everything all right?"

Anna hated lying, but not as much as she would hate telling the truth. "We're fine, just busy. That's why you're going to Maui and we're not."

"I guess I shouldn't be looking that gift horse in the mouth."

"You guys have fun, and take lots of pictures of Jonah at the beach." She looked up to see Holly looming in her doorway. "I thought you were leaving early today."

"I am, but I wanted to ask a favor." Holly sauntered in and leaned on Anna's desk, a coy look on her face. "How about coming down to San Diego tomorrow night? I think it's going to be a special weekend."

Lily stared at the address Andrew Shively had given her. Karen Ann Parker, now Karen Parker Haney, had a current driver's license that showed her living in Oakland.

Given the path she was currently on, Lily needed to see what her mother had become, whether she had beaten alcohol, or it had beaten her. But only six weeks into her four-month suspension, she couldn't go alone. As important as this trip was, she wanted to ask Anna to go with her, but she didn't think she could withstand Anna telling her no.

"Sandy? Hi, it's Lily." It was the first time they had connected outside of work since the funeral. As they exchanged pleasantries, Lily learned that Suzanne had the weekend shift in the ER, and that made her request easier. "Sandy, I need to ask a favor. A big favor."

"What is it? You know I'll do anything I can."

"I need to go up to the Bay Area this weekend . . . but I can't drive because I got a DUI and my license is suspended."

"You got a DUI? How on earth did that happen?"

Lily explained the circumstances briefly, but had already decided she wasn't going to say anything else about her situation unless Sandy agreed to drive her to Oakland.

"I can go if you can wait until after work. I have a couple of home visits to do tomorrow afternoon."

"That would be great, Sandy. I love you for this . . . I mean I love you for lots of things, but this especially."

"I feel like I haven't seen you in months. It'll be nice to catch up. Shall I pick you up at your house?"

Lily drew in a deep breath. "That's one of the other things I wanted to tell you. I've moved out. I'm living in a motel for the time being. Anna and I . . . it just wasn't good at home."

"Oh, Lily." The shock was evident in her voice. "After all you've been through, how could Anna do this to you?"

Lily had expected that Sandy would take her side where she perceived a rift. "This isn't Anna's fault. She's been there for me. I just . . . it's all me, Sandy."

As Sandy offered her support and encouragement, Lily couldn't help but feel that she didn't deserve a friend like Sandy. She hadn't really given anything of herself to anyone in months.

"When we get back from the Bay Area, you're coming to stay with Suzanne and me. I can't believe you're living in a motel."

"I don't mind it here, Sandy. You know how I am about being by myself." She listened politely to Sandy's objections, but held her ground. She wouldn't be good company right now. "There's one other thing you should know. I've been suspended from work for missing a court date."

As she let the final shoe drop, Lily took stock of how much she had lost in the past few weeks—her mother, her job . . . Anna.

Finding her birth mother seemed like her only hope of putting some sort of stake in the ground. Or it could just be the last thing she had to lose.

"Are you sure she said San Diego and not Palm Springs?" Lily asked for the second time. It didn't make sense that Anna would go to San Diego on a Friday night.

"Positive," Sandy said, tucking her cell phone into the console of Lily's X3.

Lily had persuaded her to call Anna at Premier Motors, hoping for a chance to tell her she was okay and working on things, as Anna had asked her to do. Since realizing that finding her mother was part of that quest to sort out her problems, she had grown increasingly anxious to let Anna know she was making progress.

"Maybe it doesn't have anything to do with work," Sandy said.

Lily didn't want to think that Anna was out having fun while their whole life was upside down. In the first place, she had selfishly hoped all along that Anna was miserable too, or at least concerned enough that she wouldn't just carry on with her social life as if nothing was wrong. And in the second place—a far worse place in Lily's mind—what the hell was she doing in San Diego and with whom? The last time she had gone down there was with that creep, the ad manager who tried to get her to spend the night with him.

As they made their way north on Interstate 5, she shared with Sandy the awful details about how she had come to call the Waterways Lodge home, unemployed and all alone. "Do you think I'm an alcoholic?" she asked nervously.

From the glow of the dashboard lights, she could make out Sandy's furrowed brow. "Yes, sweetheart, I think you are." As if to soften her words, she placed her hand over Lily's and squeezed.

Lily immediately turned to look out the window, not able to

face such a pronouncement. "I don't ever have to worry about sugarcoating from you, do I?"

"Sorry. You know how I am about saying what I think. As long as I've known you, you've turned to alcohol when things bothered you. Remember after you left Beverly? You went through a bottle of wine every night in your room."

Lily remembered it as a humiliating time. She had stayed with Suzanne and Sandy while saving up for deposits on an apartment and the utilities. "Oh, that reminds me . . ." She went on to add the tale of running into Beverly Adams to her list of recent woes.

"God, you're like a little misery magnet." Sandy always had a way of lightening Lily's mood, either with her humor or with her heart of gold. Tonight, she was using both.

"Beverly was a long time ago, Sandy. I eventually stopped with the nightly wine bottle. I know I can control it."

"It wasn't just that, Lil. You started drinking again when things went south after the Tahoe thing."

Lily remembered how devastated she had been when she'd seen Anna kissing Hal's friend in the kitchen.

"And how many times have you gotten drunk since Anna started working so much? Or since your mother died?"

"I get your point," she said, more sharply than she had intended. Lily needed to digest these facts and answer the question for herself. "Sometimes I do it because I know it makes Anna mad. It's like there's no other way to get her attention."

"But you just told me you waited until you knew she was gone."

Lily sighed. "It's hard to explain. If I don't drink at all, I don't sit around wringing my hands about my next drink. But once I start . . ."

"You can't stop."

That was it, she realized. "That's the part I can't control anymore."

It was after eleven before they reached Hayward, where

159

they checked into a double room at the Hampton Inn. Lily could barely sleep, knowing they would set out first thing in the morning to find Karen Parker Haney. She had no idea what she would do when they did.

Sandy located and pressed the button for the X3's automatic door locks. Though their work often took them to the less desirable neighborhoods of LA County, something about this Oakland neighborhood had both of them spooked, even in broad daylight. Using the X3's GPS, they had found the apartment complex listed on Karen Parker Haney's license. When they scoped it out, they realized they wouldn't be able to get as close as they wanted, so they found a discount store where Lily bought binoculars. Now from the safety of their vehicle, they could clearly watch the comings and goings at Apartment F.

Andrew had run a vehicle check as well and determined that Charles Haney at the same address owned an early model Oldsmobile Cutlass, even providing Lily the tag number. No such vehicle was parked at the complex, but they settled in to watch and wait.

It was nearly five in the afternoon before the Cutlass appeared and a tall thin man of about sixty wearing jeans and an Oakland Raiders T-shirt exited and went into the apartment they were watching.

"I guess we've found the right place," Lily said. "I wonder if she still lives there."

They got their answer a few minutes later when the door opened again and a woman came out and headed to the car. From the way she was dressed—black stiletto heels, black stockings and a miniskirt with a white tuxedo shirt—she obviously worked as a cocktail waitress and was ready to start her evening shift. Lily knew at once that the woman was Karen Parker.

"Follow her, Sandy."

Sandy lagged behind a little, and soon they were circling a

motel at the Oakland Airport, driving on past the entrance so as not to be recognized. They circled through airport departures and returned to the motel's parking lot, parking near the entrance to a lounge.

"So what do you want to do now?" Sandy asked. "Looks like she lives in a dump with a skinny old Raiders fan, and she works here in the evenings slinging drinks."

They sat quietly in the car for several minutes, Lily unsure what more she wanted to know.

Sandy looped her purse strap over her shoulder. "You want me to go in and check it out?"

"You mean go into the bar?"

"Sure. We can drink a Coke or something. We didn't drive all the way up to here to sit in the parking lot."

Lily weighed the idea of actually talking to her birth mother, even if it was just to order a drink. "Do you think I should talk to her?"

"What would you say?"

"I have no idea."

"Then let's just go see her up close. If you get the urge to say something, you can."

They entered the dark lounge and looked around. Lily immediately spotted a table from where they could view the whole room. Karen was already on duty, serving two men in a corner booth. As she walked past them to the bar, she said, "Be with you ladies in just a minute."

"What are you thinking?"

Lily's heart was hammering. She could practically see herself in Karen's lined face. "Right then, I was wondering if she'll recognize me the way I recognized her."

"You recognized her because you expected to see her. I bet you're probably the last person on earth she ever expects to see again."

Karen finally came to their table. "Okay, what can I get you?"

"I'll have a Diet Coke please," Sandy said.

Lily couldn't help staring at the woman, even when they locked eyes as Karen waited for her order. Karen was only forty-seven years old, but she looked every bit of sixty. Her skin was weathered and practically hanging from her skeletal frame. Her bleached blond hair was well overdue for a touch-up, as her gray roots were prominent.

"Something for you?"

Lily couldn't speak at all.

"My friend will have a Diet Coke also."

Karen rolled her eyes, making no secret of her annoyance at having them take up her table. Clearly, she preferred heavy drinkers who would run up a large tab. She silently delivered their drinks, foregoing the bowl of popcorn that appeared on the other occupied tables.

"I don't think she likes us very much," Sandy said.

"No, she probably figures we're not going to leave much of a tip."

They watched as Karen hovered over a table of middle-aged men, one of whom rubbed his hand along the back of her thigh.

"Your mother has lived a rough life, Lily."

"She's not my mother." Lily felt bad immediately for her sharp retort. "I just can't think of her that way, you know?"

"I know. I'm sorry I said that."

"It's okay." She watched Karen flirt with each of the men at the table, smiling and making small talk as she replenished their drinks. "I remember her doing that before, Sandy . . . pushing herself at men. Everyone was always drinking and smoking. Probably doing drugs too. That's what my file says about her."

"How does it make you feel to see her again?"

Lily turned her thoughts inward in search of any hint of longing or sentimentality. But only one feeling was crystal clear. "Lucky."

They nursed their drinks for almost an hour as Karen continued to ignore them.

"Think there's any chance of us getting a refill?" Sandy

asked.

Lily snorted. "I doubt it. It's funny. I was sitting here thinking how familiar this is, being ignored by Karen Parker. I'm surprised she hasn't moved us to one of the other tables and asked the men to keep an eye on us."

"She did that to you?"

"All the time. I'm not sure which was worse—that or being locked in a closet while she went out." A shiver ran up her spine. "What do you think it means that I'm sitting here remembering all that?"

Sandy patted her hand just as Karen approached. Without a word, Karen laid their check facedown on the edge of the table and walked away.

"Lily, I know it's hard to be here, but I'm glad we came. There isn't one thing about that woman or her life that makes me think of you."

Lily doubted Sandy would still say that if she had seen her getting smashed three nights ago at the Waterways Lodge. "We're not that far removed, Sandy."

"But you have to remember that Eleanor Stewart was your real mother. She's the one who made you, and she's the one who gave you the opportunity to choose who you really want to be."

Sandy's words echoed loudly in her head. Lily had always maintained that Eleanor Stewart had saved her from a life like Karen Parker's. She couldn't allow herself to squander such a gift. "I'm ready to go." She pulled out a hundred dollar bill and gestured to Karen.

"You got anything smaller than that?" Karen practically snarled. "I just got on. I can't break that yet."

"Keep it," Lily said, looking past her to the door.

Anna left her car and started toward the motel office, trying hard not to panic about the fact that Lily's car was gone. If she had found a more permanent place to live, Anna could only hope

163

there was a forwarding address on file.

She had driven to the Waterways Lodge straight from her night in San Diego, where Holly had defied her family and married Jai Ganesh, her longtime boyfriend from India. As Anna listened to their vows of love, she decided it was time to ask Lily to come home. They could work through anything as long as they loved each other.

"Excuse me. Do you have a guest by the name of Lilian Stewart?"

"Yes, we do. Would you like me to ring her room?"

Anna was startled by the reply. "No, that's all right. Tell me, have you seen Ms. Stewart today?"

The young man shook his head.

"Thank you." Lily couldn't drive except to go to work, which wasn't likely on Saturday. She hoped Lily wouldn't have driven somewhere in defiance of the court order.

From Playa del Rey she drove to Sherman Oaks, where she was disappointed not to find the silver X3 in the driveway of Sandy and Suzanne's house. She continued on to Lily's office, again frustrated that Lily's car wasn't there.

Suddenly it occurred to her that Lily might have gone home on her own. Surging with fresh optimism, she drove home to Brentwood, where her spirit deflated again to find the garage empty. It assuaged her alarm that Lily hadn't checked out of the lodge, and obviously planned to return.

The moment she opened the side door, she was bowled over by Chester, who had managed on his own overnight. A quick check of the house confirmed that he had finally adapted to his doggie door, and for that bit of good news, Anna was grateful.

"Better get your nap, Chester. We're going out on patrol again tonight."

"I won't be long," Lily said, stepping out of the car at the cemetery.

"Take your time."

This was her first visit to the cemetery since her mother died, and she was anxious about how she would hold up. Her knees almost gave way when she saw the headstone, even though she had chosen it herself and planned its inscription.

Eleanor R. Stewart . . . Beloved mother . . . Loyal friend

"Hi, Mom. Told you I'd be back." It was almost surreal to see her mother's name on the granite slab.

"Anyway, I wanted to stop in and tell you how much I miss you. I don't think I ever really expected to lose you, but then all of a sudden you weren't there. The one thing I've always known is how important your promise to me was, that you'd always love me and always be there for me, no matter what. I could sure use some of that right now, because I'm not very lovable these days."

She was filled with shame for what she would say next. "I sort of lost control of myself, and started drinking too much. I've been suspended from my job, which by the way, I haven't been doing very well lately." In the last couple of days, she began to see herself in a different light, and she came to realize that Tony had been right about her lack of focus at work.

"But the worst part is that I really messed things up with Anna. I did something she may not be able to forgive, and I honestly don't know if we'll be able to work it out. She doesn't even want to see me right now." The hard lump nearly pierced her throat as she fathomed her loss of the two most precious people in her life.

"But that's not why I stopped by today. I sort of figured you already knew all that stuff. It makes me ashamed to think you're watching me screw up like this. I came to tell you that I don't want to be like that anymore. I want to get control of my life again, and since you've always been my anchor, I plan to call on you whenever I need help."

She stood and brushed the grass and dirt from her jeans. "Thanks for always being there, Mom. I love you and I really miss you."

Chapter 13

Anna almost cried with relief when she spotted Lily's car in Sandy and Suzanne's driveway on Sunday morning. After waiting for hours last night at the Waterways Lodge and driving all over town again today, it was almost enough just to know that Lily was safe and with friends who loved her.

But she had practiced over and over what she would say—that they would take this on together, as they had the earthquake. Nothing was stronger than both of them together.

Her hand shook as she rang the bell. Sandy answered and Anna knew instantly that she was angry. "I'm looking for Lily. I need to see her . . . please."

"What makes you think she wants to see you?"

"Sandy—"

"You've got a lot of nerve showing up here, Anna. How could you do that to Lily after all she's been through?"

Anna hadn't anticipated such an attack. "Sandy, I know you're

Lily's friend, but this is between Lily and me. I just need to talk to her."

"She isn't here."

"But her car—"

"I dropped her off." Sandy stepped into her house but left the door open in apparent invitation, albeit unwelcome. Anna followed her into the living room and slumped wearily onto the couch. "Is she okay?"

"No, she isn't. She knows she's been drinking too much, but she feels like you abandoned her instead of helping her stop."

She felt tears pooling in her eyes. "I knew this would happen."

"Anna, what were you thinking?"

"I tried to help her, Sandy, but it kept getting worse. No matter what I did . . ." She wondered if Sandy knew the whole story about how bad things had been. "But I talked to someone who said I had to step back and let her fall because I was enabling her."

Sandy looked at her with sudden interest. "Who told you that?"

"An alcohol counselor. He said she had to feel the consequences before she would ever start to help herself, and that she had to do it for herself, not for me."

"So this was all a plan?"

"Of course it was. Except now I don't think it was such a good idea. I've been worried the whole time that she might think I didn't love her anymore, but I do. So I went to talk to her and ask her to come back home, and her car was gone. I've been driving all over town all weekend looking for her."

Sandy stood up and started to pace. Anna couldn't imagine why she was suddenly smiling. "And you knew all along where she was staying?"

Anna nodded. "She called me a couple of days after she left and I traced it. I've been driving by there every night with Chester." And now that she knew where Lily was, she was determined to bring her home. "But it's time to end this."

"I'm not so sure of that, Anna. I think your plan worked."

"What do you mean?" She listened with astonishment as Sandy related their trip to Oakland and the brush with Karen Parker.

"I think she hit bottom, but now she's ready to climb back up," Sandy said.

"Maybe she'll let me help her now."

"I'm more worried that she'll change her mind. Give her a couple more days. If she does this on her own, she has a better chance of making it."

After feeling that Lily had slipped away from her over the weekend, Anna was reluctant to lose this chance to talk to her about coming home. But Sandy was right that this had been her plan all along—for Lily to realize she had a problem and do something about it. It was worth a few more days to see if it would work.

"Redwood Hills. Sounds like a retirement home," Lily groused.

"Or a ski resort," Sandy said, her voice bubbly and optimistic.

"Yeah, a ski resort for retired people."

Sandy helped her stow the last of her things in the small closet. The plain look of the Waterways Lodge was positively gaudy compared to her new digs. The tiny second-floor room to which she had been assigned had a small bathroom and closet on one side, built-in drawers and a writer's desk on the other. Opposite the door and beneath the window was a simple twin bed with a bedspread in institutional green.

"The only thing missing is a cross over the bed," Lily muttered. "I wonder if Sister Bernadette carved her initials on the wall."

"Lily, you've been living in a motel for a month eating out of vending machines. Surely this is an improvement."

"At least I didn't have to talk to anybody there." Since the moment she committed to the four-week program at Redwood Hills, she had second-guessed herself. Did she really need something this intensive?

Unfortunately, it was Redwood Hills or nothing, as Judge Anston had denied her request for extended driving privileges so she could attend a day treatment program. He liked this program and thought she would have a better chance of success by giving it her all.

"I should call Anna and let her know where I am."

Sandy sat down on the bed. "Maybe you should get this behind you first, Lily. Then you can start with a clean slate."

That had been her thinking when she first moved out—that she would go without a drink for a couple of weeks on her own as proof she could handle it on her own—but she had come up short. "What if I don't get through this?"

"You will."

"But I haven't talked to her in almost a month, Sandy. Shouldn't I at least tell her I'm doing what she told me to do?"

"I'm sure she knows you're working through things, Lily. I've seen you and Anna together enough to know she loves you, and it's probably driving her crazy not to know what's going on. But this isn't about her. You have to do this for yourself."

Lily was still obsessing over Anna's trip to San Diego. If that was a sign of how concerned Anna was over her well-being and their relationship, it might all be lost already. Sandy was probably right that her only hope for salvaging things with Anna was to start from scratch with a clean slate.

She walked over to the window and peered out. She had chosen Redwood Hills from a half dozen other programs because it was set in the foothills of the San Gabriel Mountains above Pasadena. On a clear day—if she should happen to be there on such a day—she would be able see the entire LA basin from the front lawn.

Since her admission was voluntary, she was technically free to leave the grounds for a hike on the hillside. But on the advice of

169

the intake counselor, she had agreed to limit her outings, as well as her visitors and telephone contacts. With every minute that passed, she felt more isolated. "Sandy, promise me that you'll come get me if I call you."

Sandy gave her a warm hug. "You're going to be fine here, Lily."

"Promise me," she insisted. She needed to know there was a safety net, even if she never used it.

"Okay, if that's what you really want. But you promise me that you'll try as hard as you can to finish this program, all twenty-eight days."

"Scout's honor," she answered, holding up two fingers in a pledge.

"I love you, Lil."

"I love you, too. I wouldn't stand a chance in this world without a friend like you."

"You're tougher than you think." One last hug and Sandy was gone.

And Lily was all alone. Again.

"I can't tell anyone. She made me promise," Sandy said over the phone.

Anna was in panic mode again now that Lily's car had gone missing, especially after learning she had checked out of the Waterways Lodge. "Sandy, why is she hiding from me? Why hasn't she called?" More each day, Anna worried the distance between her and Lily was growing too vast to overcome.

"She wanted to call you, Anna, but I told her to wait. The way you were talking last weekend, I was worried she might change her mind and come home. She needs to do this."

For the last month, Anna had made the most of her nightly visits to Playa del Rey, feeling as if she was watching over Lily. She could only hope that wherever Lily was now, she would be safe. "Will you tell her something for me?"

"She already knows you love her. And I know she loves you too. But what she's doing now is bigger than that. If she doesn't beat this, she'll never be the partner you need, or even the friend that I want."

Yes, Lily was getting the help she needed. But Anna hadn't considered until just now that they might not survive this as a couple. "Just please tell her I love her, Sandy."

"If she calls me, I will. But you need to be patient for Lily's sake."

Anna didn't have any choice. "Can you at least tell me if she's all right?"

"She's pretty sad. But I think she's going to be fine. In fact, I think you're both going to be fine."

That was the best news Anna had heard since the day Lily left.

If it weren't for her caffeine addiction, Lily would have skipped breakfast. She wasn't yet ready to meet her fellow patients, the other "inmates" as she thought of them. She'd had no idea how difficult this first step would be.

The information packet in her room contained her daily schedule for the first week. Nearly all her time was structured, either in some sort of therapy or meeting. Added together, it totaled twelve hours a day she was expected to spend with others. Facing a program like that, Lily wasn't sure she would make it through Sunday, let alone twenty-seven more days.

Hearing voices in the hallway, she peered out and was relieved to find others dressed casually. Comfortable that she wouldn't stand out in her jeans and T-shirt, she headed out for coffee.

The dining hall was the largest room at Redwood Hills. According to her schedule, it doubled as the site of the general meetings. Four long tables, each seating eight diners on each side, were lined up perpendicular to the buffet line on one side and an elevated speaker's platform on the other.

The first person who spoke to her was a fortyish man, tall and barrel-chested, sporting a thinly sculpted beard with no mustache. "Good morning," he said, placing an arm around her shoulder with undue familiarity. "Welcome to Redwood Hills. My name's Randy. And you are . . . ?"

Lily lifted the large hand from her shoulder, letting it drop behind her where it brushed against her rear. "Good morning, Randy. My name is Lily, and I'm not really a morning person."

Spotting the industrial-sized percolator on a table at the side, Lily navigated her way around the groups of chatting "inmates" to grab a cup from the stack. As the line formed for bacon, eggs and hotcakes, she ducked out of the crowd to avoid having to interact. From her seat at the table farthest from the door, she could see the entire room. Gradually, all of the tables began to fill with diners, and soon she was joined by a beautiful woman of about fifty, her long black hair showing the first tinges of gray. As the woman briefly flashed startling blue eyes in her direction, Lily couldn't help but think of Anna, who she knew would be every bit as lovely as she aged.

"Hi, my name's Virginia. You have that 'what-the-hell-am-I-doing-here?' look that says it's your first day."

Despite her anxiety about the growing crowd, Lily was eased by the woman's smile and disarming nature. "Yeah, it's my first day. I'm Lily. Nice to meet you." She held out her hand shyly and Virginia took it.

"Lily. My grandmother's name was Lily. I even considered naming my oldest child after her, but I doubt he'd have liked that much as he got older."

Lily smiled, thinking she didn't mind conversation so much when it had nothing to do with why they all were here.

"We should hit the line and grab some breakfast, Lily. It's a long time before lunch, and there's no guarantee it'll be something you like."

She really was hungry, especially since she had stayed in her room through dinner the night before. She and Virginia filled their plates and returned to their table. "How long have you been here?"

"I finished the program three and a half years ago. Now I fill in here as a weekend counselor, and I even pull chaplain duty if they need it."

Lily was caught by surprise, but not upset. "That was pretty sneaky."

"Sorry. I always slip in on Sunday morning to help the new people feel at home. I bet you weren't even going to eat until I led the way."

"Probably not." She looked around, noting that almost all the tables were full, and people were chattering away. "So am I the only new person today?"

"Yes and no," Virginia answered with a sly grin. "There are a couple of other folks starting the program today, but they've been here before."

Lily didn't like the sound of that. "The program didn't work the first time?"

"The program always works, Lily. But the people have to work too."

"That sounds like those miracle diet pills . . . the ones that are guaranteed to work, as long as you limit your food intake to carrot sticks, and you exercise for six hours a day."

Virginia laughed. "In some ways, that's exactly what it's like. But trust me, it works."

At eight sharp, two men and a woman moved to take chairs on the platform. The youngest, a man about twenty-five years old, took the podium and announced, "Good morning. My name is Tyler, and I'm an alcoholic."

"Good morning, Tyler," the crowd responded in unison.

"God, what a day!"

Lily collapsed on her small bed. She had counted fifty-one others at each of the general meetings, concluding that "general" was a euphemism for "mandatory." Between those two meetings, there was a step meeting that focused on the first of the infamous twelve steps, admitting powerlessness over alcohol and imploring a higher power for help. Lily wasn't yet ready to admit to being powerless, or that she needed a higher power. But she couldn't deny that her life had become unmanageable.

Then there was the group therapy session, followed by lunch and more meetings. In all, she had heard nineteen testimonials, some more than once. For the most part, Lily didn't think her own story was as dismal as those told by the others. Alcohol abuse had been a way of life for them, causing them to lose their families, their jobs . . . *shit*. But none of them had told about losing their mother, or of walking through life feeling like you didn't belong to anybody.

She had shared a lot about her mom in the individual therapy session with Virginia, but she didn't feel much like talking about Anna. In fact, when the counselor had asked her if there was someone she would like to invite next weekend to take part in family therapy, she had declined, saying she had no family.

Tyler, the young man who started off the morning meeting, was her peer counselor for the week. He was starting his third week in the program. In her second week, Lily would be paired with someone in their final week of treatment. By the third week, she would be assigned to a newcomer, a notion that had her anxious already. It was impossible to imagine trying to lead someone else through this program.

Tyler had spent their hour together talking about the program, about the things he had learned and how he had come to accept who he was and what he must do to turn his life around.

At the evening meeting, all of the newcomers were asked to stand. An older guy Lily remembered as William walked around the room handing out white poker chips. The chip, she learned, was to commemorate her first day of sobriety. Counting back to the night before she was suspended from her job, Lily noted that today was in fact her eleventh day without a drink.

174

• • •

"Any chance you could make some time to have lunch with your old man?"

Anna was startled to see her father standing in the doorway of the conference room at the VW dealership. "I suppose I could arrange that."

"Good. You've been pretty hard to pin down lately."

Not wanting to have to explain Lily's absence, Anna had turned down their invitations to dinner over the last three weeks, citing her overwhelming workload. She couldn't deny that she missed seeing her family, and was glad for the chance to talk with her father again. "So how's the golf game?"

"It's getting there, I think. But I'm still kind of rusty, you know. Can't seem to remember all the swear words."

"You should hang out in our VW service area sometime. It's quite a refresher."

"I'm sure it is." He escorted her out and into his car. "Empyre's?"

"Sure." It would be nice to get away from her desk for a while. With Lily out of reach, she had been spending too much time at work.

"This retirement gig . . . it's good for the golf game. But I think Martine's getting tired of me already. She says I need more hobbies."

Anna laughed. "I bet Kim would sell you Hal's boat."

"No kidding." They reached the restaurant and were seated at a quiet table for two. "I have an idea for a new hobby." He gave her a boyish grin.

"What are you up to?"

"How about letting me take the reins at the VW dealership?"

Anna stared for a moment with her mouth agape. "You've got to be kidding! You gave all that up because you wanted to spend more time with Martine and Jonah. How are you going to do that?"

"I've learned my lesson, and you need to learn it too. Put in an honest day's work, and then go home. Premier generates enough revenue to pay two or three more managers. Let them work weekends and give yourself a couple of days off."

Anna hated to tell him she was already doing that. "But why VWs? You've been selling BMWs for thirty years."

"I'm bored."

She looked at him in disbelief. "Mom's going to kill me."

"Don't bet on it. I don't think she had any idea how much trouble I can be when I don't have anything to do."

It would be great to get back to her own office. And her father was right about the effect of more managers. At least the BMW dealership was running smoothly. "All right, Dad. When can you start?"

He opened his menu. "Let's eat first."

"I can't believe this. After all these years, you work for me now."

"Except I won't deal with the IRS anymore. Or the Chamber of Commerce."

"Fine." Hal handled their taxes now, and she had finished her term as Chamber treasurer last year.

"Oh, and we're having your birthday party next Sunday . . . two o'clock by the pool. Steak and cake, your mom says."

Her stomach sank as she realized the implications. "I don't know, Dad. After thirty, these birthdays just aren't such a big deal anymore. Why don't we wait a while until things settle down a bit more?"

"Nonsense. You have to be the one to settle down."

"I know. It's just . . ." She was prepared to lie again, to say that Lily was swamped, or that she had to leave town for a conference.

"We were going to make it a surprise party, but we haven't been able to reach Lily. Your mom left about five messages on her cell phone, and even called her a couple of times at work."

Anna sighed and leaned back in her chair, feeling guilty about her silence. "Dad, there's something you should know. Lily and I are having some problems right now. She's staying somewhere else until we can get things worked out."

Her father's smile gave way to a pained expression. "Anna, why didn't you say something? I . . . I hate this for you . . . for both of you. Is there anything I can do to help?"

"You coming back to work is going to help a lot. But Lily and I still have things to work through. She's had a really hard time with losing her mom, and I haven't helped her as much as I should have."

"I don't know what to say, sweetheart. All of us are Lily's family now, not just you. We love her, and we're there for her."

Anna could feel the tears welling up in her eyes. "Dad, that means so much to me. And it will mean so much to her too. I think a family is just what she needs."

After four days of casual conversation, Lily had begun to talk to Tyler about the series of incidents that had brought her to Redwood Hills. Despite her cynicism, she found herself listening to the testimonials of her fellow residents, noting with chagrin the similarities between their stories and her own.

The step meetings were the most agonizing, especially all the God parts. It wasn't that she didn't believe in a higher spiritual power. It was more that she didn't trust that power to intervene in her life. The way she saw it, her problems were her own, and it was unrealistic to think some spiritual being might just take them away. Lying in her bed on Friday night, Lily recalled the talk from her mother's gravesite two weeks ago. Hadn't she called on her mother for help? Wasn't it irrational to believe that her mom could help her when a higher power could not?

On her seventh day at Redwood Hills, Lily stood at the morning general meeting, speaking to the group for the first time.

"Good morning. My name is Lily, and I'm an alcoholic."

Chapter 14

Lily tipped her chair back a bit so she could get a better look at the man sitting across from her at the table. Daryl was wiry and somewhat sloppy in appearance, in his mid-fifties, she guessed. She couldn't help but think of Charles Haney, the man her biological mother had married. "I think everybody feels that way at first, like you really don't belong here. But after a week or two—"

"Oh, don't get me wrong. I belong here and I know it. I'm just saying it won't make any difference. I'm going to do the same thing I did last time—sit through all these meetings until my time's up. Then they'll fill out the paperwork for the judge so that I won't have to go to jail. And the second I walk out that door, I'll go home and find out that it's still the same fucked up place it was when I left. Then I'll stretch out on the couch with a cold beer."

Lily had been warned by Virginia that her week as peer

counselor to someone like Daryl could prove challenging. "Was it drunk driving?"

He nodded shamelessly. "Third time's a charm."

"Once was enough for me. I'll never forget that sick feeling in my stomach when all those lights started flashing in my rearview mirror. I sobered up in about a second."

"I wasn't even driving when the cops got there. I was wrapped around a light pole. I would have run off, but I couldn't get the door open because it was bent so bad."

It was hard to understand how a person could screw up like Daryl and not feel even a trace of remorse or a desire to turn his life around. "You ever try working the steps?"

He shrugged. "I admit I'm powerless over alcohol. But I like to drink. That's what makes me powerless over alcohol."

"And the other part of that step is to admit that your life has become unmanageable. Has it?"

"My ex-wife probably thinks so." He folded his hands and leaned across the table, his look smug and almost playful. "What about you? Is your life unmanageable?"

Lily had uttered the words of the first step several times during the two weeks she had been at Redwood Hills. In her testimonials, which she had shared with her group and at the general session, she had itemized all the ways her life had come apart—from losing her driver's license to losing her job, and even to losing the one she loved. What she hadn't really talked about was how these things had rendered her life unmanageable.

Her mind was repeatedly flooded with thoughts of that awful night when Anna had angrily confronted her. Had she not been drinking, it never would have happened at all. And had she not been drunk, she would not have become defensive and combative. That's why Anna had gotten hurt, because she was drunk and unable to think clearly, unable to manage. How many times since then had she envisioned that bursting gash coming from Anna's head instead of her hand? Or what if the glass had severed her thumb? Lily knew she would never accept forgiveness for something so awful.

"For me, Daryl, it comes down to hurting people." Her voice cracked with the admission. "That's the part I can't manage, because I can't just turn it off and stop caring about the people I love. And if I really care about them, the last thing I want is to see them hurt."

He sat quietly for a moment, his face now serious as if respectful of her obvious pain. "Sometimes we can't help things like that."

"But working the steps is what I have to do to get myself back in charge. If something bad happens, I don't want it to be because I made a selfish decision to drink."

"That's just the thing right there." He held up a finger. "Let's say you get out of here all cured. I know they don't call it cured, because alcohol's a demon that stays with you, whether you drink it or not. But suppose you leave thinking you don't need to drink anymore."

Lily nodded. That's what she hoped for, the conviction that she could be sober.

"Your life isn't going to be perfect all of a sudden like somebody's waved a magic wand. You won't be in charge then any more than you were before you walked in that door. The only difference is that you won't have a crutch anymore."

"I don't want a crutch, Daryl. I want to be able to walk on my own, and I can't do that if I'm drunk."

"I understand that. All I'm saying is don't expect your life to be better just because you don't drink. Everything that used to bother you is still going to be there. All the people that pissed you off will still piss you off. You still won't have enough money, or enough love or enough whatever it is you didn't have before."

She drew in a deep breath, silently acknowledging the truth of his words. The bigger truth was that stopping drinking was no guarantee that Anna would have her back. And even if she did, it would have to be on her terms. The proof of that was in the conditions Anna had already laid down. Lily would likely go home to the same insecurities she felt before, and it was only a matter of time before—

"Just wait till you try to go making amends. That's when the real fun starts."

Lily looked at the clock, feeling that was enough cynicism for one day. It pained her to realize she had a whole week of Daryl ahead.

Anna pulled into the center lane, breathing a sigh of relief that the traffic back into LA was moving at a steady clip. The drive down to Orange County during rush hour had been nothing short of excruciating, but ultimately worth it.

The online community bulletin board had listed more than a hundred Al Anon meetings in the LA area. Anna had chosen Artesia for one simple reason—she knew no one who lived there. Just because the nurse at the hospital had said alcoholism was nothing to be ashamed of, that didn't mean she wanted everyone to know about Lily. The organization's very name underscored this anonymity.

Lily might not be too happy that she had ventured out to hear how others dealt with loved ones, but Al Anon wasn't for alcoholics. It was for the relatives and friends of those with alcohol problems. Her first surprise at the meeting had been the ritual reading of the Twelve Steps. Until tonight, it hadn't occurred to her to admit that she too was powerless over alcohol, and that her life had become unmanageable. That had nothing to do with her own drinking behavior, and everything to do with how Lily's drinking had impacted her life.

She had discovered Al Anon quite accidentally after concluding from Sandy's hints that Lily had most likely entered a residential treatment program. That explained why she was gone from the Waterways Lodge and why her car was parked at Sandy and Suzanne's. A Web search for area facilities yielded a list of dozens. Not that she was trying to track her down. She was more interested in learning about what she was going through, what her days might be like and when she might be finished. That's when she had stumbled on mentions of Al Anon and discovered that others met and talked about their roles in the lives of alcoholics. She vaguely recalled the counselor at the hospital saying she was an "enabler" and she needed to understand what that meant.

Despite the realization of kinship with those at the meeting, she had not spoken up this evening. Instead, she listened as, one by one, people rose to share their stories. They were women and men, young and old, professionally dressed and casual. Yet, there was no attention to their differences, only their commonality of purpose—because someone who had a problem with alcohol had impacted their life.

Following their testimonials, there was a brief discussion about how the members regarded their own drinking behavior. From what Anna had gathered, the consensus was to abstain, though the reasons varied. One of the younger members feared he would become like his father, drunk and abusive to his children. A middle-aged woman in a waitress uniform thought it best to remove the temptation from their home, and to avoid reminders to her husband that others could drink freely.

The one who had moved Anna most was Arlene, a woman of about forty dressed in business attire not unlike her own. She described her husband's struggles in work and social settings, the times he felt the most external pressure to drink. At first, she had reasoned that since others around them were already drinking, it didn't matter if she enjoyed a glass of wine here and there too. Then one night at a party, she watched him wrestle with the urge and realized how out of place he must have felt. From that day on, she abstained, and it gave her both empathy for his efforts, and pride in his perseverance.

The best thing about the meeting tonight was that it had given Anna a sense of anticipation, an eagerness to show Lily that she was ready to help her face these challenges. When she opened the garage, she felt a wave of hope that soon Lily's car would be home.

The first order of business—as always—was Chester. He was overjoyed to see her, and followed her from room to room. After changing into jeans, she took him for a quick walk and returned to scrape together something to eat. She was off her peanut butter sandwich kick for now, and dined instead on French bread, Gouda cheese and pepperoni, and fruit salad. Sitting down while eating . . . such a novel idea, she thought.

When she finished, she retrieved the recycling bin from the garage. Then she rounded up and methodically emptied all of the wine and liquor bottles she could find and tossed them in the bin. To that, she added her entire set of leaded crystal wineglasses, the ones she had gotten as a wedding gift, along with brandy snifters and beer mugs.

With a final burst of energy, she dragged the wooden wine rack from the pantry to the garage, where she broke it apart with a hammer and stuffed it in the garbage can. By midday tomorrow, the trash collectors would take away every remnant of alcohol from their home.

Lily sipped her coffee from the worn ceramic mug, her final cup at Redwood Hills. She had passed on lunch, hoping Sandy and Suzanne would run her by the drive-through window at the In-N-Out Burger in Glendale. Her stomach rumbled, both from hunger and nervousness, as the others finished eating.

A man named Mickey was chairing the general meeting today, and he kicked it off with the familiar reading of the Twelve Steps.

"Today is Lily's last day with us, and she's asked to speak."

She rose shakily and approached the podium. "I'm Lily, and I'm powerless over alcohol."

"Hi, Lily," they murmured. Some were already smiling at her accomplishment, no doubt imagining their own farewell speeches.

She cleared her throat and took a deep breath, hoping her first sentence wouldn't cause her to cry. "I lost my mom back in June . . . at least I thought I did. When I came to Redwood Hills twenty-eight days ago, I missed her so badly, I thought I'd never stop hurting inside. After the first week or so, I have to admit I was getting pretty discouraged. I listened to your stories, and I kept thinking I could never do this on my own the way so many of you seemed to be doing. You were moving ahead . . . and I wasn't."

She made eye contact with a handful of people who had arrived within a few days of her start of the program. They had been through a lot together.

"People talked about calling on their higher power, and I started to get worried, because that sort of thing just didn't work for me. I've never been much of a religious person, but I do believe there's a spirit inside all of us that guides us to do the right thing if we just let it.

"I woke up early one morning, ready to just give up and walk out the front door. Then I heard my mother's voice inside my head. She was telling me I could do this, and encouraging me just like she always did. That's when I realized she was going to be my higher power."

Blinking back tears, she looked again at the faces of those she had come to care for over the last four weeks.

"As I leave here, I know I'm going back to a world of problems that won't change just because I've stopped drinking." She smiled at Daryl, who gave her a knowing wink. "What's changed is me, and that's happened because of the strength I've drawn from all of you, and from my mother. I can't promise I won't stumble down the road. I know it happens. But today, I feel victorious, because I've armed myself with the conviction that I can recover."

"Amen," several said, as heads bobbed around the room.

She stepped down from the podium and into the arms of Virginia, who had promised to serve as her sponsor.

"You have my number. You can call me anytime, day or

night."

"Thanks. I was lucky to find you."

Following her good-byes, she returned to her room for her things. Through the window, she could see Sandy and Suzanne waiting in the parking lot. Joy and fear fought for dominance as she pushed open the glass door and walked into the bright sunlight. Joy was winning.

Chapter 15

"You're not going to believe this, but I feel like the last three weeks just flew by," Lily said. "The first one was a little dicey, though."

Sandy laughed. "I can imagine. Every time my phone rang, I figured it was you calling me to come get you."

Suzanne joined them at the table. "You should have seen her. She never wanted to answer the phone."

"I probably would have called if you hadn't taken my cell phone. But once I got into the program, I never even considered not finishing."

"So are you done?" Suzanne asked.

"Alcoholics aren't ever really done. We just stop drinking one day at a time."

"Like the bumper sticker."

"Yeah. And one of the recommendations when you first start is to do ninety meetings in ninety days. So I have sixty-two more

AA meetings before I'll be able to set my own schedule."

"Where will your meetings be?" Sandy asked.

"My sponsor looked it up. There's a Methodist church about three miles from Playa del Rey that has one every morning at seven."

"Playa del Rey? I don't think so," Sandy said. "You can plan on staying here now."

"No offense, guys, but I haven't had a moment alone in a month. I need my space." She also needed a more permanent place to live, but for now, she liked the idea of being back at the familiar lodge near the beach.

"Fine, but I'm coming to get you for dinner at least twice a week. You don't need to be eating that crap out of the vending machines."

Suzanne added, "And you can take my mountain bike. I don't use it that much anyway."

"Boy, is that an understatement," Sandy said, rolling her eyes. "She rode it twice."

Lily laughed at Suzanne's injured look. "I really appreciate everything you guys have done for me. In fact, starting today, I promise to be a better friend to you both. I've been on the receiving end of things too long."

"You don't owe us anything, Lil. That's what we're here for," Suzanne said.

"Just humor me, Suzanne. It's part of my program. I'm supposed to make amends to those I've harmed, and you guys are on my list."

Sandy put her hand on Lily's arm. "You haven't harmed us, Lily. But it's good news if it means we're going to be seeing more of you."

"And I have to fix things with Tony, of course, and by extension everybody else in the office who cleaned up after me. I plan to call him on Monday to see if I can come back to work. But it's possible he'll say no. I really screwed up there."

"You're good at what you do," Sandy said. "There's no way

Tony won't take you back."

"Let's hope you're right." Lily had no idea what she would do if she couldn't go back to work at the clinic.

"So when will you call Anna?"

She had spent much of the last week thinking about Anna. "Eventually, but not right away. I'm just not sure I'm ready to talk to her. I have to apologize for all the trouble I caused, but I don't even know what I'm going to say."

"She loves you, you know," Sandy said.

"Yeah, I know. And I love her." Lily was still grappling with doubts about how they had parted, and how Anna had just gone on with her life as though nothing had happened. As if that wasn't enough, she had Daryl's reminders that the rest of the world would be just as she left it. If anything, Anna was further than ever from making the commitment Lily knew she needed.

"Just put all this behind you, Lily. Sometimes that's all anyone can do."

Lily nodded to show she understood, though she didn't share Sandy's optimism that love would be enough. She needed an anchor in her life, someone who would be there for her no matter what . . . someone who wouldn't bug out when things got tough. If it couldn't be Anna . . .

No, she wasn't ready for that conversation yet.

Anna smiled to herself as she walked out of her father's new office at the VW dealership. The staff had welcomed him eagerly, probably because it meant Anna would quit firing people and go back to the BMW lot. But she knew they appreciated that in only six weeks, her advertising campaign on the radio and in the LA Times had generated a thirty percent increase in traffic on all of the Premier Motors lots, and a corresponding increase in sales. In particular, used car sales had soared at the VW dealership, since the BMW dealership now had a lucrative outlet for its more downscale trade-ins.

From the corner of her eye, she noticed a man getting out of his sports car.

"Say, I hear the Passat wagon is a pretty nice ride for a family car," he shouted.

She immediately grinned at the familiar voice. "Scott!" She jogged across the lot and gave her ex-husband a warm hug. "What are you doing here?"

"Sara told me I needed a car that would hold another car seat." He couldn't hide his proud grin.

"Two car seats?" Anna asked excitedly. She was genuinely happy at his news. Despite his one-night stand with his ex-girlfriend, their divorce had never been malicious or vindictive. "I think that calls for a special deal."

"Yeah, I read in the paper that Premier had bought this one, so I had a feeling I might do better here than over at the Toyota lot."

Her arm hooked through his, she walked him into the showroom to show off her line of family cars. "How's your son, Scott?"

"I think he's perfect, but then I'm a little biased." He reached immediately for his wallet so he could show her the photos of little Matt, now three years old. "Our next one's a girl."

As he talked, her cell phone rang, but she muted it, making a mental note to check her voicemail later. "He looks just like you . . . same smile."

"Yeah, handsome devil, isn't he?" He put his wallet away. "And what about you, Anna? Any new sweetheart besides the four-wheeled variety?" He used to joke that she loved her cars far more than she could ever love a husband.

She chuckled, thinking there was probably a lot of truth to his gentle jibe. "It so happens there is someone." She reached into her own wallet and extracted the only photo she carried of Lily, a cropped version of the one taken at Yosemite Falls. Nervously, she waited for Scott's reply.

His surprise evident, he took a deep breath and blew it out

loudly. "Wow. I wasn't prepared for that, Anna."

"Yeah, it kind of took me by surprise too," she said, smiling softly. "Her name is Lily Stewart. I'm sure you remember her. She's the woman I was trapped with after the earthquake."

His face showed nothing but confusion.

"We got to be good friends, and things just evolved. I really didn't expect it."

Scott shook his head, still in disbelief. "I'm happy you've found someone that makes you feel that way . . ."

"But?" She almost laughed at his obvious discomfort. "You're wondering if my being with a woman had anything to do with you and me not working out."

"Am I that easy to read?"

"Yes." She chucked his shoulder playfully. "The answer is that I really don't know. It was over a year before we got involved with each other, so it didn't affect us that way."

"Yeah, I was the one who had the bad timing."

"This is true. But I'd like to think we're both happy now, and that our marriage to each other didn't ruin either one of us."

"Well, I am happy, and I hope you are too."

She would be—as soon as Lily came home. "I bet you'd enjoy talking to our general manager here. I know he'd get a kick out of seeing you again." She led Scott upstairs to her father's office and excused herself.

As she got into her car, she remembered to check her phone.

"Hi, Anna. Sandy Henke here. Thought you might be interested in knowing that there should be a familiar car back at the Waterways Lodge tonight."

Tony closed his office door and turned to face Lily as she stood nervously before his desk. Their deep feelings of friendship won the moment, and they embraced without a word. Lily was first to find her voice.

"You said I could come back when I'd gotten my act

together."

"How are you, Lily?"

She was touched that Tony was more concerned about her well-being than with the problems she had caused. "I'm doing a lot better. I completed a treatment program for alcoholics. It was appropriately excruciating," she added sheepishly. "But I survived it, and I'm hoping you'll give me another chance."

"You'll never run out of chances here. We've missed you."

Her eyes misted. "I've missed you guys too. And I promise I'll never give you another reason to worry about my work. I'm so sorry for putting this firm at risk. I hope you know how much this place means to me."

"I always knew. And I hope you'll forgive me for suspending you. I know you were going through a lot, but I didn't know what else to do."

"I didn't leave you a choice, Tony. And believe it or not, it helped me realize how unmanageable things had become."

He sat on the corner of his desk. "Would you be okay with coming back part-time for a month or so? Colleen picked up your caseload, and I'd like to see her follow the active ones through. You can have everything new that comes in, and maybe even work on writing a grant or two."

Lily nodded her agreement. "I'll do anything—answer phones, mop the floors—whatever you say."

He lowered his voice. "Between you and me, I'm really looking forward to that call from the public defender's office. I love Colleen, but working together is making us both crazy."

She chuckled. "At least you won't be meeting her in court."

"Lucky for us. Oh, by the way, you were right about the Esperanzas. About two weeks after they got their kids back, Miguel was arrested on a domestic violence charge. Roberto and Sofia are back in foster care."

Lily sighed. She hadn't wanted to be right.

• • •

191

Anna was elated to see Lily's silver X3 back at the Waterways Lodge. She had left Chester at home tonight, hoping she might finally talk to Lily face-to-face. They still had a lot to sort out, but the bottom line was that she wanted Lily to come home.

She climbed out of her car and walked nervously inside to the front desk, where she found the clerk watching baseball on a portable television. "I'm here to see Lilian Stewart please."

He dialed the room but got no response. "She walks on the beach a lot. I bet that's where she is."

Anna grabbed her jacket from the car and headed toward the beach, looking carefully down side streets so she wouldn't miss Lily if she was on her way back. Her heart pounded with anticipation as her head skipped ahead to the joy of talking to her again. This awful separation would be over soon.

She scanned the small crowd of beachgoers, but didn't see Lily. With the sunlight quickly fading, she thought it best to wait at the entrance to the beach, thinking Lily would most likely take this path back to the hotel. After almost a half hour, she made out a familiar figure in the distance.

Anna began walking toward her, her excitement giving way to anxiety when Lily spotted her and stopped in her tracks. Even in the waning light, she looked apprehensive. Only when they were within a few feet of each other did Lily drop her guard, and Anna closed quickly to draw her into a strong embrace.

"Lily."

"I'm so sorry you got hurt because of me."

Anna had forgotten all about her injured hand. "I've missed you so much," she murmured above the roar of the surf, her hand tucking Lily's head against her shoulder.

"I've missed you too." But Lily abruptly broke away and stepped back. "How's Chester?"

"He's good. He misses you too." Tears of joy filled Anna's eyes and she pushed them away. "We want you to come home."

Lily shook her head. "I don't think I can."

Anna hadn't expected a miraculous return to bliss after all that had happened, but she was confident they could repair the chasm between them. "I was wrong about everything, sweetheart, and I'll do whatever it takes. No more working weekends. We'll get away together, anything you want."

Lily looked away, her jaw quivering as if she were biting her tongue. "There's a lot you don't know, Anna." She turned back toward the airport and began to walk, pushing her hands into her pockets as if to withdraw from physical contact.

Anna fell into step beside her. "I know that I love you."

"And I love you," Lily said flatly. "But I don't feel like I can trust you anymore."

The words hit her like a slap. "Of course you can."

Lily stopped and spun toward her, her eyes tinged with anger. "What can I trust? I know what I did was wrong, and I'm sorry. But you practically kicked me out of the house. How do I know you won't do that the next time I do something you don't like?"

"I didn't kick you out. I came home and you were gone."

"I left because I figured you couldn't stand the sight of me. But when I tried to come back, you said no."

"I never said you couldn't come home. All I said was—"

"I remember it, Anna. You laid down your list of conditions. I could come home as long as I was willing to jump through your hoops. In case you forgot, my mother died. And instead of helping me cope with that, you pushed me out the door and told me to deal with it."

"That's not what happened. I had only one condition—that you get help for your drinking problem. And I told you I'd do whatever I could to help." She was careful this time not to use the word "support," since Lily had taken that to mean financial support.

"That may be how you see it, Anna, but it didn't feel that way to me," she said sharply. "Put yourself in my shoes. I lost my license, my home . . . my job. And you—"

"Your job too?" No wonder Sandy had said Lily hit bottom.

"Everything. And the one person who should have stayed with

me through it all told me instead to help myself." She brushed past Anna and began stalking back toward the lodge.

Anna grabbed her elbow. "I tried, but nothing I did made a difference. The counselor told me I had to step back and let you feel the consequences for yourself."

"You talked to a counselor about me?" It was more of an accusation than a question.

"It was at the hospital, when I—" She stopped herself, knowing that a reference to that night would only make things worse. "I didn't know what else to do. He said I had to stop protecting you."

Lily glared at her. "But you were supposed to protect me, Anna. That's what people who love each other do."

She had run out of words to make Lily understand. "Lily, pulling away from you was the hardest thing I've ever done in my life, but I did it because I love you." She let go of Lily's arm and drew a deep breath. "I don't know what else to say to make you to believe that."

Lily glanced at her briefly, but then looked away. "It doesn't change the fact that you let me down."

"Then how can I make that up to you?"

Their eyes met, and it looked to Anna as if Lily was about to cry. "I wish I knew." Then she turned and walked briskly in the other direction.

Anna knew she had the whole staff at Premier Motors walking on eggshells with her persistent bad mood, but she couldn't seem to snap out of it. She was consumed with thoughts of how she might convince Lily to come home, and was growing more discouraged by the hour.

"Poor Chester," Holly said as she appeared in Anna's doorway at the end of the day. "He waits at home all day for a happy face and he gets your grouchy mug instead."

"Am I that bad?" Anna asked, dreading the response. She

hated to think the people around her were speculating about her sour mood.

"I think it's safe to say everyone here is avoiding you. They can't wait for you to leave next week."

Anna was scheduled to fly out on Wednesday morning for the annual auto show in Detroit. "Glad I can accommodate them."

"You don't scare me, though. Is something going on?"

Anna sighed with frustration. She had tried to keep this to herself, but turning it over in her head for three days had gotten her nowhere. She felt she could trust Holly, but she feared her emotions would get the better of her if she allowed herself to open up. "I'm dealing with some heavy-duty personal issues right now, and everything I do seems to make it worse."

"I can tell you're going through something. Is it anything I can help with?"

She shook her head. "It's one of those things I don't want the whole world to know about."

Holly stepped in and closed the door. "You were there for me when I needed you, Anna. I'm here now if you want to talk about it."

"Thanks, Holly. I just . . . I've been sitting here thinking about it, and I can't believe what I've done." She pushed her hands through her hair as the first tears gathered in her eyes. She took Holly through recent events, glossing over the details of how bad things had gotten at home before Lily left. "Over and over, I put this business in front of what Lily needed. I even left her in San Jose by herself after her mother died so I could get back here and sign the Sweeney deal. What kind of partner does something like that?"

Holly handed her a tissue, and she wiped her eyes.

"She told me it didn't matter and I believed her. But then the Kimble thing came up and she asked me if I could wait a while. 'Oh, no,' I said. 'We have to move now or somebody else will jump in and bid.'" Her head bobbed back and forth as she mocked herself.

195

"But that was true, Anna. If you hadn't moved on Kimble when you did, someone else would have."

More tears burned her eyes. "So what if they had, Holly? She needed me, and I wasn't there for her. Instead, I was out gathering my little auto empire. Now I have it, and look what it cost me."

"Are you at least talking to each other? Because if you are, there's still hope things will work out."

Through all of her ruminations, Anna wouldn't let herself imagine their relationship was over. "She doesn't want to come home. But at least she hasn't . . . as far as I know she hasn't found another place to live. Until she does that, I keep hoping she'll change her mind."

Holly nodded assuredly. "Maybe she just needs a little time."

"I can't just sit here on my hands and wait for her. I need to make her understand how I feel."

"Any chance she's just playing hard to get?"

"I don't think she's playing anything. She says she doesn't trust me anymore, and I can't earn that back if I can't even get her to talk to me."

"You don't have to make her talk, Anna. You just have to make her listen. Tell her over and over if that's what it takes."

Anna sniffed and wiped her eyes one last time. Then she drew in a deep breath and tried to lighten the mood. "Maybe I should take Chester to see her. Those droopy eyes of his are hard to resist."

"If you want my opinion, I think you should go home tonight. You look like you could use a little rest." She reached across Anna's desk and closed her appointment book. "All of this will wait. Just go home and relax a little. Have a nice dinner, soak in the tub, then give her a call. No pressure. Just let her know how much you care about her."

Maybe Holly was right, she thought. Her direct approach—asking Lily to put it all behind her and come home—had already been rebuffed. She couldn't expect Lily just to forget about all

196

she had been through in the last two months. Earning her trust again would take time.

Admitting to herself that she was exhausted, she called it a night and went home. A check in the mirror confirmed what Holly had seen, a drawn face with dark circles under her eyes. No wonder her mood was so bad.

As she took Chester out for his walk, he tugged her toward the garage.

"Not tonight, fella. We're going to bed early, but we can give her a call. What do you think of that?"

As Chester took his time sniffing around the grass median in front of their house, Anna let her mind wander, going over in her head what she would say. Maybe Holly was right that she just needed to be persistent. What better way to convince Lily that she would always be there than to always be there?

Determined to relax, she scanned her mail while eating a dinner of canned soup and crackers. Then she took a leisurely steam bath to clear her head. The last thing she wanted was to let her earlier mood bleed over into her talk with Lily.

Only when she was ready for bed did she finally pick up the phone. Chester wandered into the room and settled at the foot of the bed. "Here goes nothing, boy."

She dialed the number for the Waterways Lodge and paced nervously as the front desk clerk rang through to Lily's room.

"Hello." The television played loudly in the background.

Her heart raced at hearing Lily's voice. "Hi."

"Anna . . ."

"How are you doing?"

"I'm okay. You?"

Anna's first instinct was to answer that she was lonely, but she held that in check. "I'm all right. Getting ready for bed. Chester's already sacked out."

Lily chuckled slightly as the background noise faded. "On the bed, I bet."

"You got it. He's taken over the place." She gave the dog a pat.

"Holly thinks I ought to bring him to work with me. If she could see him now . . ."

"Holly . . . she's your friend from San Diego, right?"

"Yeah." Anna rolled her eyes at the frivolous conversation. Why couldn't they just talk? "I hope I'm not calling too late."

"No, it's okay."

"Good. I was worried you might be in bed."

"Well, I am, but that's because my only choices are the bed or the bathtub."

Picturing Lily in the motel room, Anna bit her tongue again to keep from asking her to come home. She didn't want to ask for anything at all—not even if they could get together and talk again—for fear that Lily would say no. "I just . . . I wanted you to know that I was thinking about you. Pretty much all the time."

Lily was quiet for several seconds. "Anna, I—"

"And I'm sorry. I let myself get caught up in all my big plans and lost sight of what really mattered, and that was you." She took Lily's silence as a confirmation of her blame. "It's okay. You don't have to say anything. I just needed to tell you that. I love you. Good night." Anna's heart sank, and she pressed the button to end the call before Lily could protest.

"Admit it, Lily. You like eating real food once in a while," Sandy said, gesturing toward Lily's empty plate.

"Yours especially. At least I'm driving into work again every day, so I can get a decent lunch downtown."

Back at Sandy and Suzanne's on Saturday night after her first week out of the rehab center, Lily felt good about her progress. She had ridden Suzanne's bike to an AA meeting each morning, and made amends to Tony and the law clinic staff. On Thursday, she had returned to Judge Anston's court, this time entering a not guilty plea for a client charged with resisting arrest. The judge had been pleased to see her, and filled with praise that she had completed the program.

"Have you talked to Anna this week?" Sandy asked.

"She came by the motel on Monday night. How do you suppose she knew where I was?" She made no secret of her suspicions that Sandy had tipped Anna off.

"Did you ask her?"

"No." Her shoulders slumped. "She asked me to come home."

Sandy and Suzanne exchanged looks, and Suzanne spoke. "So what are you doing still at the Waterways Lodge?"

She shook her head. "I don't think I can't go back home. I need to start looking for a place to live."

"What do you mean you can't go back home?" Sandy left the dishes on the counter and returned to the table. "Why not?"

"It doesn't feel right. It's like I'm just . . . I don't know, postponing the inevitable."

"What's inevitable? Don't you two still love each other?"

"I do," she said. "And Anna probably thinks she loves me too. But I don't think she's really thought through all of this."

"Thought through what?" Suzanne held up her hands in apparent dismay. "She loves you. She wants you to come home. End of story."

"End of story until something else comes up," Lily answered with a snort.

"What's that supposed to mean?" Sandy asked.

"I can't get past it, Sandy. I wish I could. I know I was a little out of control, but Anna turned her back on me. She said so herself, that she let her business take priority. She said she was sorry, but if she'd thought about me as a partner, it never would have happened in the first place. I need somebody who's going to be there for me, no matter how hard it gets—not somebody who's going to wash her hands of everything that"—her voice turned sarcastic and she rolled her eyes—"interferes with Premier Motors."

Sandy looked at her sternly. "From what you told me, you were more than just a little out of control."

199

"That's not the point. Would you have thrown Suzanne out of the house?"

"If I ever need my ass kicked, Sandy better be the one to kick it," Suzanne said sharply. "That's what I count on her for."

"But you know as well as I do that she isn't going to let you fall on your ass," Lily said. But the anger in her voice was for Anna, not Suzanne.

"Anna didn't let you fall either, Lily," Sandy said. "She was there for you every step of the way."

"That's bullshit. She was out with her new friends."

"It's not bullshit. That first time you called her, she traced it to the Waterways Lodge. Then she went down there every night to keep an eye on you and make sure you were okay." Sandy was getting louder by the second. "And that weekend we went to Oakland, she came over here freaked out because she didn't know where you were."

Lily was shocked to learn that Anna had kept tabs on her. "She was watching me all that time and didn't even try to talk to me?"

"She didn't want to interfere, Lily. She was trying to get you to help yourself, but she wasn't going to just sit by and let you fall apart. She was there for you all along. You just didn't know it."

Lily thought back to what Anna had said on the beach about talking to a counselor. She knew from the testimonials she had heard at Redwood Hills that letting a loved one "bottom out" was the impetus for getting many of them into treatment.

"And when we got back from Oakland, I had to stop her from going to get you. She wanted you to come home that weekend."

Myriad emotions ran through Lily—frustration, gratitude, even a little hope—but the one that came out was resentment. "Why did you stop her, Sandy? You saw how miserable I was about going into that place, and the whole time I thought she didn't care at all. You could have saved me from that."

Sandy looked hurt. "Yes, I could have. In fact, I gave her hell about how she treated you until she told me why. And then I realized she was right. It didn't matter what kind of partner you were, or what kind of friend. What mattered was that you beat this thing."

"So this whole time, all of you have been pulling my strings like a puppet. 'Let's see if we can get Lily to do this.' Everyone's in on the secret but me."

"Is that what you think, Lily?" Suzanne asked, her tone indignant. "That this was all some big game for everybody?"

"No," she answered meekly. She didn't have the strength to deal with a pissed-off Suzanne. "Of course not. I just wish I'd had a choice."

Sandy patted Lily's arm. "Lily, I'm sorry I kept things from you. But when we got back from San Jose, you'd already made up your mind to get help, and you were doing it for yourself, not for Anna. Can you honestly say you would have gone into that program if you could have gone home instead?"

The answer to that question was obvious to everyone.

Chapter 16

Lily flipped open her cell phone for the third time, gathering her nerve to make the call. It had been a thought-filled week for her as she studied on the things Sandy had told her about Anna. Through it all, she heard Daryl's voice in her head, taunting her about how nothing would change, how she was coming back to the same fucked up world she left.

She could feel herself falling again into a state of agitation. Two months ago she would have reached for a drink, and justified it with her anger. Now she had no choice but to face it down.

The culprit, as always, was her insecurity. It was easy to blame that trait on her transient childhood in foster care, but she had no excuse for holding on to it at thirty-one. Eleanor Stewart had shown her she was worth caring for her, and Anna had professed her love and devotion in hundreds of ways. Instead of accepting what Anna had given her so freely, she had sabotaged their relationship with unrealistic expectations, convincing herself that Anna couldn't possibly want her forever.

From her searching and moral inventory, the fourth step in her recovery, Lily knew the dangers of letting her insecurities rule her life. She couldn't magically set aside her intrinsic anxiety about being abandoned, but she could learn to have confidence in knowing that it wouldn't be the end of her, and that with the help of her higher power, she was strong enough to survive.

Armed with this modicum of self-assurance, she looked anew at her feelings about how Anna had pulled away and let her fall. It made perfect sense that Anna would seek help once things grew out of control. She didn't let problems languish the way Lily did. The clandestine watchful eye and now the open plea for her to return home were all consistent with the Anna she knew and loved, while the one she had conjured as selfish and aloof was a stranger.

Besides the revelations from Sandy and Suzanne, Lily found even more reasons from her AA program to re-examine what she wanted with Anna. Despite her progress with overcoming alcohol, her life—which still included lonely walks on the beach and a tiny room at the Waterways Lodge—remained unmanageable. Her path became clear at Thursday's step meeting, where they had spoken of making amends with those who had been wronged by the alcoholic's behavior. The leader of the group had implored them to be honest with themselves, and in that moment, Lily realized all the ways she had wronged Anna with her drinking. She had hidden things from her for weeks, and even let her take the blame when things had spiraled out of control. Though she had blurted out a lame apology when they first saw each other, she had never faced the music for the shameful night Anna had been hurt.

At the beach, instead of thanking Anna for taking action to help her, she had lashed out in anger. By forcing her to help herself, Anna had saved her every bit as much as Eleanor Stewart had when she stepped forward to give her a home. The question wasn't so much if she could forgive Anna, but if Anna could forgive her.

She pressed the button for Anna's cell phone and was startled when it went to voicemail right away. She disconnected and dialed the number for the house. After four rings, that one too rolled over to voicemail and she hung up. Anna didn't usually work on Sundays, but nothing about their lives was normal these days. Though she dialed directly into Anna's office, the weekend receptionist answered.

"May I speak to Anna Kaklis please?" she asked, injecting a formal tone so her voice wouldn't be recognized. She didn't want people at Premier Motors gossiping about the call.

"I'm sorry. She's out of town. May I take a message?"

Lily bristled uncontrollably to think Anna might be off again with her new friends. "When do you expect her?"

"She's in Detroit for the auto show. I believe . . ." There was a long pause. "The schedule has her back at work on Tuesday."

Lily hung up and sighed with relief to know where Anna was, or rather, where she wasn't.

Anxious to get out of the motel room, she skipped down the stairs to the storage closet where they let her keep her bike. With Anna in Detroit for two more days, this was her first chance to go back to their Brentwood home. She had a right to be there, she told herself, even if it was just to pick up her mail, which she hadn't collected in months.

The ride through heavy traffic took her an hour and a half, and she was especially relieved when she pulled off busy Sepulveda Boulevard. She smiled as soon as the Spanish-style home came into view.

Lily pushed the bike around back, parking it inside the gate next to the garage. The pool was sparkling, a sign that the pool service had been by in the last couple of days, and the landscaping was freshly clipped and groomed. She dug out her key and walked back out to the side door to enter through the family room.

She was surprised by the strong emotional response she got from being inside the house. It was full of clues about how Anna had lived her life over these past few weeks. The table next to the couch was stacked high with *Car & Driver*, which meant Anna was behind on her reading.

She spotted her mail in a cardboard box on her desk. A quick perusal told her there were no unpaid bills. Apparently, Anna had taken care of them, just as she had after the funeral. She chuckled with irony to realize Anna had paid her credit card bill, which included over forty nights at the Waterways Lodge.

Uneasily, Lily mounted the stairs to the master bedroom suite. Oddly, she felt a bit like a trespasser, even a voyeur looking in on Anna's private life. Their room was unchanged from when she had left, neat and clean from the housekeeper's recent visit. She couldn't help but smile as her eyes came upon the framed picture on the nightstand, the one from Yosemite. It was touching to see that Anna had brought the photo up from the family room to her bedside. What lay beside the photo moved her profoundly—a book she recognized from the library at Redwood Hills, the story of a woman who had guided her husband into recovery after years of alcohol abuse, and how their love had flourished from the shared ordeal. Maybe Anna understood more about her recovery than she had thought. If she could read that woman's horror-filled memoir and still think they had a chance . . .

The last four days hadn't been the respite Anna had sought from the worry and sadness that were now her constant companions. The annual event in Detroit was usually one of the highlights of her year. But even the most stunning innovations in automotive engineering had failed to interest her this time. Instead, she found herself imagining the emptiness of a life without Lily. She thought about her at every turn, wondering if she was still at the lodge, and if she had thought any more about the plea for her to come home.

Somehow, Anna had to strike the balance between patience and perseverance. She wanted to give Lily the time and space to heal, but not enough to allow her to think she didn't care anymore.

"Would you like something to drink before we land?" the flight attendant asked gently. From her nearly untouched dinner, he had apparently sensed her somber mood.

"No, thank you." She turned back to the window, searching the fading red desert below for signs of civilization. They would be in LA soon.

Bored with the auto show and preoccupied with thoughts of Lily, she had changed her travel plans to return a day before schedule. She smiled as she thought of her penchant for coming home early, mostly engineered to surprise Lily. There would be no reward waiting this time.

At least Chester would be there. She planned to call as soon as they landed to ask Holly to bring him to the house. It would be a very long night indeed without the pooch to keep her company.

And once she settled into bed, she would call Lily again.

Distracted by her mail, Lily lost track of time, realizing with irritation that she would have to ride back to the lodge in the dark. She considered leaving Anna a note, but her presence would be obvious from the empty box on her desk, and the paper in the trash can. When she got back to her motel room, she would leave a message on Anna's cell phone. Stashing a couple of cards from her mother's friends into her small backpack, she headed out the side door, and then through the gate to retrieve her bike.

Again in the backyard, Lily was overwhelmed with homesickness as she looked first at the pool then at the hot tub. She and Anna had spent many relaxing evenings out here, not to mention many romantic moments.

It suddenly occurred to her that she didn't have to go home in the dark tonight. Anna wasn't due home until tomorrow night, and she didn't have to be at the law clinic until noon the next day. She could stay the night and ride home early in the morning. It would even be against the traffic flow, which was safer anyway.

She let herself back into the house and went into the bathroom off the family room. There she deposited her backpack and traded her clothes for one of the guest towels. The backyard was dark and private, visible only to someone nosy enough to pierce the dense crape myrtle hedge that grew five feet high around the property. Wrapped in her towel, she waited in a nearby chair at the far end of the pool while the water heated in the spa. When the steam began to rise, she cast her towel aside and slipped into the tub.

As she relaxed, she thought back to the last time she was out here with Anna, the night they returned from Joshua Tree. Though she hadn't realized it at the time, she and Anna were holding on by a thread. The last time they had been really happy together was at Yosemite, before her drinking had gotten out of control. If Sandy was right that she turned to alcohol in times of stress or depression, something about Yosemite must have set her off.

Carolyn and Vicki being pregnant . . . Anna saying that kids were a commitment, and she didn't want any. And Anna teasing that she wasn't a lesbian. That conversation had been playful, but the bottom line was clear: Anna wasn't ready to commit to a life together, and while Lily had vowed to herself not to ruin things by putting pressure on Anna too soon, she had fallen instead into a pattern of escape and self-pity, made worse by the death of her mother.

She settled deeper into the tub, determined to move past the dismal place in her head. The churning water was soothing, the lull of the pump peaceful, and she relished it until her skin began to wrinkle . Stretching across the deck, she threw the on-off levers for the heater and pump that were mounted discreetly under a nearby bush.

Out of nowhere, headlights appeared in the driveway, freezing her in place, half in, half out of the circular tub.

"Go ahead, Ms. Kaklis. I'll bring your bag in," a man's voice said. From the businesslike tone, she guessed it was a chauffeur.

Fuck! That meant Anna was home. Lily was too surprised to move, and not sure where she would go if she did. She couldn't just waltz through the back door naked.

"Thank you, Henry."

Yes, that was definitely Anna, she realized. She saw the light go on in the family room, one she had intentionally turned out so as not to illuminate the patio. She could barely make out Anna's figure through the French doors.

Lily gauged her options. There was no way to avoid a face-to-face encounter, unless she waited for Anna to go upstairs so she could rush inside. At least that way she could get her clothes back on.

Settled on this strategy, she watched and waited from her position in the tub. But as soon as the limo pulled away, a second car appeared, this one parking next to the garage and turning off the lights.

"Come on, boy. Let's go see mommy!" The woman's voice was familiar, but Lily couldn't place it. Whoever it was had obviously kept Chester while Anna was gone.

"There's my boy!" It was Anna's voice again at the side door. "Hey, fella."

"I'd say he missed you."

"I missed him too. Thanks for bringing him tonight, Holly. Come on in."

Holly. Lily's stomach roiled with jealousy that Anna had seemingly filled the void in her life with new friendships.

The light came on in the kitchen and Holly walked through. Anna followed and lifted the panel on the doggie door. Within seconds, Chester dashed out from around the side of the house. He ran through the yard while Anna and Holly stayed in the kitchen to talk. As Anna ducked her head into the refrigerator, Holly walked outside through the French door Lily had left unlocked.

Lily slid lower into the tub so she wouldn't be seen.

"Look at him go. I wonder if he'll find anything interesting," Holly said to Anna as she came out.

Oh, fucking hell! Lily peered toward the house where the women had taken seats at the umbrella table. On a night as warm as this one, they might sit and talk for hours. Her skin would be pruned by then.

She was startled by the sudden arrival of Chester, who began to growl and yip playfully. "Go away!" she whispered.

Instead, he darted forward and back, as if expecting her to throw a toy.

"Chester, if you ever loved me . . ."

Anna stood and clapped her hands. "Chester, come here!"

As he dashed back to Anna, Lily blew out a breath of relief. She couldn't hear what the women were saying, but they briefly embraced and kissed each other's cheek. Her feelings of jealousy about their friendship gave way to relief that Holly was leaving.

Holly stopped at the gate and turned. "Are you going to come in tomorrow, or should I pretend I haven't seen you?"

"Let's play it by ear," Anna said. "If I don't come in, you didn't see me."

"It's a deal. Welcome home, boss. So long, Chester." Holly patted the dog's head and walked out through the back gate.

Lily rejoiced momentarily in her reprieve, though she still wasn't sure how she would get into the house for her clothes. Even if Anna went back inside, she would have to wait for her to go upstairs. Suddenly Anna stood and peeled her shirt over her head. *Oh, fuck!* Lily realized with horror that she was probably coming to the hot tub.

But she wasn't. Anna tossed her slacks over the chair and stepped slowly into the shallow end of the heated pool.

Lily craned her neck to watch as the shapely form disappeared inch by inch beneath the surface. Sliding slowly around the rim of the hot tub, she positioned herself where she could watch with a low risk of being seen.

Mesmerized by the sight, she thought back to the times they

swam together late at night. Often, they played and teased one another in the water until things turned serious. Caught up in the memories, Lily almost got up the nerve to slip over the small waterfall that divided the pool from the hot tub.

But after only a few laps, Anna stood at the shallow end and stepped out of the water. She gathered up her clothing and walked toward the house. "Come on, boy. Let's go to bed."

Things were more complicated now, Lily realized, because it would be awkward to explain why she had stayed hidden. She would definitely have to sneak in and get her clothes without Anna knowing.

But that option vanished as soon as Anna walked back into the kitchen—and locked the door.

Oh, shit! Lily suddenly remembered that her house key was in her backpack, inside the now locked house. She watched as the lights downstairs gave way to those in the master suite. Her skin now wrinkled, she climbed out of the hot tub, retrieving her towel from underneath the bush where she had thrown it earlier. After tiptoeing to the house, she verified that the kitchen door was indeed bolted, as was the door leading to the family room.

On the off chance that Anna had left the side door open, Lily slipped outside the gate into the driveway. Suddenly, the motion detector on the porch light illuminated her presence for the neighbors or anyone who might be driving down the street. With mounting frustration, she decided she didn't care who saw her wandering around outside wrapped in a towel, as long as it wasn't Anna.

Shit. That side door was locked too.

Returning to the backyard, Lily weighed her options. She could start pounding on the door, but then she would have to explain what she was doing out there without her clothes. And worse, she would be hard-pressed to come up with a good reason for not announcing herself earlier. Why hadn't she just called out when Anna and Holly had come outside?

Because she was out there naked and she didn't want to look

like an idiot in front of Anna's new best friend.

The kitchen window! Anna usually left it cracked to allow the fresh air in. Lily slinked around the side of the house to test her theory.

Damn. The place was like Fort Knox. The kitchen windows were the only ones on that side, and there were none in the back of the house. Her only other options were the windows along the well-lit driveway or those in the front yard. Out of choices, Lily started toward the front of the house.

Then she saw it, like a gift from the heavens. There along the ground was exactly what she needed—Chester's doggie door. She stooped down to feel the opening. Anna had left the panel out so Chester could come and go at night. The hole was small, but she was sure she could fit through it.

Gripping the towel in front so it was tightly wrapped, Lily knelt down and poked her head through the opening. The house was completely dark downstairs, and she could barely make out the sound of the hair dryer running in the master bath. She couldn't have asked for a better scenario. Anna wouldn't hear her, and she could slip in and out without her even knowing she had been there.

She tried to get her shoulders through the hole, but it was too small. She backed out and started through again with her arms straight ahead. The door was taller than it was wide, so she turned on her side to make it easier. Pushing with her feet, Lily made slow progress. The towel was part of the problem, bunching up and creating a logjam just underneath her shoulders. Again, she backed out.

She pulled off the towel and shoved it through the hole, and then started through again, confident she would make it this time. Arms first, then head, then shoulders. Once she got both shoulders all the way through, she would be home free.

"Grrrrrrr! Rrrraaaarff! Rrrraarrff!"

Fuck!

Viciously protective of his turf at first, Chester calmed

211

immediately when he recognized her. Then he began to pounce around the kitchen, barking with enthusiasm.

Lily's heart stopped about the same time as the hair dryer.

"Chester!" Anna called from upstairs.

Fuck! Lily squirmed, not sure whether to go forward or backward. Not that it mattered. She couldn't seem to move either way.

"Chester!"

Anna remembered the panel on the doggie door. The installer had suggested she close it at night, just in case any raccoons or stray pets wandered up. She could hear the struggle in the kitchen. Whatever it was, it sounded as though Chester had it cornered.

Filled with apprehension, she pulled on her robe and headed back down the stairs, stopping to grab a broom from the hall closet between the kitchen and family room. Shaking with anticipation, she reached for the light switch.

Nothing on earth could have prepared her for the sight that greeted her. Chester was sitting in the middle of the room, wagging his tail with glee, barking excitedly at Lily, who seemed to be . . . naked . . . and halfway through the doggie door.

"This isn't what it looks like," Lily quickly said.

For the life of her, Anna couldn't imagine what it was if it wasn't what it looked like. "It looks like you're crawling into the house naked."

"I'm not crawling anywhere." Lily's face was beet red. "I'm stuck."

"And the naked part?"

"I guess that is what it looks like." Lily stretched out for the towel to cover herself. "I can sort of explain all of this."

"Should I go get a chair?" Anna couldn't help her irreverence. She was overjoyed at having Lily this close, and while any explanation for this scene would be forgotten someday, this image was forever.

"Very funny. Do you think you could trouble yourself to help me out of here?"

Anna thought about it for a second or two. If she pulled Lily all the way through, she would wrap up in the towel, tell her story, and then probably get dressed and leave. At least this way she was captive. "I get the whole story, right?"

"Whatever."

"Well, since you asked so nicely, do you wish to be pulled into the house, or pushed out of the house?"

Lily squirmed to gauge her condition. "In, I think."

Anna reached down and took hold of Lily's forearms and pulled her gently until she finally cleared the opening. There was a small scrape on her side, but other than that, she seemed no worse for the wear.

Lily stood shyly and wrapped the towel tightly around her torso. "Thanks." Still red in the face, she started for the family room.

Anna caught her elbow and pulled her back. "Oh no, you don't! Now I get an explanation."

Leaning against the counter, Lily sighed and ran a hand through her hair. "This is humiliating."

Anna suddenly felt ashamed for taking advantage of the situation. The last thing she wanted was to make things worse. "Go on, then. Get your clothes," she said. "If you want to talk, I'll listen. If not . . ."

"I do, Anna. I do want to talk."

With guarded hope, Anna nodded.

"I've been thinking about that night you came to the beach. I wasn't in much of a mood to listen, but I heard the things you were saying."

Anna was prepared to say them all again, especially to affirm her love. And she was ready to accept her share of the blame for putting her work first, and for not making it clear from the beginning that she wanted Lily to come home.

"I tried to call you this morning, but they said you were gone to Detroit. And you're not due back until tomorrow night, by the way."

Anna gave her a small smile, still unsure of where this was going and what it had to do with Lily standing naked in their kitchen.

"Anyway, I came over this afternoon on my bike because I thought, well, I just wanted to be here again. This is the first time I've been here, I swear."

"This is still your home, you know. You're allowed to be here."

Lily's serious look brightened, if only a bit. "Yeah, okay, so I was going through my mail and it got late. I thought about going back to the lodge, but it was dark and I didn't want to ride down Sepulveda. So I decided to stay the night. I was going to leave you a note or call or something to tell you I'd been by."

"It's all okay, Lily. You don't have to justify being here." She eyed Lily's towel and took a step toward her. "But I know you didn't ride over here like that."

Lily rolled her eyes and almost smiled. "I was out in the hot tub when you got home."

"Why didn't you say something?"

"Because I was going to come in when I saw it was you, but then Holly got here with Chester. So I stayed down low in the tub waiting for her to leave."

"And then I went swimming."

"And then you went swimming," Lily said, looking away guiltily.

"So why didn't you join me then?" She took another step closer.

"I . . . I thought about it. But I didn't want to scare you. I thought I should just get my clothes and get out of here. But then you locked all the doors."

"You could have knocked." Another step.

"I was sort of hoping I could get away without you knowing I

214

was here. I didn't know how to explain why I hid. I'm not really sure why . . ."

"I don't care why." Anna closed the distance between them and lowered her head. "All I care about is that you're here now." Her lips closed over Lily's as she pulled their bodies together. The kiss had to say everything in her heart because she wasn't sure she would get another chance.

Several seconds passed before Lily responded, and when she did, it was with the fervor of new love. "God, I've missed you so much."

Anna squeezed her eyes shut and savored the feel of Lily's arms as they went around her neck. She couldn't live without this. "I'm so sorry I hurt you, Lily. I should have paid more attention to what you needed. I was selfish."

"No, I was wrong to blame you, Anna. If it hadn't been your work, I would have found another excuse." Lily's hold on her grew tighter. "I just lost control. You didn't do anything wrong."

"I wanted to help you."

"You did, Anna. I know that now."

They stood quietly entwined for several minutes. For Anna, it was a return to stasis, a place where all her world was balanced. The familiar stillness that life with Lily had given her crept over her as her mind slowly emptied of the turmoil that had plagued them for months.

"I'm so sorry for all I put you through," Lily said, her voice cracking as though she might cry. "Will you ever be able to forgive me?"

Anna kissed the top of her head. There was only one thing she wanted from Lily. "Marry me."

Lily pushed back to see her face, clearly shocked by the words.

Anna took a deep gulp of air, not sure what to say next. "I've wanted to ask you ever since we went to Yosemite, but I kept waiting for the perfect time. That's what Maui was supposed to be about."

"Anna . . ."

"You don't have to answer me now—unless you want to say yes. You can do that now."

"I . . . I can't believe you still want me as fucked up as I am."

"I don't care about anything that's happened." She gripped Lily's shoulders harder. "You could never do anything to make me not want you."

Lily buried her head against her chest and began to cry. "Yes."

Epilogue

"Where's your leash?" Lily asked animatedly, sending Chester off in a rush to the family room. She caught up with him and clipped the leash into place. George would be there any minute and she wanted to be ready to go.

Chester dragged her to the door.

"Not yet, hound dog. And I hate to break it to you, but you're going to stay with Holly for a week." Lily remembered with embarrassment hiding from Holly and Anna in the hot tub. That seemed like ages ago, when in fact, it had been only three months. They could have pulled this off sooner, but then Anna had gotten the idea to wait until today, the third anniversary of the earthquake. Some things were just too perfect to pass up.

She shuddered to think how close she had come to losing the wonderful life that she knew lay ahead, though Anna continually assured her she would never have let go. There had been other close calls in her life, she realized, decisions or events that had

217

changed her profoundly. Rescue from her birth mother, her adoption...the earthquake. She chuckled softly as she recalled another, when she had asked Beverly to commit to her. How different her life would have been had Beverly said yes.

Through the side window, she saw a black BMW sedan pull up.

"Let's go, Chester. There's our ride."

George was already out and loading Chester's crate in the backseat. "You couldn't have ordered more perfect weather," he said.

The sky was blue, but there was a nip in the air, not unusual for February. "Hope you brought a jacket."

Lily had on pale yellow linen pants with drawstrings at the waist and ankles. She wore a matching shirt and a loose pullover sweater. She guided Chester into his crate as George held open her door on the passenger side. "I think it's so funny that Martine insisted on us not seeing each other today until the ceremony."

"What can I say? She's old-fashioned."

"I think it's kind of sweet." She was pleased to see George dressed casually for the ceremony on the beach. "And it's pretty sweet of you to offer to drive me over. You're supposed to give Anna away, not me."

He shrugged. "I already gave Anna away. She came back."

Lily laughed heartily and so did he. It was nothing short of amazing how far he had come in his acceptance of her in Anna's life. "You know, George, I got a card from my mom after her last visit down here. She wrote it just before she died, so it's something that means a lot to me. One of the things she said was how much she enjoyed meeting you and Martine. I know she meant that, and"—her voice began to crack—"I know why."

He smiled at her warmly and reached over to clasp her hand. "You make my daughter happy. That by itself would have been enough for me...once I got over being pigheaded." They both laughed again, and he went on. "But there's more to you than just who you are with Anna. I've seen the kind of person you are—the kind we all want to surround ourselves with."

Lily was almost embarrassed by the praise. "Even after all that trouble I caused last year?"

"You got through it, Lily. As far as I'm concerned, that only adds good things to who you are."

They pulled into the parking lot at Leo Carrillo State Beach. Anna's car was there, and Lily recognized several others belonging to Kim and Hal, Sandy and Suzanne, and the people from her office.

George came around and opened her door. "You ready for this?"

"I've been ready for this day my whole life." She let Chester out and gave him a long lead on his leash. "I wish Mom could have been here."

"Something tells me she is." He held out his arm, and together, they walked toward where the small crowd had congregated.

Kim took her hand from her pocket and laid her palm on Anna's forehead.

"What are you doing?" Anna asked, folding her arms to ward off the breezy chill.

"I'm checking to see if you're sick. You're supposed to be nervous."

"Hmpf!" She gently pushed her sister's hand away. "What I am is cold." Like Lily, she had chosen linen pants and a high-collared sweater, both in teal blue, for their ceremony.

"You picked the beach in February. What did you expect?"

"It's a special day and a special place." Anna smiled to herself, remembering the afternoon she and Lily had skipped out on work and brought Chester out to play. "One thing I didn't expect was so many people. I would have thought they had their fill of watching me get married."

Kim shook her head. "Most of these people are new."

They were, Anna realized, and many of them were Lily's

friends—Sandy and Suzanne, the people from the law clinic, and Virginia, Lily's AA sponsor and, for today, their minister. They were huddled together talking and laughing as they waited for Lily to arrive.

On Anna's side was Carolyn, who had made the trip alone from Seattle, leaving Vicki at home with their newborn daughter. She was talking with Holly and Jai, who had come to return Anna's support, and to take Chester home once the ceremony was over. Hal and Martine each had one of Jonah's hands and were walking with him near the shore.

The only other person in attendance was a friend of Hal's who had come along to take pictures. He had wandered all over the beach, snapping several candids of the group.

"I'm really proud of you for doing this," Kim said.

Anna looked at her skeptically, expecting a trademark wisecrack to follow.

"I'm serious. It's a big step."

"But it's the right one this time."

"I know. But I'm proud of you for knowing that." She looked past Anna's shoulder. "And don't look now, but your better half just got here."

Anna spun around to see Lily walking toward them across the beach on her father's arm, with Chester pulling them toward the water's edge. Utter joy welled inside her as they drew closer. From this day forward, she and Lily would be one.

Holly took Chester's leash and tugged him over to the circle they had formed. George and Lily arrived to stand in front.

"I've brought you something," her father said with a wink, depositing Lily's hand into hers.

Anna smiled and kissed him on the cheek. "Thanks."

"You have the best ideas, Amazon," Lily said, too low for others to hear. The shake in her voice was barely perceptible.

"Are you nervous?" she whispered.

"Yes. You?"

"Nah, this getting married is a breeze once you get the hang of it."

Lily chuckled. "Just don't make a habit of it."

They turned to face their friends and family, all of whom were grinning broadly.

"Good morning." Anna was pleased that Sandy had already taken the initiative and made introductions. "We asked you here because we love you all and wanted you to be a part of this special day. So thanks for coming, especially Carolyn, because she had to tear herself away from her new daughter."

Carolyn smiled warmly. She had already made it clear that she wouldn't have missed this day for the world.

"I also want to thank Holly and Jai. They probably don't realize it, but their wedding last fall was an inspiration to me. They were so brave for stepping up and making a public commitment when it wasn't the easiest thing to do."

Jai put his arm around Holly, who smiled back at Anna with a look of genuine friendship.

"And to my family..." She looked at each one. "Thank you for your love and patience, but most of all, for always being there when I needed you."

Lily took over the welcome. "For anyone who hasn't met Virginia yet, she deserves major kudos for helping me deal with a few demons. She's also here today to preside over this occasion."

Anna could see only hints of her resemblance to Virginia that Lily had described, though the woman had long, dark hair like hers, and bright azure eyes.

Lily acknowledged the people from her office for seeing her through both the saddest and happiest days of her life. Then she addressed Sandy and Suzanne.

"If I had one wish for everyone in the world, it would be that they had friends who stood by them the way you two have stood by me. It thrills me to have you both here today, and to know that you share my joy as if it were your own."

With their backs to the pounding surf, Anna gripped Lily's

hand tightly and spoke in a clear, unwavering voice. "We cherish you all, and we hope you'll accept the duty we ask."

Lily, who had been watching her intently, turned to the group. "To Anna and me, you're all a part of this promise now, and we're asking each of you to help us fulfill the pledge we'll make today."

"Three years ago today in a moment of fear and doubt," Anna said solemnly, "I was trapped in a dark place, both real and symbolic, entertaining thoughts that my life might be over. Little did I know that it was just beginning."

Lily spoke. "Since that day, I've known tremendous sadness and daunting personal trials. But with Anna at my side, I have also known happiness beyond what I ever thought possible."

Virginia cleared her throat. "Like all of you, I am honored to be here today to help set Anna and Lily on their path together. Since you know these women so well, it should come as no surprise that they've planned their own vows."

Anna held out her hand to Kim to receive one of the woven gold bands they'd had made especially for this day. Then she turned to face Lily, tuning out the others. "Lily, I want you to wear this ring so you'll always remember the promises I make to you today." She held Lily's left hand and slid the band onto her finger. "I will be with you to my last breath, and put my love for you in front of everything else in my life. I will stand with you to face whatever comes, and to make your challenges my own. And I vow to you that the deepest part of my heart will always be your home."

Lily looked at her hand and wiggled her fingers, her eyes sparkling with unshed tears. "Wow." Smiling and clearly giddy, she held it up and playfully showed it off. "Oh, wait. We're not finished."

Everyone laughed at her nervous antics, and Sandy stepped forward to place the other ring in Lily's hand.

"Anna, you can never know how much it means to hear you making promises like the ones my mother once made, the ones that anchored my soul and made me feel safe and loved."

Now it was Anna's turn to fight tears. A comparison to Eleanor Stewart put her importance in Lily's life in perspective.

Lily then placed her ring on Anna's finger. "I promise to love only you forever, and to support you in everything you do. And I pledge to you that I will do my best to never let you down."

Anna, and perhaps the others, understood that as a coded reference to Lily's struggle with alcohol.

"You can kiss me now," Lily said.

She did, sweeping Lily into her arms as their friends and family clapped and hooted.

Lily settled into the soft leather of her first-class window seat, still riding high on a wave of exhilaration. Their day had been perfect, from the sun-filled ceremony on the beach to the celebratory luncheon that followed at Empyre's.

"What are you thinking about?" Anna asked, sliding in beside her.

"What a beautiful day it was."

"It's not over yet. We should be at our hotel by ten."

"Ten in Maui will be midnight for us."

Anna leaned over and whispered, "I hope you don't plan on sleeping."

"Not until we're back in LA."

"You were so beautiful today. When I saw you walking across the sand with Dad, I almost cried."

"Your father said the most wonderful thing to me. He said he thought my mom would be there."

"Did you feel her?"

"I did. And I know…" Her eyes filled with tears. "I know she would have been so proud of us."

"And especially of you, Lily." Anna dabbed at Lily's tears with her knuckle. "I'm in awe sometimes at what a solid person you are. You've been through so much adversity in your life and you've beaten it all."

Lily sniffed. "Mom gave me that strength. And now I'll get it from you."

Anna gave her a gentle smile. "There was something else I wanted to promise you today, but not in front of everyone. This one's just between us, but I mean it every bit as much as the others."

"You already promised me everything I'll ever need."

"But I want you to know that I don't expect you to be perfect forever. People slip, and if that happens—not that I think you will, but if you ever do—I'm going to be right there beside you. You won't ever have to worry about me pushing you away."

Lily felt they had healed and moved on from the events of last year, but realized that Anna's new promise was in response to hers about trying not to let her down. "Honey, you don't have to help me get through forever. You just have to help me get through today."

"And I will."

"But what you did last year when I let myself lose control... it was the right thing. Suzanne made me realize that. I asked her how she'd feel if Sandy had handled her the way you handled me. And she said she expected Sandy to kick her ass if she ever needed it, that it was her duty as a partner to do that." She met Anna's skeptical look with an assuring smile. "If I ever need it, you're the one that has to do it. That's how you can support me."

"I love you madly," Anna said.

Finally, Lily knew how it felt to hold forever in her heart.

Publications from
BELLA BOOKS, INC.
The best in contemporary lesbian fiction
P.O. Box 10543, Tallahassee, FL 32302
Phone: 800-729-4992
www.bellabooks.com

WITHOUT WARNING: Book one in the Shaken series by KG MacGregor. *Without Warning* is the story of their courageous journey through adversity, and their promise of steadfast love. 978-1-59493-120-8 $13.95

THE CANDIDATE by Tracey Richardson. Presidential candidate Jane Kincaid had always expected the road to the White House would exact a high personal toll. She just never knew how high until forced to choose between her heart and her political destiny. 978-1-59493-133-8 $13.95

TALL IN THE SADDLE by Karin Kallmaker, Barbara Johnson, Therese Szymanski and Julia Watts. The playful quartet that penned the acclaimed *Once Upon A Dyke* and *Stake Through the Heart* are back and now turning to the Wild (and Very Hot) West to bring you another collection of erotically charged, action-packed, tales. 978-1-59493-106-2 $15.95

IN THE NAME OF THE FATHER by Gerri Hill. In this highly anticipated sequel to *Hunter's Way*, Dallas homicide detectives Tori Hunter and Samantha Kennedy investigate the murder of a Catholic priest who is found naked and strangled to death. 978-1-59493-108-6 $13.95

IT'S ALL SMOKE AND MIRRORS: The First Chronicles of Shawn Donnelly by Therese Szymanski. Join Therese Szymanski as she takes a walk on the sillier side of the gritty crime-scene detective novel and introduces readers to her newest alternate personality—Shawn Donnelly. 978-1-59493-117-8 $13.95

THE ROAD HOME by Frankie J. Jones. As Lynn finds herself in one adventure after another, she discovers that true wealth may have very little to do with money after all. 978-1-59493-110-9 $13.95

IN DEEP WATERS: CRUISING THE SEAS by Karin Kallmaker and Radclyffe. Book passage on a deliciously sensual Mediterranean cruise with tour guides Radclyffe and Karin Kallmaker. 978-1-59493-111-6 $15.95

ALL THAT GLITTERS by Peggy J. Herring. Life is good for retired Army colonel Marcel Robicheaux. Marcel is unprepared for the turn her life will take. She soon finds herself in the pursuit of a lifetime—searching for her missing mother and lover. 978-1-59493-107-9 $13.95

OUT OF LOVE by KG MacGregor. For Carmen Delallo and Judith O'Shea, falling in love proves to be the easy part. 978-1-59493-105-5 $13.95

BORDERLINE by Terri Breneman. Assistant prosecuting attorney Toni Barston returns in the sequel to *Anticipation*. 978-1-59493-99-7 $13.95

PAST REMEMBERING by Lyn Denison. What would it take to melt Peri's cool exterior? Any involvement on Asha's part would be simply asking for trouble and heartache . . . wouldn't it?   978-1-59493-103-1 $13.95

ASPEN'S EMBERS by Diane Tremain Braund. Will Aspen choose the woman she loves. . . or the forest she hopes to preserve.   978-1-59493-102-4 $14.95

THE COTTAGE by Gerri Hill. *The Cottage* is the heartbreaking story of two women who meet by chance . . . or did they? A love so destined it couldn't be denied . . . stolen moments to be cherished forever.   978-1-59493-096-6 $13.95

FANTASY: Untrue Stories of Lesbian Passion edited by Barbara Johnson and Therese Szymanski. Lie back and let Bella's bad girls take you on an erotic journey through the greatest bedtime stories never told.   978-1-59493-101-7 $15.95

SISTERS' FLIGHT by Jeanne G'Fellers. *Sisters' Flight* is the highly anticipated sequel to *No Sister of Mine* and *Sister Lost, Sister Found*.   978-1-59493-116-1 $13.95

BRAGGIN' RIGHTS by Kenna White. Taylor Fleming is a thirty-six-year-old Texas rancher who covets her independence. She finds her cowgirl independence tested by neighboring rancher Jen Holland.   978-1-59493-095-9 $13.95

BRILLIANT by Ann Roberts. Respected sociology professor, Diane Cole finds her views on love challenged by her own heart, as she fights the attraction she feels for a woman half her age.   978-1-59493-115-4 $13.95

THE EDUCATION OF ELLIE by Jackie Calhoun. When Ellie sees her childhood friend for the first time in thirty years she is tempted to resume their long lost friendship. But with the years come a lot of baggage and the two women struggle with who they are now while fighting the painful memories of their first parting. Will they be able to move past their history to start again?   978-1-59493-092-8 $13.95

DATE NIGHT CLUB by Saxon Bennett. *Date Night Club* is a dark romantic comedy about the pitfalls of dating in your thirties . . .   978-1-59493-094-2 $13.95

PLEASE FORGIVE ME by Megan Carter. Laurel Becker is on the verge of losing the two most important things in her life—her current lover, Elaine Alexander, and the Lavender Page bookstore. Will Elaine and Laurel manage to work through their misunderstandings and rebuild their life together?   978-1-59493-091-1 $13.95

WHISKEY AND OAK LEAVES by Jaime Clevenger. Meg meets June, a single woman running a horse ranch in the California Sierra foothills. The two become quick friends and it isn't long before Meg is looking for more than just a friendship. But June has no interest in developing a deeper relationship with Meg. She is, after all, not the least bit interested in women . . . or is she? Neither of these two women is prepared for what lies ahead . . .   978-1-59493-093-5 $13.95

SUMTER POINT by KG MacGregor. As Audie surrenders her heart to Beth, she begins to distance herself from the reckless habits of her youth. Just as they're ready to meet in the middle, their future is thrown into doubt by a duty Beth can't ignore. It all comes to a head on the river at Sumter Point.   978-1-59493-089-8 $13.95

THE TARGET by Gerri Hill. Sara Michaels is the daughter of a prominent senator who has been receiving death threats against his family. In an effort to protect Sara, the FBI recruits homicide detective Jaime Hutchinson to secretly provide the protection they are so certain Sara will need. Will Sara finally figure out who is behind the death threats? And will Jaime realize the truth—and be able to save Sara before it's too late?
978-1-59493-082-9 $13.95